A PHANTOM LOVER

In the dream, a warm wind swept across her body, like fingertips barely grazing the surface of her flesh. It aroused her and made her desirous and more. Its silken touch pleased her. Her body had spent the totality of its existence in ignorance of carnal pleasures. Contradictory feelings collided within her mind. The body was to be a pure temple to the Lord. That's what the Bible taught—and yet, there were such longings inside her, desires long concealed and repressed that now demanded satisfaction. Her body in the dream had yielded to temptation and began to writhe about as the wind increased its intensity and commenced kneading the flesh of her breasts and thighs. Moving, rocking, hands reaching out, fingers caressing the hidden crevices of her body, the Lea of dreams allowed her carnal desires to overcome her. The phantom voice made sounds of pleasure, moaning low as she twisted back and forth.

WORSHIP THE NIGHT

MARY VIGLIANTE

LEISURE BOOKS ❧ **NEW YORK CITY**

A LEISURE BOOK

Published by

Dorchester Publishing Co., Inc.
6 East 39th Street
New York, NY 10016

Printed in the United States of America

WORSHIP
THE
NIGHT

CHAPTER I

The day was devoid of color. The sky was gray, its fragile clouded mist reaching down to touch the earth. The air hung heavy with the damp cold of death. How appropriate it all appeared.

Lea stood underneath the branches of a maple tree, somberly watching the activity going on within her line of vision. Aunt Evelyn had begged her not to linger at the cemetery, but for some reason, she felt unable to tear herself away. It had happened so quickly that she had not yet adjusted to the fact that her mother was dead. Lea had always known that the woman had high blood pressure; but she had never, in all her horror-filled imaginings, thought that the condition was as serious as it, in fact, must have been. She was overwhelmed by her loss, yet she could not blame God. It was a merciful death, a massive cerebral hemorrhage. Mama had felt nothing, no pain, no agony, nothing at all.

When Lea had received the news at the library, she had taken it quite well. Mama had been a good

Christian; going to services, Sunday school, Bible class, and all the rest. She was a truly holy woman and God wanted her to be with Him. Lea had no doubt that her mother's soul now rested in Paradise. She had fought temptation all her life, didn't sin, either in thought, word or deed. There was no way that Mama could be suffering in the fires of perdition, feeling the tongued flames of Hell. The thought comforted Lea. Mama had long ago taken Christ as her savior and God; and, through the strictness of her teachings and her unbendable moral code, she had led Lea along the same path to righteousness.

There were tears gently trickling down the pale, bespeckled, face. Lea tried to control them but she couldn't. This was not a day for mourning, but rather one for rejoicing. Mama was in Heaven. That was what the Bible said, that was what she believed; yet she found herself engulfed in a sea of loneliness and morbidity. She would miss Mama terribly. It was the old woman who had made the decisions, laid down the laws of conduct, watched over each aspect of Lea's life to insure that temptation could not make inroads, that Satan would not find in her a place to take refuge. Now she'd have to care for herself, ensure that her heart was a pure temple of the Lord.

Lea was only thirty-three, yet she acted, dressed, and appeared much older. Her hair was cut short in an unflattering style. Her plain, matronly dress hung loosely in a shapeless mass from her shoulders. She was a frail, petite, little being, barely over five feet tall. Lea's eyes were blue in color, but they never sparkled like those of other women her age. Her pale face was colorless, ashen.

Painting one's face was a sign that the body contained no grace. Those who tinted their faces with rouge and spread color above their eyes were creatures of Satan, having yielded to the sin of vanity. Within such a person there could be no purity.

Once, when Lea was very young, perhaps thirteen years old, she had borrowed lipstick from a friend and drawn it over her mouth. Strange—the act had not made her feel sinful, until Mama had caught sight of the faint hint of color. She had strapped Lea soundly and had made the girl memorize passages from the Bible which concerned vanity, fallen women, and sin.

Lea had spent her entire life in fear of her mother's wrath. She had been a hard woman, to say the least. She had taken painstaking steps to assure Lea's purity. When Lea was in high school and short skirts were all the rage, Lea was not allowed to wear them. They showed too much of the anatomy and were, therefore, sinful. Let other people's daughters play the harlot. No daughter of Beatrice Eaton was going to be accused of such things. Lea was forced to wear loose-fitting cotton dresses which fell at least two inches below the knee. The bodices were not fitted, giving no hint of the firm, full, breasts that lay beneath.

During high school, being garbed in such a manner made her an oddity. Lea had spent the entire four years with no friends, being laughed at for her manner of dress. She had never been invited to a pajama party by the other girls. They had kept their distance from her, afraid that she would try to proselytize.

None of the boys had ever looked at her then. Her Mama had insisted that that was because they had the sin of lust on their minds and it was quite apparent, from the way she looked and acted, that Lea was pure, virginal; that was why the boys had left her quite alone. Dates were a thing that other girls engaged in, but not Lea. Even if anyone had ever asked, Mama wouldn't have allowed it. When members of the opposite sex were alone together, it placed them in Satan's grasp; it laid open the way to temptation.

At thirty-three, she had had but one date in her entire life, and that had come when she was twenty-seven. It had been with a man from their church; but even at that, Mama had disapproved, giving Lea a detailed description of the degrading things that men did to women. The date had been to a church social, well chaperoned. It had been enjoyable enough although Lea had found herself at a loss for words, not knowing what to talk about several times during that evening.

In the end, Mama had been proved right. The man had tried to kiss Lea. From all that her mother had told her, Lea knew that such things, although not a sin in themselves, if done in pure heart, were preliminaries for acts of fornication. First the kiss, then fondling of the breasts, caressing of thighs, and finally intercourse.

Even in marriage the act was dirty and only to be done for the sake of procreation. Mama had told her that next to childbirth it was the most painful thing a woman had to endure. It was a way for men to appease their animal urges. It gave them pleasure, but not the woman. For her it was painful and humiliating. Such things were the punishment that God had meted out to women in retribution for Eve's original sin. Purity and virginity as a life-long pursuit were pleasing to God. Those who would not give in to their base instincts were surely bound for Heaven.

12

Lea had always listened closely to her mother when she explained the origin of her knowledge on the subject of men, women, and sex. Beatrice had been married as a young girl, barely eighteen. She had not been saved then, had answered the degrading wants of her body, and had, in the end, paid the price. She had lain with her husband and had conceived Lea.

At that time, Beatrice had been a foolish, sinful, girl and had seen no harm in what she had done. But, when Lea was almost five, his want and lust for her having been spent, he left. It was then that Beatrice had turned to the church and its strict moral code for salvation. Through religion, she had found the strength to go on alone and to raise her young daughter.

Lea had racked her brain on several occasions, trying to remember her father and what he was like, but the memories did not seem to be there. She knew that he was a bad man, not a Christian. Whenever she did something that was not to her mother's liking, Lea would be told that not only did she look like her father, but she was just as far from grace as he had been. She had no recollections of his deserting them, nor for that matter, of anything that occurred before her fifth birthday.

It was a subject of much internal agitation to her. Even though she knew that he had been sinful, Lea wanted to know more about him. Every time she tried to draw the memories out of her brain, she would begin to sweat profusely and her hands would grow hot, burn, almost as if they were being held over a fire. Then there would be nausea; wave after wave of it. Beatrice always told her that God was causing the symptoms because He didn't want her to think about her past, that He only wanted her to think about Him and His holy mercy.

There was much confusion in Lea's mind about the burning sensation in her hands and the nausea. There were other times too, when she would experience such manifestations. They came, most frequently, in connection with her own body. If she was undressed and would catch a quick glimpse of herself in the mirror or if she would touch the intimate parts of her body while bathing, the feelings would start. Lea knew that nakedness was an abomination to God and that it was a sin to stare at an unclothed body, even if it were your own. And touching one's self, in anything other than the cursory manner needed to assure hygiene, was self abuse and sinful in the eyes of the Lord.

Over the past few years, there had been periods when the symptoms had been very severe and had necessitated her going to doctors; but their diagnoses had always been the same: there was nothing physically wrong with her. The malady was created in her mind. One doctor had suggested that Lea seek psychiatric help to discover the cause, but Beatrice had forbidden such action. Playing with the human mind was done by devils. The brain was the estate of God, controlled and directed by His will. Psychiatrists and their analyses, which washed the mind of guilt and expunged the conscience, were the rituals of demons. Guilt was placed in the mind by God and, therefore, it was a good thing, a necessary form of mental torment. When the sickness would overtake Lea, Beatrice would hand her the Bible and tell her to read it. That brought some relief, but not enough to make all things right. Lea suspected that deep down inside her there was some sin, one that she could not recognize nor identify, one inadvertently committed, which caused her malady.

14

God was punishing her for something; yet she could not understand what it was that she had done to offend Him.

Lea watched as the men begain to throw shovel after shovel of dirt into the open grave. The tears became more copious. Who was going to watch over her now? How was she going to maintain her place in God's favored light? Lea was so used to being told how and what to do, she was unsure if she could manage on her own. There was direction which could be sought from the church, true; but Mama had always insisted that the church was lax in certain areas, not demanding a strict enough code of conduct and morality.

It had been her contention that it was the Reverend's fault. He was fairly young and less adamant about adhering to every aspect of the Bible and its teachings. As Mama always said, "The Bible was written by God a long time ago. It was right then, and it's right now." Mama's biggest denunciation had to do with the way the minister allowed the Sabbath to be violated. There were church picnics and pancake suppers on Sundays. To Beatrice, this was sin. According to her, the only things that one could do on Sunday were to pray and read the Bible.

Lea couldn't turn to Aunt Evelyn for direction, for she was damned—at least, that's what Mama had always said. Evelyn was Beatrice's younger sister, by about four years. She was not a member of their church, nor for that matter any church. She smoked and drank, wore fashionable clothes and makeup, swore on occasion, loaded her body down with jewelry, splashed on expensive perfume, went to movies, had a television that was on all the time, and worst of all, after her husband Uncle Adam had died, she dated other men, sometimes going away on weekends with them. She was a fornicator, perverse and depraved.

Through the years, Mama and Lea had joined hands innumerable times, in prayer that Evelyn would turn from sin and join God's flock; but all the invocations in the world could not change her. Evelyn liked her life just the way it was. There had been a time when her aunt had been barred from coming to visit, Beatrice feeling that her sister was a bad example for Lea, showing the young girl wordly ways. In the end, however, it was decided that even though she was sinful, there was always the possibility of redemption. Prohibiting her from entering the house would only make her stray further and further from the paths of righteousness. It would have been unchristian to not attempt to lead her to salvation.

When Lea was about sixteen, Evelyn began coming to the house regularly again. They'd read to her from the Bible and try to get her to recognize and repent her sins; but to no avail. Mama had always said that she'd die happy if Evelyn would declare herself saved, but unfortunately that never happened. The mantle of purpose had fallen now to Lea; but she was not sure that she was capable of such a task, such a holy undertaking.

There had been loud and vociferous arguments between the sisters over the years, centering mainly on Lea. It was Evelyn's contention that Beatrice should loosen up the reins on the girl, that Lea's life was being wasted because of her zealot mother's religious fervor. The arguments were worse at Christmas and on Lea's birthday, when Evelyn would bring her presents, forbidden things. There were fashionable blouses or dresses, perfume, jewelry, makeup; but their purchase had been a waste of money. Beatrice had never allowed Lea to keep any of them. When she was younger, wanting to be like other girls she knew, desiring those things, Lea would retreat to her room in tears, mourning the fact that God had required her to be so very different. In later years, however, realizing the inherent sin in such objects, it had been Lea herself who had thrown the objects out or who had returned or exchanged them in favor of less worldly articles.

Regardless of how sinful she was, Evelyn was kin. Next to the father who had long ago deserted her, whose whereabouts were unknown, Evelyn was Lea's only other living relative. Because of the family ties that bound them together, she would have to continue seeing the woman. Lea just hoped that she would not be tainted and made less pure by the continued contact. She would have to guard against her aunt's exerting any influence over her. Lea would have to exemplify purity and righteousness, just as her mother had. She would continue the work of Evelyn's salvation that her mother had started. It was the Christian thing to do.

Life would be difficult now. Lea would have to make her own decisions on the rightness or wrongness of things. Mother had not prepared her well for such an undertaking. She knew instinctively that all the answers to all the questions ever formulated lay within the covers of the Bible. It was just a question of finding the correct one before the sin could be committed.

There were certain things that Lea knew to be sin without needing to consult the Bible; but then there were others that fell into a large area of gray. Mama contended that television was sinful because many of the programs depicted immorality and held up non-christian homes as examples of the typical American family. There had been occasions, however, when she had been visiting Aunt Evelyn, that Lea had watched tv and seen a game show or the news. Those did not appear sinful to her and she saw no harm in them, nor did she feel guilty for having watched them. It was within such gray areas that Lea would find it difficult going.

Now that Mama was gone, she'd have to read the Bible more closely, paying strict attention to the meaning of every single phrase, so that she knew without a doubt that she was doing God's bidding. From now on, she'd spend an hour on her knees every night, praying for guidance, rather than the normal fifteen to thirty minutes as had been her custom.

The dirt had formed a mound over the once open pit. It was almost finished now. A few more shovels-full and her mother's body would be forever committed to the ground. For a moment, Lea closed her eyes and thought about Jesus and Lazarus, how they had risen from the dead. She clasped her hands tightly around her Bible and began praying with all her might that the grave might open up and that her mother might once again walk amid the land of the living.

She held her breath, drawing it in deeply, and blinked her eyes open, staring in the direction of the gravesite. Nothing happened. Her prayers had not been answered. It was not God's will that He should perform a miracle today. It was by His decree that she should be left alone to make her way to Him.

The workmen were placing the floral arrangements over the top of the grave. The largest by far was the basket of red roses with the banner in big letters that spelled out the word "Mother." It was Lea's final gift to Mama, the very last thing that she could do for her.

There was sorrow in Lea's heart for all the unkind things that she had ever thought about the woman; all the times that she had resented her strictness, thought her punishments unfair, circumvented her authority to get her own way. For those and a host of other real and imagined indiscretions, she was truly and deeply sorry. Lea hoped that her mother was looking down at her from Heaven, listening, and finding it within her gentle heart to forgive her sometimes wayward daughter.

The men were walking away, having completed their day's labor. The gravesite was now deserted. Lea moved across the green carpet of grass, past the large gravestones, to the place where Beatrice now rested.

She approached slowly, the tears falling faster than ever, a large lump in her throat. It was not only her mother who lay beneath the chill soil; but also her teacher, her nurse, her companion, and most of all, her best friend. There had been times when they had been unable to communicate, when Lea had thought her mother cruel and uncaring, too stern and unbending, but now she yearned to have her back.

As she was standing next to the flower bedecked mound, she bent and plucked a single red rose from the arrangement she had provided, opened her Bible, and pressed the blossom within the Book of Psalms, her mother's favorite passages from the Good Book. It was only fit and proper that a remembrance should be kept there to remind Lea of that dear departed soul every time she scanned its pages.

She knelt in the soft earth and stared downward. "I love you, Mama," she said in a barely audible whisper, the words straining to exit her tightening throat. "I'll miss you terribly. You know that, don't you Mama?" With that her body shook with uncontrollable sobs. "I'll be good. I'll really be good. I'll remember everything you taught me and I'll read my Bible and I'll say my prayers. I'm going to try to be the best Christian I can be, Mama. You'll be proud of me. I won't be bad. I won't ever be bad. I'm going to be good just like you were. I'll be saved. I won't let Satan into my heart. You'll see Mama, I'll be in Heaven with you. I'm not going to burn in the fires of Hell. I'm not going to burn!" A feeling of fear, far sweeping apprehension, surrounded and engulfed her. Did she really have the power to be good without someone making her? Could she avoid the sinful temptation of the world? Was her resolve strong enough?

Lea bent to the ground, pressing her lips into the loosely packed earth. It was her final kiss, her final act of affection to the woman she had loved so well. Strange, during her tenure on earth, Beatrice had never allowed the child that. There had been no exchange of affection between them, no warm embraces, no kisses, no gentle hugs. Ever since the earliest time that Lea could remember, it had always been so. You demonstrated love and affection to only one, and that was the Savior. Touching among people, even mother and child, made the mind stray from thoughts of the Lord; and such mental meanderings were reserved only for those who were damned.

She rose to her feet, the movement taking great effort. Her grief and mourning weakened her more than was already the case. She had been a frail, sickly, child and had continued so in her adulthood. Lea dusted off the hem of her dress and her knees beneath it. It was time to leave. Mother was no more.

Lea turned from the grave, taking small steps, crying uncontrollably. Now she was her life's keeper, guardian of her own soul and its destiny.

CHAPTER II

Lea was pushing her book-laden cart through the ceiling-high stacks. This was one of her favorite jobs—returning books to their place, knowing they had done their job, had imparted knowledge to someone. She was replacing them on the shelves so that still another could benefit.

Lea liked her job at the Albany library. As her mother had always told her, "Being a librarian is a fitting and proper vocation for a single Christian woman." There was little temptation here, unless, of course, you read forbidden volumes; but Lea never did. She knew from the synopses what the books were about and read only those that dealt with appropriate, wholesome, Christian topics.

During her college years, she had been forced by her professors to read books that dealt with the seamier side of existence; but after having done so, she would always fall on her knees and pray for forgiveness. Since she had graduated, however, she had stayed clear of anything written that could possibly have been interpreted by her mother as being less than decent.

Lea was more than a little confused today. She had arrived late, having stopped first at Mr. Grayson's office for the reading of her mother's will. Aunt Evelyn had been there and so had Reverend Daniels. As expected, Aunt Evelyn had received a few mementos that had once belonged to Lea's grandparents. They were of little worth, except for their sentimental value. The church had received a bequest of four thousand dollars, which was to be used however the Reverend saw fit. The rest had gone to Lea.

Her inheritance had consisted of several thousand dollars of her mother's savings, plus an account which had been held in trust for Lea, and the house, the small clapboard structure where she had been raised. It was just what she had expected; but there had been something more, another piece of property that she had never realized existed.

According to the will, Lea was now the owner of a mountain cabin and fifty acres of land that was just outside the Adirondack Mountain town of Big Moose, not far from the Stillwater Reservoir. Lea found it hard to believe that her mother had actually owned such a vacation retreat, for she had never once mentioned it to Lea.

Strangely, when the lawyer was talking about this unexpected piece of real estate, Lea had suddenly envisioned a small log structure, nestled amid pines, sheltered on all sides by grandiose mountains, with something large and blue shimmering in the distance. The scene had only flashed in her brain for a fleeting second, then disappeared. Was it an illusion of what

26

Lea thought a mountain retreat should look like, or had she actually seen it? She struggled through her wealth of memories, sorting them out, trying to remember if she had ever been there; but it was all a misty blur.

Lea left the lawyer's office in the company of her aunt. As they walked down the street, she had questioned Evelyn about the cabin. Her aunt had informed her that her father had bought the property a year before Lea's birth.

"Beatrice and Jack were crazy about that place," Evelyn enthused. "They used to take their vacations up there fishing and relaxing, and they'd make the drive just about every warm weekend to spend their Saturday and Sunday mornings in the mountains."

Lea had found it a little hard to believe that her mother would be driving and fishing on the Sabbath rather than being in church. "Was I ever there?" she asked.

"Oh sure you were, when you were a very little girl. Even your Uncle Adam and I would go up there, every once in awhile, with your Mom and Dad."

"Strange, but I don't ever remember being there. Until just a few minutes ago, I wasn't even aware that Mama owned such a place. It seems unlike Mama to own something so obviously frivolous." Lea mulled it over while her aunt stood staring.

"That, my dear child," her aunt said, raising her eyebrows high on the pudgy, round, face, "was before your mother got religion. She used to be a hell of a lot of fun back then." Evelyn's eyes misted as the recollections of her sister came back to her. "You don't remember being there because you were so little when you stopped going. One weekend when you were four or so, your

27

Mom and Dad went up there together. Your mother never talked about it much, but I assume that they must have had one bad fight. He packed his bag and left your mother and you up in the woods and took off for parts unknown. After that, your mother never went back there. I had thought for sure that she must have sold it years ago. It's funny, but I always figured Jack would come back, if not to see Beatrice, at least to see you. He was crazy about you. Wherever you were, he'd be. Your Mama, though, insisted that he'd never turn up again, said he didn't give a damn for his family or his responsibilities.''

Lea's face showed shock. She couldn't in her wildest dreams imagine her mother using profanity.

"You look a little funny, is something wrong?" her aunt asked.

"No, it's just that I wish I could remember. You know, Mama used to talk about my father sometimes and she'd say that he was evil and he would be damned to hell because of it. All the times she spoke, I'd try to remember what it was he looked like; but nothing came back to me. I know he hurt her badly and she destroyed everything in the house that was his, but still as bad as he was he's still my father and I should be able to remember him. Don't you think?" Her voice belied the inner struggle that was going on in her heart. By wanting to learn more about her father was she somehow slighting and hurting the woman who had raised her?

"I used to have a picture of him, but when your mother found out about it, she took it and burned it." Evelyn shook her head at the memory. "She couldn't bear to be around anything that reminded her of him.

For the first year after he left, she never went out of the house. It was as if the two of you lived in a dark cave. You know," she said, cocking her head slightly to one side, "She wouldn't even let me in the house."

Lea had vague recollections of that time. She could remember her mother sitting and crying all the time. That was the year when Lea should have been in kindergarten, but instead had been kept home. She had begun school the following September, going straight into first grade.

"Your Uncle Adam and I used to try to get her to come out with us. We, quite frankly, were worried that she might consider doing away with herself; but she'd never budge."

Lea had a hard time believing such a statement. Her Aunt had been talking about suicide and that was a sin. Your soul was forever damned to Hell for such action. Only God could take life.

"Then," Evelyn had said in disparaging tones, "your mother turned to religion, with a vengeance. Now you know that I never agreed with her on that," she avowed, looking over at Lea sternly. "If all people believed like your mother, we'd never make any progress, never have any fun. Everything was a sin to her. Now don't get me wrong, I don't begrudge her the beliefs she held; it was something that she needed to keep going. My quarrel was not with what she did to herself, she was an adult and could do as she damn well pleased. I got mad at what she did to you. Look at you, you're a pretty little thing, but she always made you look like somebody's mother. You should have been going out and having fun. If she hadn't been such an uptight bitch, you would have had boyfriends, probably been married by now with some kids of your own. For that I can't forgive her!"

Lea had held her temper as she looked at the short, plump woman with the greying hair, rouged face, and form-fitting clothes. She was the complete opposite of her own mother. It was hard to believe they were sisters. "Aunt Evelyn," she spoke those words in measured tones, "Please don't talk about my mother that way." With that, Lea started to cry, the magnitude of her loss still weighing heavy upon her.

Aunt Evelyn apologized and then they parted, each going their separate ways, to live their lives in their own fashion.

Lea was placing the books carefully on the shelves, assuring that they were in their appropriate area; but her mind was somewhere else. It was disturbing both that Beatrice had never mentioned the cabin, and that she had never confided in Lea the circumstances surrounding her father's leaving. Lea had always gotten the impression, from the way she had spoken of the man, that Mama held him in great contempt. Yet, according to Aunt Evelyn, her mother had been overcome with grief after he left her. It seemed odd that if her mother did, in fact, love her father, she had managed to keep it a well-hidden secret from her daughter.

Aside from the fact that her mother and father weren't divorced, Lea had always assumed that her mother stayed away from men because she had an intense dislike for them. It had always been her mother's contention that males had an insatiable sexual desire and that their thoughts were ruled by the wants of their penises. Such carnal, lusting, thoughts were the results of males' basic inability to withstand the temptations of Satan. It had also been Mama's belief that males had a harder time finding salvation because of this.

Lea had always gotten the impression that her mother hated any and all sexual relations she had engaged in with her husband. Intercourse had demeaned, degraded, and humiliated Beatrice in her own eyes. That concept of sex, dirty and vile, had always disturbed Lea. In the Bible, it said that people should marry, be fruitful, and multiply. The very statements contained in the Holy Book were the opposite of what her mother preached, or at least so it seemed. Sex outside of marriage was fornication; but within the confines of wedlock, between husband and wife, it was considered a sinless and loving act.

Lea shook her head, trying to cast the thoughts from her brain. She shouldn't be thinking such things. Since she wasn't married nor planning to be, she had no right to allow such thoughts of sex to linger in her mind. It took very little to change thoughts of such physical encounters from the decent to the salacious, the prurient. She had to remove the temptation from her mind immediately or risk committing sin. She began to quote Biblical passages in a low whisper, in an attempt to wash the distasteful sensual thoughts away.

She was rounding a corner of the stacks, pushing her little cart ahead of her, when she spied him. He was young, perhaps twenty-two or twenty-three, very tall and lean, with a handsome face, and a thatch of dark curly hair. He looked up at her for an instant and smiled, then his focus returned again to his book. Lea stared at him for a moment. He had a nice face, strong and masculine.

As if a power stronger than she was in control, her

eyes began to move downward. The shirt fit tightly around his massive chest. It was unbuttoned almost midway, revealing dark curly hair. Lea's eyes lingered there a moment and then continued their steady descent.

The waist was small, as were the hips. The pants were tight, outlining his thighs, pulling close against them. Her eyes were trying to avert their gaze yet they were drawn as if by a magnet to the ample, rounded bulge of his pants.

For a moment, she stood there watching him. Suddenly she began to feel it. Her hands were warming, it was as if all the heat in her body was being concentrated in them. Her stomach was beginning to convulse and she could feel the sweat on her brow. She had committed a sin, one of lust, and God was punishing her.

Lea turned and began running in the direction of the ladies room. Her hands were burning. It felt like she was holding glowing coals that were blistering and searing her flesh. Cramps seized her stomach as wave after wave of nausea washed over her. She was beginning to gag. The sweat, the constant outpouring of fluid, moistened her clothing, causing it to adhere to the curves of her body.

She was running blindly, bent over, one hand holding her stomach, the other pressed against her mouth. She felt dizzy, almost as if she had stepped off a cliff and was journeying through some hideous black abyss. From the left, she heard someone call her name loudly, fearfully. Then came the footsteps, running toward her. She could barely make out the face of Ruth, the head librarian, as she neared, offering help. Through tear-filled eyes, Lea looked up at her, mumbled something incoherent, and then collapsed on the floor.

She was falling, falling into hell. There was no one to stop her, no one to save her. Around her a gray blur had formed. She could see nothing, save for the distorted shapes that bent around her. There was pain, knife-like, cutting at her insides, and there was fire, burning her hands and arms. Finally, as if the punishment was deemed sufficient, mercifully there was blackness, calm and quiet.

CHAPTER III

Lea lay on the bed, observing the willow tree swaying listlessly in the warm breeze outside her window. She had languished long enough in the confines of her room. She wanted to get up, move around, go back to work; but the doctors and Aunt Evelyn wouldn't hear of it.

Lea felt like such a fool. The episode at the library had effectuated her admittance to a local hospital. She was diagnosed as having an acute case of nervous exhaustion prompted by her irrational grief. Lea had remained in the psychiatric ward four days, floating through a half conscious, drug induced stupor, being closely observed like some crazed animal. The doctors had told her that, for a while at least, they thought it best for her to continue at the hospital as an out-patient. They said that it would enable her better to deal with the reality of her mother's sudden death. Lea declined, remembering her mother's admonitions concerning the sinfulness of psychiatry. At first they thought, because of the severity of the stomach pains, that she had been afflicted with some sort of physical ailment; but after a few tests were conducted, they determined that her symptoms were just a manifestation of her profound mourning. Lea didn't disagree with the doctors, nor tell them what had caused the strange complex of pain.

Confession was a good thing, at least that was what Mama had always said. When Lea was a little girl and Beatrice would punish her, she had always forced the girl to recount her sins, prior to feeling the sting of the strap on her buttocks. To confess to the doctors that the pain was punishment for the sin of lust, however, would have served no useful purpose. It would have humiliated and degraded her to admit it and they probably wouldn't have believed her anyway. After all, the God of physicians was the false messiah of science, not the Lord God Jehovah. Besides, she didn't want to give the medical people an excuse to keep her in the hospital any longer than absolutely necessary.

She had been discharged six days ago with a stern recommendation that she have sufficient amounts of bed rest and quiet. Lea had disregarded it but Aunt Evelyn hadn't. Mother had been reincarnated in the form of her aunt.

When she left the hospital, instead of going home, she was whisked away to Aunt Evelyn's. Lea had protested, but to no avail. She was so used to demonstrating absolute obedience to older women that she found the same attitude of quiet compliance spilling over into her relationship with her aunt. Evelyn had never had any children of her own, and so she looked upon Lea's presence as an excuse to let all her latent maternal instincts surface.

Immediately upon arriving, Lea had been stripped of her clothing, put in a nightgown, and forced into bed. She had accepted her sudden return to childhood with grudging resignation, but had drawn the line when Aunt Evelyn attempted to disrobe, bathe, and spoon-feed her. Lea would have none of such things.

The quick, hysterical onslaught of pain caused Lea less consternation then it did anyone else. She viewed it simply as being a just punishment for a sin committed against God. Lea accepted it, willingly, as being the baptism of pain which would wash her soul clean. If Mama had taught her nothing else, she had educated her in the punishment meted out by God, the wages of sin. He was a stern and demanding God who accepted nothing less than perfection in those whom He had created. When His beings strayed from the path of righteousness, He seized on them with wrath. This was what Lea had been taught and what she fervently believed. She had sinned and was punished, and that was that.

Lea wanted to be left alone with her Bible and her prayers, but Evelyn seemed to feel that such solitude was unhealthy. Consequently, she was continually bursting into the room, trying to interest Lea in a variety of inane conversations. It mildly angered Lea, but there was really little she could do about it. She knew that her aunt was well intentioned. Of course, the road to Hell was paved with good intentions. The statement was exemplified in the person of Aunt Evelyn.

This was the longest period of time that Lea had ever spent in her aunt's company. Lea had always realized that Evelyn had cared for her, but she had never before realized the depth of her feelings. If one disregarded the fact that she was not a church member, with its implications of damnation and continual sin, one could have easily interpreted the woman's actions as being a font of Christian charity. She was generous, kind, and understanding, possessing all the needed virtues for salvation. All her life Lea had been taught that her Aunt Evelyn was one of Satan's own; but now, seeing the inherent goodness in her, Lea began to question the validity of her mother's vilifications. Regardless of what Mama had said, Aunt Evelyn seemed more saintly than demonic.

Lea was listening to the gentle chirping of a bird when she heard the door to her room begin to creak open. Aunt Evelyn was once more about to intrude into the private world of her thoughts.

"Well dear, how we are feeling this afternoon?"

Lea's stomach knotted in irritation. For some strange reason, Aunt Evelyn insisted on addressing her in the same sing-song manner that one directs toward a toddler. Her head peered around the edge of the door, only half her face visible. It looked like she was attempting to play a game of peek-a-boo with her almost middleaged niece. This behavior disturbed Lea. She wasn't a child and she resented being treated like one. For a split second she thought about responding with a cutting remark, but then decided against it. The Bible demanded that one respect one's elders, under any and all circumstances. This was one of those times when she really wished that the Good Book hadn't been so specific.

"I'm feeling much better," she said, smiling sweetly, trying to mask the ingratitude and annoyance of her true sentiments.

"Oh, that's wonderful," the woman gushed. "I have a surprise for you," she stated emphatically, eyes twinkling.

Lea stared at her for a moment. To Aunt Evelyn, everything was a magnificent surprise; yesterday's was chocolate pudding for dessert. She really couldn't show any enthusiasm for what today's might be.

"Don't you want to know what it is?" Evelyn's lips pursed together, head turning from side to side trying to arouse Lea's interest.

Lea really didn't want to play this ridiculous guessing game, but under the circumstances she had little choice. Besides, she couldn't be nasty to Aunt Evelyn, not after all the woman had been doing for her. Lea curled her lips into a plastic smile, tried to look excited, and emitted a hollow, "Yes."

"I talked to the doctors today."

Lea's eyes narrowed. If Aunt Evelyn was once again going to try to convince her to go to group therapy, they'd surely have an extremely unpleasant debate on the subject. "They told me that by tomorrow you'll be up and about, feeling as good as new." There was genuine happiness in Evelyn's voice at her niece's evident return to good health.

The news made Lea's eyes open wide. That was what she had been waiting for. Now, she could go back to work; but best of all, she could go home to peace, quiet, and blessed solitude.

"Now Lea dear," Evelyn began," I want you to listen to me for a few minutes. I have something that I want to discuss. You promise you won't interrupt?" Aunt Evelyn was looking at her, concern evident in her face.

Something was bothering her.

Now what? Lea thought. Her aunt's manner was strange. Was it her imagination or were they actually about to have an adult conversation? It would be the first one since Lea's arrival.

"The doctors say that you're in need of a rest. A long one. We all feel that perhaps it would be best if you went away someplace for a month or so. A change of scenery would do you a lot of good. Maybe if you're away from the house, you'll be better able to adjust to your mother's death." Evelyn's eyes glowed with warmth and caring, her voice was gentle and soft, taking on the tones of velvet persuasion. "You can't expect to get over your loss, if you insist on going home every night to a darkened house that holds so many memories. After a month away, you'll be better able to cope with it, dear. Everything won't be so vivid to you."

"Aunt Evelyn, I can't do that," Lea stated categorically. "I have a position at the library to maintain. I can't just up and leave for a month. My superiors would never allow it."

"That's all been arranged, dear," Evelyn countered, closing off the first means of escape, crumbling Lea's argument.

"What?" Lea asked incredulously, her eyebrows moving higher and higher on her forehead. What had the meddlesome old biddy done?

"I've taken the liberty of contacting Mrs. Weston at the library. I explained the situation to her over the phone. She told me that you have some four months of accumulated vacation time. She said that you've never once taken a vacation, in all the years you've been there." Evelyn's voice demonstrated her disbelief.

42

"Dear, all work and no play makes Lea a very dull girl."

Lea was already angry, and throwing in a stupid cliché only served to increase its intensity.

"Mrs. Weston is such a nice person, so very understanding. Oh and Lea, she's so fond of you, so concerned! You're really quite lucky to have a boss like that." Evelyn paused for a moment, trying to determine how best to phrase her words. She didn't like to interfere in other people's lives but in Lea's case it was a different story. The young woman had never learned to do for herself, to take care of her own needs. If someone didn't take the time to give her some adequate direction, to make her slow down and view her mother's death in the appropriate perspective, the girl would wind up in an institution, suffering from a nervous breakdown.

"Now, Mrs. Weston and I have worked out a little plan which we feel will benefit you. She's going to take this past week or so off your sick leave and then starting Monday, that's the day after tomorrow dear. . ." She said the words slowly, attempting to clarify and assure that Lea understood. Evelyn didn't know if her illness had caused Lea to lose track of time. Lately it seemed that the young woman was living the totality of her life in memories, in the past.

"On Monday," she repeated, "Mrs. Weston is putting you down for four weeks vacation. You don't have to be back till August fourth. She said that you could even have an additional week or two should you require it. Isn't that wonderful?" She tried to give the words an uplifting spirit, as if it were the most exciting thing that could happen.

All the while, however, Evelyn was watching Lea's face for her angered reaction. The young woman was anything but delighted and her face showed it. Her cheeks were flushed, eyes set in a disdainful glare.

How dare she do such a thing! How dare she call Ruth and arrange this behind her back! What right did she have to interfere in her life without at least first consulting her? Lea's lips parted to say something, but she held back, afraid of the vicious barrage that she might hurl against her aunt. When were people going to learn to leave her alone, let her be her own person? The whole thing seemed so very futile, why say anything at all? The damage had already been done. Her colleagues at work probably thought her an incapacitated psycho. Lea wanted to scream out her rage, to let it fly, take joy in it; but she couldn't. It would have been a sin. Unleashed anger was wrong. It was an unkind act and, after the episode in the library, she could ill afford arousing God's anger. How could she be saved and sure if she kept committing sins?

Finally, words came from Lea's mouth, but they did not mirror what was going on inside her. Instead of loudly shouted epithets, the words were a mask of calm tolerance. "You needn't have gone to such trouble for me, Aunt Evelyn." The phrases might have provided a facade for her to hide behind, but the look on her face revealed the true emotions, hidden so well within the depths of the frail body.

"Now dear, you know I wouldn't think of interfering in your life, but really you do need a rest and I know how conscientious you are about your work. I knew that if I didn't do it, that you wouldn't! You're so bound up in this idea of duty and responsibility, that sometimes you're unable to see what harm it can do to you." Evelyn stared at her for a moment, to see if Lea had been moved, if the words had swayed her. It didn't appear so. "I was only acting in your best interest." The words had a half-pleading sound.

"I know you were." If the statement was supposed to give comfort to her aunt, it did not. The face was set in stone and the eyes resembled ice. "The only problem now is that I have no place to go." The words were snapped from the lips with no concern as to how they would be received.

"You're going to think I'm a terrible meddler, I know," her aunt said, hanging her head just slightly as if in embarrassment.

Lea continued the reproachful stare, thinking to herself that truer words had never been spoken.

"But I called a real estate agent up in Big Moose. He used to be a fishing buddy of your Uncle Adam's. I arranged for him to have someone go up and clean out the cabin; get the water, lights, and phone turned on. I hope you don't mind. It's really quite beautiful up there; you can hike, and fish, and swim. It will do you a world of good. I mean, after all, the place was just sitting up there falling into ruin. You might as well derive some benefit from owning it. Besides, what cheaper vacation is there than staying in your own little cabin in the woods, right?" She began to giggle, not out of mirth but from nervousness. Evelyn was afraid that she was about to have a confrontation with Lea over the cavalier way that she had moved in and begun taking over the younger woman's life. If she hadn't been so sure that she was doing the right thing, she wouldn't ever have attempted such action. To ride roughshod over Lea had been Beatrice's life's work. Evelyn felt a little guilty about continuing the same course of action that her sister had begun.

Of all the unmitigated gall! First she interferes with my work, then she sends me packing to the north woods! Lea looked at her aunt for a moment, not knowing what to say; then the barbs began to fly. "Aunt Evelyn, I'm not the outdoor type. I've never fished in my life and, in case you weren't aware of it, I don't know how to swim. Running around in a scanty bathing suit hardly corresponds with my religious beliefs. I really feel that the effort you've expended in planning this whole thing has been entirely wasted."

Evelyn moved away from the door, walking slowly across the room, finally stopping by the bed. She sat down next to Lea and put her arm securely around the young woman's shoulder. She stared squarely into Lea's big, blue eyes. "If I were in your shoes right now I'd be damn mad. Some old biddy trying to horn in and tell you how to live your life, is hardly what anyone wants. Look, I understand how you feel. Maybe I did overstep the bounds a little, but I thought I was doing right by you." Her voice was beginning to crack and moisture was beginning to build up in the corners of her eyes. "Lea, I love you very much." With that she placed a gentle kiss on the side of Lea's cheek.

For a moment Lea was taken aback. Such open, demonstrative displays of affection were not in her realm of experience. Yet it seemed that Aunt Evelyn was truly sincere. Perhaps Lea had acted unjustly in being angered by the woman's actions. Didn't the Bible teach that a person's intentions were what counted? Aunt Evelyn was certainly well-intentioned. Perhaps Lea had neither reason nor right to find fault. It was Christian charity to forgive the woman her misdirected concern.

"We are all that's left of our family, just you and me. We have to look out for one another and care about each other. If we don't, then who in hell is gonna?" She forced a weak smile at her niece and tried to continue. "I know you don't want me to get sick and I feel the same about you. If you stick around here any longer, you're on a one-way street to the lunatic asylum. I know you miss your mother terribly. For all these years, it was just you and her; but now, honey, it's just you. You've got to get that straight in your mind and accept it. That isn't going to happen if you insist on staying here." She opened her eyes wide. A tear began to trickle down the wrinkled cheek; then, as if an idea had just made itself known, her face burst into a big grin. "Does it say any place in the Bible that taking a vacation is a sin? Huh, does it?"

Lea giggled. Her aunt had her on that one. She began to shake her head from side to side.

"OK, it's no sin. Enjoying the sunshine is no sin either! The air is clean up there, no pollution. Does your Bible have a dictum on that?"

Lea convulsed with laughter. Her aunt was quite the character.

"Can't answer me, huh? I thought not. There's nothing in that Book that says what I want you to do is wrong. Even your wearing a bathing suit isn't wrong. You may not believe it, but I've read the Bible too! And, there isn't anything in there that addresses itself to such questions as proper bathing attire. The test of sin is doing something because you *want* to be bad. Your true intentions are the determining factor. Isn't that so?" she asked seriously.

47

Lea stopped laughing for a moment and stared at her aunt. It was hard to believe that the woman had ever opened the Holy Book, let alone read it. Grudgingly, she nodded her head in agreement. "If you wear a bathing suit or shorts and your intentions are not to be immodest, then you've committed no sin. Providing, that is, that they cover enough of your anatomy not to outrage public decency. Regardless, the cabin is quite a way off the main road and nobody is gonna see you anyway, except maybe a couple of racoons and a stray bear. So where's the harm?"

"Bears?" Lea questioned incredulously, between an outpouring of girlish giggles.

"Of course bears, dummy," Evelyn laughingly chided her, "Where the hell did you think you were going? New York City?"

At that, both burst into loud, riotous laghter. It was not usual for Lea to find profanity humorous, but in this case it seemed like such a *little* sin and besides, she couldn't help herself.

Lea put her arm around Evelyn's shoulder pulling her near. It was nice to feel the warmth of another human body next to her own. For a moment, she was truly touched by the tranquility she felt, even though the action was foreign to her.

When she was little, and had observed the way that other mothers held and fondled their little ones, she had sometimes gotten the feeling that her own mother disliked her, hated her; but, of course, now that she was older, she knew that to be a fallacy. It had just been Mama's way of doing things. Sometimes Beatrice's interpretation of Christian scripture was hard to take; but Lea supposed that it had been necessary. Still, being close to Aunt Evelyn didn't seem wrong. Their exchanging little signs of affection did not make her love God any less. So where was the sin in it? Lea sat, relishing this pleasure; the warmth and the caring, the feeling of being loved.

In a softly whispered voice, her aunt again began to speak. "You will go up to the cabin won't you? You'll go for me, won't you?"

Lea moved her head up against her aunt's cheek, turned, and quickly kissed her. "Yes," she said in mock resignation, "If that's really what you want, then I suppose it won't kill me to try it."

"Don't worry about getting lonely, because I'm going to call you every night; and maybe, in about two weeks or so, I'll come up and spend the weekend with you. I'll even teach you to fish. How'll that be?"

"That will be fine, just fine, Aunt Evelyn." Lea's eyes searched the woman's face. What a shame it was that she'd never borne children. She would have made a kind and caring mother.

"Now we need to get some things to take with you. I'm going to give them to you as a present," she announced. "Let's see, a bathing suit, some shorts and tops, sneakers, a fishing pole, tanning lotion. . . . Oh well, we'll think of the rest as we go along."

Evelyn rose from the bed and began walking around the room, pacing, as she worked out the time frames. Everything had to be accomplished and the girl on her way by Monday morning. The worst hurdle had been overcome—Lea had agreed to go; now, only the little incidentals remained to drive her crazy.

"You can go to the bank Monday morning and get enough money to take with you. I think traveler's checks would be best," she observed, thinking aloud. "We can go shopping tomorrow for the things you need. Most of the shopping centers will be open."

"Aunt Evelyn, really! We can't do that; tomorrow's the Sabbath!" It was one thing to agree to go on vacation, that didn't violate her religious beliefs; but it was quite another to not keep the Sabbath holy.

Aunt Evelyn gazed at her ruefully. Her plan of battle would have to be changed. It was unnerving to realize that ministers and their wives went shopping on Sundays but that her own niece refused. It was Evelyn's contention that religion was not wrong in itself, really quite the opposite, in fact; but the creed that her sister had followed and forced her daughter to adhere to was not ordained by God. It was rather the bitter, cruel prejudices of a woman who hated everything and everybody. Someday Evelyn hoped that she could make Lea realize that.

"I'm sorry," Evelyn stated matter of factly, not really meaning it, "I forgot." She paused a moment, thinking how best to overcome this momentary setback. "Do you feel well enough to do a little shopping?" she asked, taking note that Lea seemed chipper, had color in her cheeks, and appeared to have regained her strength.

"Yes, I think so," Lea responded, a hint of excitement now noticeable in her voice. She was looking forward to getting out of bed and out of the house into the warm summer sunshine. The reason why mattered little to her, nor the destination.

"Why don't you take a nap while I make us an early dinner. The shopping centers will be open until ten tonight so, if we leave after dinner, we should have enough time to get everything accomplished." Evelyn moved toward the bed, bent, and gently kissed Lea on the forehead. "You get a little rest now, you hear!"

Lea nodded her head, watching as her aunt left the room. It really wouldn't be that bad, being up at the cabin. Maybe Aunt Evelyn was right. Perhaps she really did need to get away. Her only concern now was how she'd keep from going crazy up there, for a whole month. A weekend could probably be tolerated; but four weeks seemed too much to ask.

She snuggled against her pillow, thinking about her coming period of forced relaxation. Lea remembered Evelyn speaking to her of her father's love for the area. Maybe, just maybe, being up there would bring back some recollections of the man and what he'd been like. If she could just remember even a little, then the month's exile would be worth it.

CHAPTER IV

She was rounding the corner, onto the deeply rutted, dirt, road. It wouldn't be long now. Everything had worked out much the way Aunt Evelyn had said it would. Lea was outfitted and set for a month's relaxation, whether she wanted it or not.

She had lessened the tedium of the drive, some five hours, by singing favorite hymns. It had actually been rather nice. There was something uplifting to the spirit in singing loud praises to the Lord while passing the majestic Adirondacks. For some reason, the scenery, the air, the greenness surrounding her, made Lea feel closer to God. Perhaps she had been too hasty in dismissing the whole concept of a vacation. If she viewed it as being a retreat of sorts, a time for spiritual renewal, the whole idea seemed more palatable. In fact, when she took the time to think it out logically, it seemed quite worthwhile. The only thing still disturbing her, however, was how a group of heathens, the doctors and Aunt Evelyn, had come up with such a summarily blessed plan. But it didn't really matter how the whole series of events had come to pass; only that God had ordained and decreed it to be a useful way in which to bring Lea more securely into His flock.

Lea stopped in the small village of Big Moose and found Ronald Penn's office. The real estate agent was helpful, informative, and really quite nice. He provided her with directions to the cabin and had expressed the desire that some evening, after she was settled in, she should come to his house for dinner to meet his wife and family. Lea couldn't believe the friendliness of the man. The unsociability of people in Albany was a far cry from the hospitality of the mountain dwellers of upstate New York.

He explained to her that everything was set for her arrival. The utilities had been turned on, the walls scrubbed down, and, as far as possible, the furniture made serviceable. Almost thirty years of disuse had taken its toll on the contents of the cabin. Rats had chewed and nested in some of the furniture, necessitating its being discarded. The rodents had also done a job on some of the appliances and interior wiring.

Ronald had taken the liberty of replacing the refrigerator, the mattress and box springs, the couch in the living room, and having some needed repairs made to the electrical system. When he presented her with the bills for the purchases and his services, she had been slightly taken aback. It really wasn't very much, only five hundred dollars. Most of the things purchased had been second hand and the wiring was done by a local handyman. All told, she determined that the cost was not exorbitant at all. It was well worth it, to have a clean and Godly place to reside and, furthermore, should she decide to sell the property at some later date, it would serve to increase the asking price. Lea paid the bill immediately. She didn't like making others wait for their due.

When Lea left the office, Ronald called after her, telling her to contact him should she require anything. Lea didn't know whether she'd like the area, but certainly had to be impressed by the neighborliness of its inhabitants.

She strolled through the village, staring into the tiny shops and purchasing the commodities needed to see her through the next few days. Everyone smiled and seemed friendly. In her travels, Lea came upon a small white church, the Big Moose Community Church. She was not sure which denomination it represented, nor its degree of Biblical adherence; only that it was Protestant and had Sunday morning worship. Whatever dogma it espoused, it was a good place to spend the Sabbath, as it was a temple to the Lord.

She'd expected that the tiny streets would be filled with tourists, refugees from the cities, descending on the north country to flush their lungs of pollution and let their spirits soar amidst the marvels of nature. It had not, however, been so. Except for a few backpackers, who came to walk the trails surrounding the Stillwater Reservoir, the area was devoid of outsiders.

Perhaps it was the ruggedness of the geography that kept the vacationers away. The area was wilderness in the true sense of the word. She had been told by Ronald that beyond her cabin, there wasn't another permanent structure for fifteen miles. Her property bordered on state land, what was referred to as a multiple use forest. The area was primitive, but held some attraction for experienced hikers who knew what they were doing and wanted to get away from it all. For miles on either side of the logging road, cutting through the forest, there was nothing except tall stands of timber, an abundance of streams, and a whole host of wild creatures both big and small. North of her, the closest residence was at the other end of the sixteen mile reservoir, the lonely ranger's station.

Lea was informed that on several occasions people had wandered into the forest and been enveloped by it, never leaving alive. In many instances, the bodies hadn't been found.

The area was just too large, too dangerous, even for the locals. When they explored the forest, they stayed within a mile or so of the road, never venturing further in. They left such bravado and blatant idiocy to the hikers from the city. The locals had a healthy respect for the mountains. They didn't want to tame them, but rather to live in peaceful coexistence with nature. The intruders from the city, however, had it in mind to conquer the forest. Therein lay their mistake. It was their bones that the small creatures gnawed.

Ronald cautioned that she not venture too far from the cabin and that she always remember to walk in the direction of the reservoir rather than up the mountains. If she could keep that in mind, she wouldn't become lost, for the road was never more than a scant mile west of the mass of shimmering, blue water. Lea took heed of his warnings and promised to abide by them. Besides, she wasn't all that adventurous. Although Lea wasn't particularly impressed by the worldly things of life on earth, she had no desire to shorten the duration of her time here.

She had been told by Ronald to prepare herself for some unwelcome night visitors. It was not unusual for bears, racoons, and skunks to scratch around the cabins at night, looking for easy food sources. Lea was told not to be frightened. They wouldn't hurt her unless she tried to scare them away. It was not wise to provoke them, for they took easy offense at even the slightest act of inhospitality. Lea laughed at his admonition, telling him that she had no intention of meeting a bear in face-to-face confrontation. They could take what they wanted, providing, of course, that they let her be.

The speed of her travel had slowed considerably. If she moved faster than ten miles an hour, she ran the danger of hitting a rut and ripping out the undercarriage of her car. There was a certain strangeness about the road and its surrounding area. When she had been on the main road, the sun was out full strength, lighting all that its rays touched; but now, under the canopy of trees, it appeared as if she had entered a land of perennial dusk. In a way it was eerie, but then what could one expect in the wilderness? The only things indicating that she hadn't totally left civilization were the power poles that stood by the side of the road. They attested to the fact that someplace at the end of her journey there was a structure that contained all the amenities of modern living.

Lea had been told that her cabin lay about a mile from the road, yet it seemed much further than that. She had been traveling down this rutted track for at least ten minutes and still hadn't come to it. As she passed the deep, green foliage, Lea tried to concentrate and remember. Had she walked this path in early childhood? She couldn't recollect. Nothing looked even vaguely familiar.

Lea was turning her head from side to side, admiring God's handiwork, when on the left, her eyes came to rest on a scene of rare beauty. Barely one hundred feet from the road stood a fifty-foot waterfall. It cascaded down a rock ledge, which hovered over the pine forest.

Lea brought the car to a halt, got out and began moving toward the sylvan beauty of that place. In all her days, she had never seen anything quite like it. She stood watching as the water rushed over the cliff, forming a clear deep pool below it. She bent near the water's edge, gingerly thrusting in her hand. The clear liquid was numbing to the touch. It looked so inviting, yet to submerge one's self in the frothy cascade might be to invite pneumonia.

Lea stared down at the shimmering pool, suddenly taken by an all-consuming urge to discard her clothing and stand naked under the falls; to let the icy droplets caress her warm flesh and arouse it with their tingling touch.

Mindful of the sensual character of her thoughts, the possible sinfulness, danger, inherent in letting her brain wander so, she moved away from the bank. Why had she conceived such an idea? Lea waited for her mind's answer, but it did not come. As Aunt Evelyn had explained, there was nothing sinful in exposing the human body, as long as it was done with innocent intention. Yet, there had to be something wicked in the very act of being naked, for the body and all its functions were vile and filth. Although Lea couldn't identify nor give name to it, she was sure that in some manner nudity offended the Almighty. Not wanting to be tempted by thoughts that seemed impure, Lea

60

returned to her car, resuming the last leg of her journey.

The further along the road she went, the less light seemed to penetrate. Lea knew that it must be nearing sundown, yet one couldn't be sure. It had been dusk since she entered the forest. It was as if the sun never kissed this place, avoided it as though something evil existed here. She dismissed the strange feeling. Never having been to the mountains before, she had no basis for comparison.

From the time that she was a very little girl, Lea had feared the darkness, been apprehensive of the things that lived within its realms. To this day, she always had a night light burning in her room. There was something that soothed her soul in even the tiniest ray of light. In many ways, she still possessed the fears of a child. When she was little, she'd believed that monsters inhabited the blackness. Now, although she was an adult and knew that such things didn't exist, the darkness still terrified her. The fear was so ingrained that before going to the bank this morning, Lea had stopped at the supermarket and bought a nightlight for her room at the cabin. She had tried to resist this foolish, fearful whim, but in the end had decided that the month was meant to be a relaxing vacation, not a test of whether she could or could not overcome her childhood fears of being alone in the dark.

The muscles in her back began to ache. Lea tried to convince herself that it was the long drive, but deep inside she knew that it was caused by the realization that time here would be spent in semi-dark solitude. She chastised herself. She was a grown woman, demanding to be treated as such. Lea had complained bitterly and often about being treated like a child; but how could she expect to be treated otherwise, if she herself refused to act like a grownup, like a rational thinking adult? Was it normal for a thirty-three-year-old to still be afraid of the dark? She hardly thought so. Besides, what was it she was so afraid of? Wasn't God always with her, protecting her, keeping her safe from harm? True, but no matter how hard she tried, Lea seemed unable to wash the apprehension from her mind.

Three hundred feet ahead, the road came to an abrupt halt in what appeared to be a small grassy clearing. Lea strained her eyes to locate the cabin, but she couldn't find it. Ronald hadn't mentioned that it was located well off the road.

She brought the little white Pinto to a halt. Right now, the most pressing thing on her mind was the proximity of the cabin. She'd have to unload the car alone. That would be quite a chore in itself; but to move each cumbersome suitcase and box over the span of, say, a few hundred feet, would be extremely difficult and physically taxing, to say the least. Besides, it was getting late and the blackness of night would soon be upon her. She had no particular desire to trudge past the bears and other night creatures that Ronald had told her about. If possible, Lea wanted to get everything moved in and unpacked tonight so that she could spend all day tomorrow recuperating from the long drive.

Lea stood in the clearing moving slowly in a circle, trying to find the outline of the cabin amidst the woods that surrounded her.

With each pass, she felt her heart throb. What would she do if she couldn't find it tonight? Where would she sleep? Bedding down in the car would not provide her the protection she required; there was too much glass.

Things could see her. She'd be vulnerable. Suppose animals wandered by or, for that matter, people who might mean her harm. Where could she hide? Where would she be safe and secure?

It was on her third scan of the area that she spotted something darker than normal, in the woods to her right. Lea couldn't make out clearly what it was, but thought that perhaps it might be the cabin.

Returning to the wheel of her car, she drove into the high, green grass of the clearing, toward the shadows. There were nerve-shattering sounds of metal scapping rock, as the car's bottom dragged across stones hidden in the tall mountain grasses.

As she neared the darkened hulk, Lea breathed a sigh of relief. It was a structure. The closer she drew to the building the more surprised she became. The cabin was larger than she expected, much larger. It was hewn from dark logs and covered perhaps thirty-five feet in width. One side of the bottom floor had a fairly flat roof, but on the other was a small peak, and in its uppermost point, a tiny glass window. In a way, it resembled the momentary vision she had had when its existence became known to her. Perhaps it was just coincidence. After all, she couldn't see the blue water that had been a dominant portion of her imagined scene.

The exterior appeared to be in good condition. It had weathered the past years of abandonment well. There was a small porch outside the front door and on it stood log benches. The scene was rustic, with a primitive beauty that she found both breathtaking and calming. Tall evergreens surrounded the cabin and the ground around it was covered by a thick, spongy layer of pine needles, causing the earth to appear a burnished brown.

All her fears dissipated. Something about the mountains, the forest, and the cabin excited her. Perhaps being here alone for a month would not be so bad after all.

The closest she could get to the cabin without crashing the car into a tree, was perhaps a hundred feet away. Lea put on the brake and looked at her surroundings. There didn't appear to be much remodeling or repair for her to do, at least not to the outside. Even the windows seemed to have been recently washed.

Lea got out of the vehicle and began walking toward the cabin's front door. She was immediately aware of the sweet smell of pine, like a heady perfume that made one's head swim and swirl with rapture. Except for the soft crunching, crackling noise of her own feet on the needles and cones, there was no other sound to be heard. Lea looked up, trying to find a break in the tree cover, so that she could see the sky; but the darkening blue above could only be viewed in small, segmented patches. Her eyes were drawn to the small second story window. Something appeared to be glinting up there. A chill ran through her. Lea had the distinct feeling that she was being watched. She ceased moving and stood stone-like, staring up at the window. It was the only one visible in the cabin that appeared not to have been washed. A heavy film of dirt caused distortion and blocked the interior from view. Lea felt her heart pound. Was it her imagination or was there, in fact, a grotesque form with glinting eyes, glaring down at her from above? For a moment, she continued staring, afraid to move a muscle.

Then, as if by magic, the flickering specs of golden light disappeared and were reborn in a downstair's window. Her heart calmed, the palpitations slowed. It wasn't anything to be feared, just an optical illusion, for nothing could move that fast. The focus of her eyes shifted to scan the treetops above. The sun's rays were filtering through the leaves of the trees. The glints of light had been the last dying reflections of the sun's glow. Lea breathed in deeply, amazed at her own timidity and stupidity. How could anybody possibly be in the house? The locks had just been changed, and she had the only key. Ronald had assured her of that. She was creating ghosts where there were none.

Lea had thought that the monsters had long ago left her, that the horror-filled, fantasy world had ceased to exist; but it now seemed that they had not totally abandoned her. She might have physically grown older, but the fears and dreads of childhood still inhabited her mind.

She ascended the stairs to the porch, bouncing slightly on each one, assuring that the boards had not been weakened by years of disuse. They certainly seemed sturdy enough.

Lea crossed the floor, reaching into the pocket of her jeans, pulling out the key which would grant her entrance. No matter how hard she tried, Lea couldn't feel comfortable wearing the things. She had never before worn trousers. Mama had always insisted that they contradicted God's Biblical canons concerning the distinction between the sexes. It was Mama's contention that if God had wanted women to wear pants and look like men He would have created them male.

Aunt Evelyn and Lea had argued fiercely about buying them, but as seemed the norm of late, her headstrong aunt won out. Evelyn had insisted that being in the woods and wearing a skirt or dress were mutually exclusive.

"You've got to keep your legs covered when walking in the woods," Aunt Evelyn had cautioned her, "or your shins will get eaten alive by bugs and cut to pieces by the pricker bushes. God doesn't want his flock, his littlest lost lamb, torn and tattered, does He?"

Lea was grudgingly forced to agree, finally asceding to Aunt Evelyn's wishes. It was easier to obey than argue with the willful woman. It was becoming more and more evident to Lea, as time went on, that her mother and aunt were truly alike, cut from the same bolt of cloth as it were. Apparently, both saw in Lea a being ripe for domination. To see and know one of the sisters was precisely the same as having stood in the presence of the other. For all the disparity in their life styles, they were, in actuality and irrefutably, one and the same.

Lea retrieved the key, slowly inserting it in the lock. Waves of apprehension like those that had previously enshrouded her, were once again her companion. Lea turned the knob, hearing the mechanism click; then with one thrust, she pushed it open, being sure to maintain her footing on the threshold. The door creaked as it swung inward, revealing the dark interior. As if she had just opened a refrigerator, a blast of cold assailed her body.

Lea peered in and with uncharacteristic bravery, stepped over the threshold. For a moment, she stood disbelieving her own eyes, thinking that she had entered the wrong building and this wasn't her cabin after all. The interior was not as Ronald described. There was nothing ramshackle about it. The walls appeared freshly painted and the furniture was homey and comfortable, with a large overstuffed sofa and big wooden rockers. Even the draperies looked new. The coffee and end tables were of heavy wood, displaying high gloss that she couldn't imagine had withstood the period of abandonment. For a moment, she thought about leaving the building and searching for a second structure, the one that she owned; yet Ronald had given her the impression that the cabin was situated wholly alone in the woods. She stared down at the key, still held firmly in her hand. If this wasn't her property, why did the key work? It had to be hers, yet it wasn't what she'd been led to believe would be here.

Her eyes were drawn to the deep, pile rug that lay before the couch. It was made of a fur-like fabric giving it the appearance of an animal pelt. She knew that fabrics such as this were a relatively new development, not available in the 1940's. Where had it come from? Ronald had told her that he'd bought some second-hand things very cheaply to replace the furniture which had been damaged, but none of this appeared to be used. The cost of the rug and couch alone would have far exceeded the five hundred dollars that the real estate agent had billed her. So the question remained, where had it all come from?

Lea mulled over their possible origin, but couldn't figure it out. They weren't a present from Aunt Evelyn. She didn't have the extra funds to expend for such niceties. They obviously weren't the remnants of an earlier time, so how could she explain their present placement in her living room? Lea racked her brain a few moments longer, finally shaking her head, thinking there must be a logical explanation. The hour, however, was late. She'd do better to free her brain for other pursuits.

She moved from the living room into the kitchen. It was large, with handmade maple cabinets, really quite quaint. There was an ancient gas range and a small white refrigerator. In the middle of the room stood an old-fashioned black and white kitchen table; not particularly attractive, but serviceable nevertheless. The shine emanating from the tile floor gave her pause for thought. Whoever had taken the responsibility for cleaning the cabin must have been an exemplary worker. The walls were clean and white, and the floor shone with several coats of wax. Even the tiles and fixtures around the sink were sparkling brightly.

From the kitchen, she moved to the bedroom. The furniture there appeared old and valuable. The bed was massive, covered by a comforter and sheets made from red satin. Lea ran her fingers over the fabric. It felt strange to her, so smooth and luxurious. She had seen such things in stores, but never before had she seen satin in this particular color red. Its hue was that of fresh blood, a bright, mesmerizing crimson.

There was a large dresser in the room and above it hung a large, carved, wood framed mirror. Across the room was a matching highboy. Her eyes surveyed the area. Although the furniture was massive, it hardly filled the room. The space looked empty, almost as if something else belonged there. In an area approximately twenty by fifteen feet, three pieces of furniture tended to look lost.

Except for a strange looking wall hanging, secured above the headboard, the walls were devoid of decoration. Lea neared the hanging and observed it closely. In the center was a five-pointed star, surrounded by depictions of what looked like tiny men and women worshiping it. They were naked, some alone, some locked in sensual embrace; all with arms outstretched toward the black outlined star. Lea studied it, unable to determine its significance. Her eyes lingered there, unable to move away. What form of pagan ritual did the scene show? Something in the picture stirred her. Lea's hands shook, her palms sweating profusely. The longer she gazed at it, the more the hanging came to life. The little figures seemed to move across her field of vision, touching, caressing, succumbing to their naked lust. It was almost as if she were viewing their cavorting through a thick haze of fog.

She jerked her head to the side and broke the object's spell. Lea was shaken. Perhaps she was sicker then she thought. Maybe she really did need a rest. How, other than illness, could one explain the movement of inanimate objects? It had to be her imagination, or perhaps she was overtired from the long, exhausting trip. Whatever the reason, the experience served to frighten her.

Lea moved from the room, searching other areas of the cabin, looking for the second bedroom, the place where she had slept as a child. She retraced her steps through the house but couldn't find it. Lea opened all the doors she encountered, revealing a myriad of cupboards and cubbyholes; but no evidence of her childhood room.

When she checked the area three times over, Lea moved to the back door and opened it, letting the warming breeze blow through the cabin. Turning, she noticed that there was an area, large enough to be a door, covered over with thin strips of grey planking.

She knew immediately that it hadn't been part of the original construction of the building. The color and texture of the wood was different from that on either side of it. Strange, but it appeared that someone had wanted to seal off one area of the house. Lea moved toward the spot, reaching out to touch the boards, checking to see if any were loose enough to pull away, revealing what lay concealed behind them. There was a preponderance of nails at either end of the planks. None were the least bit loose. As her fingers touched the rough hewn wood, a feeling of extreme cold ran through her body. Lea's skin puckered into goose flesh, as the frigid waves swept over her. She shrank away from it at once, almost in fear. An ominous feeling came with the chill, giving her the impression that some horror-filled evil lay just behind the wall. For a few seconds, she stood staring, trying to decipher all the different emotions that were swirling through her. Lea tried to think of her childhood, to search for a reason for the strange reaction. Did the fear stem from something that had happened long ago, an event so terrible and frightening that it couldn't be recollected, could not be brought out of the dimness into the realm of conscious thought?

Lea wished that she'd never allowed Aunt Evelyn to talk her into this. Something about the place frightened her, caused her mind to take flight in grotesque fantasy. She was already upset and distraught over Mother's sudden death. She didn't need anything else hacking away at her brain.

Lea pushed open the back door and moved outside, away from the fear, away from the cold. She stood a few paces from the cabin and tried to regain her fast crumbling composure. Her eyes scanned the exterior,

70

and came to rest on the second floor. Perhaps that was the area that was closed off. In her wanderings, she had found no means of access to the second story. There were no stairs, no ladder, no anything. From its outside appearance, she could tell that it wasn't just an attic. Why would anyone want an attic in a cabin and, why would anyone put windows in it? It must have been the other bedroom, but then why was it sealed? Even more intriguing was conjecturing who might have done such a thing. It had to have been done a long time ago. Following that basic assumption, there were only two people who could have sealed it off; one was her mother, the other her father. Things her aunt had said about Beatrice's reaction to the breakup of her marriage suddenly came back. Perhaps her mother had done it after Daddy left. Perhaps the upstairs room had been the one her parents had shared, not the one on the lower floor as she had originally thought. Mayber her mother had been so overcome with grief after being deserted, that she had sealed off the room, unable to face the memories it held for her. It seemed a logical conclusion, but then why her own hysterical reaction to the planking and the feeling of doom she had felt concerning what lay on the other side of the wall? Lea searched for a reason. Could it be that there had been a fight that night, that it had been vociferous and vindictive, and had sorely frightened the little girl who once lived here? Aunt Evelyn had said that Lea and her father had been extremely close. Perhaps his desertion had profoundly traumatized her. Just because she couldn't remember, didn't mean her subconscious did not. If her parents had argued and she had heard, couldn't that account for her fear of the room? Wouldn't a little girl, now grown to adulthood, fear the place, a room, where loud screaming and arguing had gone on? The more Lea thought about it, the more she was convinced that that was, in fact, what had probably happened. It was just a little girl's fear coming to light.

Lea shook her head at the idiocy of her fears. For a woman of thirty-three, she often acted like a small, panic-ridden child. At some point, she'd have to learn to live with her own foolish phobias, and now seemed as good a time as any. She'd spend her month of quiet solitude here, learning not to fear the darkness, not to fear being alone. For most people, growing up, self reliance, abolition of childhood fear and fantasy, were an inevitable by-product of the aging process. However, it had not been so for Lea. Perhaps a month of confrontation with her anxieties, thinking them out, and finally laying them to rest, might be the best thing that could happen to her. It was the type of rest and recuperation that a psychiatrist might have recommended as being valuable therapy.

Lea walked around the side of the house, toward the front yard and her car. It was getting late and she wanted to unload it before nightfall. As she speeded her pace, her head turned from side to side admiring the wonders of nature that surrounded her. It wouldn't be so bad here. It might, in fact, turn out to be an enjoyable and enlightening experience. Lea tried to reassure herself that all would be well, to be convinced of it; but, although one facet of her being agreed, a strange child's voice echoed in her mind, whispering, "Run!"

CHAPTER V

Lea dipped the last of her bread into the thickened mass of sauce. For some curious reason, she was ravenous. The anorexia, as the doctors called it, the severe, unexplained, loss of appetite that she had suffered since Mother's death, had disappeared. Normally, she hated the taste of canned food, eating it only when necessity dictated; but tonight was different. The ravioli tasted so good that if she had had more, Lea would have wolfed that down too. Perhaps it was the clean, crisp air that caused her appetite to increase. Regardless of what it was, she was grateful that it had occurred. For the longest time, Lea had been fearful that she'd waste away to nothing. Now, that was one less worry that she'd have to contend with.

She chewed the crust voraciously, savoring the spicy flavor of the sauce. Lea was quite pleased with herself. She had moved all the suitcases and boxes into the cabin and had managed to unpack every piece of assorted junk that she had carted up here. Now, there was nothing pressuring her, no work to be done, no necessary exertion; only relaxation, deep and contemplative.

Lea leaned back in the chair, allowing herself to revel in the full feeling of her belly. She was content, yet not wholly at peace with herself. The last three hours in the cabin had caused her some degree of consternation. She'd touch something and a lightning-like vision of a long ago scene would appear in her brain; but it would linger only a second, causing more questions than it answered.

Lea knew that she had been here before, was familiar with all the various nooks and crannies, yet she seemed unable to recollect that portion of her life. Was it really that she couldn't remember or that she just didn't want to? Maybe the past held too much hurt to allow her conscious mind to retrace the steps, to relive or remember those times. The recollections were locked away in her brain, she knew that. Lea had been allowed momentary glimpses, but that was all. Her inner most being was keeping secrets, guarding them, maintaining them deep within her forgotten subconscious, denying her the complete knowledge of her past. Strange—Lea had always thought that she knew and understood herself well, was conscious of all aspects of her being; but perhaps she had deluded herself.

Lea shook her head with a certain degree of amusement. For a person who always spoke of psychologists and psychiatrists in only the most deprecating terms, in her own amateurish and inept fashion she was one and the same with them. Perhaps if she could convince herself to concentrate less on the past and what had gone before, the memories would come forward of their own volition. Constantly forcing her mind to relive scenes of her childhood would accomplish nothing. With the passage of time and her body's physical movement over paths once walked, her memory might respond. If not, she'd just have to accept the fact that that portion of her life would be lost forever. In the end, her mind ruled and was master, it held sway and power over her; not she over it.

Lea was tired. She rose slowly from the chair and looked down at the dirty plate that lay on the table in front of her. Should she leave it till tomorrow or take the extra few minutes and clean up the minor mess that she had created? It was out of character for her to allow any chore to be postponed. Procrastination was the equivalent of idleness and that, as the Bible said, was an open invitation for Satan to come into one's heart. The notion of relaxation was fine, but changing her mode of conduct, life style, perception of required duties and responsibilities was not so easy. It would take more than one day of a vacation to change such ingrained patterns of behavior. Lea might be exhausted, but the dishes had to be done and the kitchen cleaned before she'd allow herself any rest.

She picked up the plate, fork, and soiled napkin and began carrying them in the direction of the sink. Lea stopped for a moment, wondering whether or not she had had the presence of mind to bring some dish detergent. She drew a complete blank.

In some things, Lea was wholly responsible; but in others, she was totally lacking in that quality. Mama had always told her that she'd have long ago lost her head if it wasn't attached. Through the years her mother had given continuous and unending lectures on this most obvious shortcoming; Lea's memory, or more aptly put, lack of it. Lea was far more absentminded now, than she had ever been before. Perhaps it was because she no longer had Mama to remind her of every minute detail.

Forgetting the detergent was a minor disappointment to Lea. She was quite proud of herself and the manner in which the whole matter of the vacation had been handled. Of course, she had to give Aunt Evelyn a great deal of the credit, but still, a lot of the little details had been remembered and accomplished by Lea herself. Mama would have been proud!

Lea washed the table and stove with plain tap water, but she required soap for the eating and cooking utensils. She scraped and neatly arranged them in the sink, waiting for a brainstorm to tell her how to clean them. At this point any soap would do. Lea was tired and wanted to get it done so she could get some sleep. She was on her way to the bathroom to get a bar of face soap when she was struck by the idea that perhaps the cleaning person might have left something appropriate behind. Lea turned and went to the sink, bending to open the cabinet which lay beneath it. Sure enough, there was a bottle of dishwashing liquid that was three-quarters full. The cleaning lady must have used it to wash the china and silverware. Lea reached in and pulled the plastic container forward, smiling to herself, pleased at the discovery.

She bent a little lower, attempting to see what other useful things might be contained in the cabinet. Then, suddenly, the expression on her face changed from one of happiness to that of terror. Her mouth emitted a long, shrill scream as her eyes fell upon the object. Her hands shook so severely that she dropped the detergent.

The longer Lea stared at it, the more her body was convulsed with fearful sobs. It was a thing of pain, an object of hurt. From deep within came a little girl's voice, crying out, "No!" Unconsciously, she began backing away from the small dark cubicle and its hidden instrument of torture; the heinous, yet innocent-looking scrub brush.

She grew still, paralyzed with fear. It appeared to be moving out of the confines of the cabinet, coming toward her, ready to attack the vulnerable, frail form that was Lea.

There was fire. It was coming from within her body, burning out of her insides, searing the flesh of her hands. Again the screams began as the pain took hold. Flames of excrutiating agony lashed at her long thin fingers and pale white palms.

The demon thing, the long, rectangular, plague of pain, was moving closer to the opening of the cabinet. Soon, it would drop to the floor and begin crossing the tile, trying to get her, to cause her harm.

Lea fell to her knees, pulling her hands close against her breasts, in an attempt to somehow make the pain subside. As the thing drew closer, she hung her head and closed her eyes tightly, in a vain attempt to shut it out of her consciousness. Her mind exploded into a gigantic screen, where vibrant colored scenes of horror were unfolding.

The predominant color was blood red. Shades of crimson, moving, swirling, spurting; first thin, then becoming a thick, gelatinous mass. It filled the screen, covered it. Then, something small and pink came into view. At first it appeared vague and out of focus; but

79

then the image cleared. It was the hand of a child.

It was from this small piece of flesh that the crimson came. Within the little one's palms were thin, long, lines, each one spreading and wounding the soft, pink tissue. Every cut appeared as a small rivulet, a stream of bright blood. Lea's ears resounded with the piercing reverberation of screams and cries, but not her own; they were coming from the child. It was a girl, young, very young, barely more than a baby. She was pleading with someone, but the fear and hysteria that possessed the little girl caused the words to flow out in one indiscernible mass. Lea could not distinguish where one word ended and the other began.

From amidst the blood, came a larger hand. Its thin, boney fingers grasped the small wrist and held it firmly as the scrub brush moved into view. Unmercifully, it began slashing back and forth at the soft, tender flesh.

The tormented little voice screamed louder still, as did Lea. She could watch no longer. She had to open her eyes, to make it stop, to eradicate this obscene vision. Her lids burst open and once again she came face to face with the actuality of the scrub brush. Lea's hands, still burning, felt like fire, just as the child's had. What was happening? What strange nightmare had she witnessed? Her chest heaving with terror, Lea reached out her hand, the arm shaking from the constant severity of the pain, and hit the cabinet door, forcing it closed with a loud bang.

Lea's chest continued straining up and down as she attempted to calm herself. She was hysterical, just as the little girl in the vision had been. Was she hallucinating or were these strange things really happening to her? Had the scrub brush really moved, or had it only happened in her imagination?

For a time, her heart pounded, feeling as if it had come to rest, with painful effect, in the center of her throat. Lea remained on her knees, but began rocking back and forth in the vain hopes that somehow the constant, continual, movement might somehow serve to alleviate the pain.

Her gaze lingered on the cabinet door. Like a small child watching fearfully for the bogey man, she waited for the door to begin frantically banging, for the thing to escape the dark confines of its prison and attack her. She watched and waited, finding herself becoming more and more calm as the moments passed without incident.

After ten minutes, the rocking motion ceased, her breathing became less strained and her heart returned to its normal rhythm. Once the blind panic subsided, it would be easier to look at the horrifying event and the occurrences that surrounded it with a cold, clinical eye. She wondered, though, if fear and its causes were so easily analyzed.

Slowly and with great effort, Lea rose from the floor and moved to the chair by the table, all the while keeping a watchful eye on the cabinet. The object that had terrified her so was only a scrub brush; a common, ordinary, household tool, useful and innocuous. Over the years, she had seen many such implements, but they had never effected her like this. Lea racked her brain. Had she ever touched one, used it, been pricked by the bristles? She thought not. The fear was irrational, having no basis in logic. Why should a person who has never been hurt by an object suddenly fear for her life when in that object's presence? What kind of encounter could engender such fear?

Lea stared at the door, deciding that the movement of the scrub brush within was something that her panic had created, an illusion, not something that had actually occurred. To prove it, she'd have to open the door and confront the object.

Lea rose and began walking hesitatingly toward the sink. Bravery had never been her strong suit; but if she didn't want to have a breakdown right here, right now, she'd have to nip this fear, this panic, in the bud. If she allowed herself this aberration, let it happen this time, then tomorrow it could be a soda bottle, or a bed sheet, shoes, even her own hand which could terrorize her.

Scrub brushes don't move of their own volition. They are not demons. They can do only what a human bids them. Those thoughts kept repeating over and over in her brain.

Lea moved more slowly toward the cabinet, wondering if perhaps there were things that existed outside the realm of logic and reason, things that rose from the bowels of Hell to convulse the Godly with dread and terror. Could the demon scrub brush be one of those things?

Enough of this childish trepidation. Somewhere during the course of the last few minutes, Lea had become phobic to the point of almost driving herself over the edge of sanity. The stupidity had to stop. Hobgoblins did not inhabit the cabin. No ghoulish, grisly, macabre creatures waited within the darkened corners to pounce and devour her. Such things did not abide in the real world; they existed solely in the morbid confines of her mind. If it was sickness, then it must be purged. Those that were righteous always prevailed.

Isn't that what the Bible said? If she was good and followed the pathways of the Lord, then who could harm her? With the Lord God Jehovah as her champion, how could she perish? The words gave some small measure of solace and imbued her with the strength she needed to examine the occurrence and its causes.

Her pace quickened and her walk became purposeful.

"If God is with me," she whispered in a barely audible voice, "Then who shall have the strength to be against me?"

Lea stopped two paces from the cabinet door, staring down at it with dread. After a second, her eyes began darting from side to side, determining what the best plan of retreat would be should nightmares have the ability to become reality. After assuring herself that, if necessary, she could be out the back door in a matter of only a few seconds, Lea was ready to begin.

She bent and wrapped her fingers loosely around the handle of the door, allowing them to linger a moment, waiting to see if the burning sensation returned. After assuring that the pain response had something to do with visual contact with the object, she mustered all her bravery and pulled the door wide open. As she laid eyes on the brush, her first rection was to bolt, escape; but she didn't. Instead, she stood her ground, closely scrutinizing the object. It didn't look very frightening from her present vantage point.

As the seconds melded into minutes and still nothing occurred, Lea became more bold, kicking at the bristles with the toe of her shoe. As it did not respond with an attack, she grew even more contemptuous in her treatment of it, finally picking it up with the tips of her fingers and flinging it hard against the floor. Still, it didn't move. The monster had lost its power. Convinced that it had all been just a trick of her own imagination, Lea breathed a great sigh of relief.

Calm and happy, but most of all proud of herself for facing her fears, Lea moved to lift the brush and examine it more closely. As her fingers encircled it, she was suddenly conscious of its weight. Its size was deceiving, it was really quite heavy. Rows of even bristles were attached to the thick piece of hardboard. From its appearance, the washed out look of the wood and the splintered ends of some of the bristles, she could tell that it was quite old. Perhaps it had remained here, hidden away in the dark cubicle, since the time her parents occupied the building. Examining it closely now, she was without fear; yet only minutes before, it had aroused her to the epitome of panic; why? What was it about this utensil that caused her to deem it a threat, view it as an implement of torture? Where in her realm of experience had she encountered one before? She couldn't remember. Mama had never kept one in the house, neither did Aunt Evelyn. Lea's thoughts focused on the nightmarish vision of the little girl's hand being scrubbed raw by the brush. Had she ever seen such a thing happen? If so, its memory eluded her. What kind of monster would hurt a tiny child that way? Certainly no one she knew.

As Lea turned the object over and over again in her hands, observing it from all the various angles, she was startled to find herself staring more at her own flesh than at the wood and bristle structure of the brush. Why had the burning sensation developed in her hands? The pain began prior to shutting her eyes and seeing the little girl's blood. Why should she associate pain with a scrub brush? Why should she be fearful of it, unless she'd experienced its hurt, unless Lea was the child who'd called out? The thought disturbed her greatly. If such a traumatic thing had, in fact, happened, she would have remembered—wouldn't she? Lea pondered a moment, then realized that perhaps she wouldn't have; after all, most of her early life was a mystery.

Lea shook her head roughly from side to side, trying to scatter the thoughts and fling them out of her brain. How could she possibly conceive of herself as that pitiful, tormented child? She'd been raised strictly, corporal punishment being the directive of God; but what she had envisioned was pure torture. The larger hand in the scene belonged to a woman. Lea could tell, from its shape and the smoothness of the skin. There had only been two women whom she had been close to during her lifetime. One was her mother, and the other Aunt Evelyn. Her aunt, however, had never so much as yelled at Lea; that left only Mama.

Her mother had always been the sternest of disciplinarians. Over the years Lea had had her mouth washed out with soap, had her backside hit with paddles, hairbrushes, switches, belts, and a razor strap; and often, as she got older, her mother would force several quarts of warm soapy water into her as punishment for misbehavior. It was discipline in its most severe form, but it was not torture. What had happened to the little girl was nothing less than hideous, blatant abuse. There had been many times in the past when Lea had disliked, almost hated her mother, feeling that she was cruel and uncaring; but even at those times, she could not have thought her mother guilty of such an act. The little girl could not have been Lea! Her identity would have to remain a mystery.

She was exhausted, and standing here contemplating pieces to unsolvable puzzles was bringing her no closer to the rest she needed. Lea put the brush back under the sink and began mechanically and methodically to start the dishwashing process. All the while, the focus of her thought remained on the identity of the child. If only Lea had been able to see the frail little thing's face, then perhaps she might be able to identify her.

By the time the dishes had been washed, dried, and put away, she was no closer to an answer then she had been before. When the last task was done, Lea, needing some kind of mental resolution to her quandry, decided that long ago she must have had a nightmare about the little girl. The sight of the scrub brush today brought back the vivid scenes of her dream and Lea, not understanding the source of the fear, had panicked and began to hallucinate. It sounded logical.

To wipe her mind clean of unpleasant thoughts, she began singing "Onward Christian Soldiers," in the loudest voice she could muster. Who could be fearful with such inspiring words pouring forth from her lips?

Lea moved toward the bathroom. A cool shower would feel very good. Her body was soaked in perspiration, not just from the scare, but also from the heat. The temperature of the cabin seemed unstable. When she had first come in, it seemed cold and dank; but now, only a few hours later, it felt as if she were living inside an oven. She really needed a cooling off.

Dressed in her plain, cotton, nightgown, she emerged from the bathroom and padded softly into the bedroom. If possible, it seemed hotter than the other rooms. How would she manage to get any sleep in this inferno?

Lea set about removing the satin comforter and top sheet. There was no need for any manner of covering tonight. The cool, crisp night air of the mountains that she had been told about certainly wasn't in evidence this evening.

When the bed was made ready, Lea gently lifted her Bible from its place on the bedstand and opened it. With the utmost reverence she got down on her knees to begin her nightly devotions.

Lea had just bowed her head in prayer when she felt a blast of hot wind scorch her face. The intensity of the heat seemed to suck up all the air around her, making her dizzy and light-headed. She couldn't breathe. It felt like the room was swirling, pulsating around her. She struggled to her feet, unable to determine the reason for the strange increase in temperature. With great effort, Lea pulled herself up onto the bed, holding her Bible outstretched in her hand. She'd have to say her prayers on her back this evening. Lea hoped that God would understand. She just wasn't feeling well enough to attempt it on her knees.

Even lying down didn't seem to ease her strange feeling of weightlessness. Her vision was blurring, as if she were about to pass out. Objects no longer appeared clear.

Across the room, in the window's upper pane, two pinpoints of yellow appeared to be watching her. At first Lea tensed her muscles, preparing herself for yet another frightful experience; but then, remembering the earlier incident with the attic window, she calmed. Lea's eyes tried to focus on the glints of light. Perhaps it was a reflection of the lamp or the mirror. It could be any of a myriad of logical explanations. This time there would be no panic, could be none. She was too tired and too dizzy to go running, screaming, from the room. Besides, she was beginning to feel that her hysterical outbursts were totally unwarranted. Justifiable fear was one thing, but this was ludicrous.

As if something heavy had settled on her, Lea felt her forearm bend backward toward the floor, and with it, the precious Bible. She tried to tighten her grip on the Holy Book, but in vain. It was slipping from her fingers. When her strength faltered and she could no longer retain it, the Bible fell to the ground with a thud. Something was not right, not right at all. The sound made by the falling book was that of an object being hurled down from a great height, not one which had dropped but a few feet.

In her daze, Lea leaned over the end of the bed to survey the damage. As she had somehow sensed, the Book had been almost destroyed. The covers had torn off as the back binding struck the floor. They had pulled away from the pages. The glue that had once held it all together, now appeared as a powder, lightly dusting the surface below. At least the pages were still in order. She had that to be grateful for.

Lea moved as far toward the edge of the bed as she could, trying to reach out for what remained of her Book. She didn't dare attempt standing, for fear that she'd topple over.

Just as her fingers reached the well-worn pages, a strange night wind poured through the open window. It was cool and calming to her, almost sensuous. The wind ripped wildly against the pages and tore them one from another, dispersing them throughout the room and into the hallway.

Lea was startled by its magnitude and force; but more so by its origin. She turned her head in the direction of the window. Outside, the wind was blowing hard, bending and shaking the trees. Her eyes darted up to the top pane. The pinpoints of light were still there, staring down at her.

There came a roar of wind, rolling through the room, toward her. The force of its gust chilled her feet and lifted her nightgown away from the smooth naked flesh that was hidden beneath it. As the coolness caressed her legs and gently kissed her thighs, Lea was conscious of nothing, other than the feelings it brought her, the physical pleasure of taut, excited, flesh. It billowed the nightdress and moved along her breasts.

Suddenly, unable to stay awake, overwhelmed with fatigue, the lids of her eyes began their descent. Lea was shrouded in darkness, covered by a new and enchanting void. For a moment, she was conscious of what she was feeling; but then she descended into the solitary, inviting blackness of sleep.

CHAPTER VI

Morning was definitely not Lea's best time. Under ideal conditions, it took her an hour or more before the sleep was totally rubbed from her eyes and she was ready to face the new day's challenges. Today, however, was not typical, not the norm. She had been tossing and turning since the first light of dawn streamed through her window. Without a clock, it was difficult to determine the precise hour, but she suspected that it was nearing six-thirty.

Lea was unsure as to whether or not she should get up. If she stayed in bed, perhaps she might be able to doze off again; but no, she was too restless for that. If she got up and made coffee at this early hour, she'd be tired the rest of the day. Her eyes snapped open and shut several times, allowing the sensitive pupils to become accustomed to the light.

Lea was startled, for a moment unaware of her surroundings. Then, it all came back. She was in a cabin, in the most desolate area of the Adirondacks.

Like a rush of wind, scenes of the previous evening began to reappear in her mind.

She leaned over the edge of the bed, searching for the Bible which had been damaged the night before. What greeted her gaze was wholly unexpected. In her foggy memory of the previous evening, she recollected that the pages had become separated and had whirled around the room, but what she saw now indicated that something more had occurred; much more.

Her Holy Book was not just damaged, it had been irreparably destroyed. The pages had been ripped apart—in half, thirds, and in some cases even shredded. How could the wind have done such a thing? From the evidence that surrounded her, it appeared that a gale had blown, full force, through the window after she had fallen asleep.

Lea's eyes surveyed the room. On the dresser, stood a stack of library books, mostly paperbacks, that she had brought from home. They had not been disturbed. How could that be?

Her eyes moved from the window to the books. They weren't in direct line with one another. Still, if the wind had been wild enough to tear one book to shreds, it should have at least blown the others open. There was, however, no evidence of that. The pile of books seemed to have spent the night in calm tranquility rather than in the midst of a whirlwind.

Lea rose from the bed slowly, wanting to see, close up, the extent of damage done to her treasured possession. Its sentimental value was beyond calculation. Mama had given it to her when she joined the church. No Bible on earth, could replace this particular one.

As Lea walked through the room, bending to take a

closer look at the torn paper scattered on the floor, tears began to fall. Not one of the pages remained intact. There was no way to salvage any part of it.

Lea's hands began shaking. How could she exist without her Bible? It would have to be replaced quickly, today. A Christian, unable to read and refer to the teachings of the Bible, was like a plant without water; for lack of one, the other dies. In the case of the human being, the physical entity did not die; but something far worse occurred—the slow death of the soul, and that meant damnation. After breakfast, she'd drive into town, go to the little church, and get another Bible.

Lea was nervous, too nervous. The peculiar happenings of the last two days had frightened her, true; but there was something more, something she couldn't pinpoint or easily identify. She was on edge. Certainly the Bible had been important to her; but God's word had not been destroyed, so why was she crying?

Lea thought that perhaps when she returned home, it might be wise to consult a doctor and get a prescription for tranquilizers. She had never before believed in such things but now, anxiety ridden, she felt differently. Something was wrong with her, really wrong. It was not that she felt herself unstable, just that of late she was becoming too easily excited and upset over the most piddling matters. Everything seemed to overwhelm her, and that was not normal.

Mama had always told her that the good Lord never sent a person more trouble than he could handle. That's why tranquilizers bordered on heathenism. But that, like a whole host of other things, had been Mama's parable, not God's. If such was the case, how had it come to pass that mental institutions were filled to capacity? Evidently their occupants couldn't cope with the crosses the Lord gave them. Besides, Lea reasoned, God made doctors. Since things of His creation prescribed the calming pills, how could the mood-altering drugs be ungodly? Did her reasoning make sense? She wasn't quite sure. Something in her, in the frail, woven tapestry of her nervous system, was being pulled tauter than a rubber band. With every day that passed, the thin thread of sanity was coming closer to snapping.

She stared at the torn pages scattered haphazardly about her feet. What did one do with a ravaged, desecrated Bible? You couldn't throw it out with the trash, for that would be overt sacrilege. Bury it perhaps? No, that didn't seem right either. The animals might cart it off bit by bit, to make their nests in it. It depressed her to think that some small animal might urinate upon the psalms. For a moment, Lea stood unmoving, helplessly wondering what she should do. Then it came to her. She would burn the sacred remains. That way, there could be no desecration of the Holy Book. It must be done now, before the first taste of hot, aromatic, coffee passed her lips. To her, God's work had priority. It came before man's simple, mundane pleasures.

Lea scoured the room and hallway, bending low to pick up the fragmented pages which held the words and phrases of scripture. When her task appeared complete, she surveyed the room once more to ensure that none of the holy writings had been overlooked. After satisfying herself that that was the case, she moved in the direction of the back door, carrying her precious Gospel cargo.

When she was out and away from the house, Lea began to search for a place that could be used as a firepit. About one hundred feet from the cabin, she found such a spot. There were several flat stones strewn about the area. A few were stacked one on top of another, leading her to believe that, perhaps a long time ago, someone had set the rocks in place for just such a purpose.

Lea knelt in the soft pine needles. Slowly she began emptying the contents of her nightgown, laying the mangled pieces of paper and cloth gently on the ground.

After the task was completed and she was satisfied that she had exercised the proper degree of reverence, Lea began assembling all the rocks she could find, forming a circle. When the structure's walls were approximately five inches high all around, she stopped, stepping back to take a critical look at her handiwork. It appeared that the creation was serviceable and could safely contain a fire.

Resembling a priestess taking part in some ancient sacred ritual, one by one Lea gathered up and then dropped the fragments into the pit. When all was ready, she ran back into the house, getting the matches which would spark the holy pyre.

Upon her return, Lea stood beside the pit, staring down at the remnants of her Bible. How was it that last evening there had been a gale force wind blowing; yet now, the trees were as fixed as statues in stone? Perhaps the wind was quietly mourning what was to come.

Again Lea knelt beside the pit, suddenly aware of the silence that surrounded her. The birds were not singing, the buzzing of insects had ceased, and nowhere, amid the great vastness of the forest, did the leaves rustle with movement. Once again, apprehension seized control of her body. What was it in the aura, the mood of this place that made it seem so eerie, so ominous?

Unwilling to let this feeling of dread run rampant through her mind, bringing the demons once more to life, Lea tossed off the event as unimportant. It was simply a natural phenomenon, she assured herself, an unusual but explainable happening that sometimes occurs in the wilds of the forest.

What did Lea know about nature and its workings anyway? She was a girl from the city whose life had been spent trying to ignore the constant drone of traffic, the screams and yells of neighbors, the ever present cacophony of blaring televisions and stereos. It was no wonder that she found the sound of silence so strange and petrifying. This was the first time in her entire life that Lea had been exposed to such a thing.

Grateful that she had managed to control her fear before it caused a major emotional upheaval, Lea knelt beside the fireplace. Folding her hands over the book of matches, she offered a prayer of thanks.

When Lea had completed her devotions, she quickly struck a match, watching it explode into a thin line of flame. As she gazed at the tongue of orange, Lea was overtaken with a feeling of profound mourning. It was as if she were attending the funeral, or rather cremation, of an old and dear friend. A single tear moved down her cheek as she allowed the match to fall from her fingers into the waiting mass below. It touched the wrinkled corner of a page and slowly began to char it, changing the color from neutral parchment to black, and, finally, to a myriad of undulating reds, golds, and oranges. The fire spread quickly, engulfing all that was in the pit in a matter of seconds.

Lea stood, mesmerized by the leaping flames. Some words should be spoken over this holy inferno. Something scriptual, perhaps. She wanted to deliver a fitting and appropriate eulogy. The only phrase that came to mind, however, was "Dust to dust, ashes to ashes." The statement referred to the decomposition of human remains, not the incineration of a Holy Book. Lea pondered a moment longer, trying to find the words which would express her emotions; but nothing she came up with could fulfill the needs of the moment. In the end, she decided that it was best just to fold her hands in silence, rather than say something which God might find offensive or inane.

When the Bible had been reduced to a pile of ashes, Lea retreated into the cabin for a cup of warming coffee and her morning ablutions.

She could hear the sound of the percolator as she stepped into the bathroom. She was experiencing minor cramping in her lower abdomen—nothing excruciating, but just irritating enough to keep it in the forefront of her consciousness. It was probably nothing more than that her bladder was too full. Normally she went to the bathroom immediately upon rising, but this morning, feeling that disposing of the Bible had been more important, she postponed her urination till now.

Lea lifted her nightgown and sat squarely upon the seat, waiting for relief, for the uncomfortable cramping to cease. Her eyes drifted down to the cloth of her gown. There were small circles scattered randomly across the front of it. They were red-brown in color, resembling spatters of dried blood. For a moment Lea stared at the puzzling stains, wondering how they came to be. Perhaps her period had started and she just hadn't realized it yet; but no, that couldn't be, it wasn't due for at least another two weeks.

As Lea continued to contemplate this, the latest minor mystery, the muscles of her bladder relaxed allowing the urine to pass. A wave of pain engulfed her. The burning sensation spread throughout her genitals, making her flesh feel raw and wounded.

Stunned, Lea pulled her nightgown up, attempting to reveal the source of the pain. She gasped audibly as the smooth pink of her flesh was exposed to view. Lea's inner thighs were a mass of long, thin, scratches. It was as if some sharp-clawed animal had attacked her while she slept.

Lea raised the gown further, exposing her most tender flesh. There she found the worst of the damage. The pink-brown tissue had been assaulted with something small and sharp. Her eyes began darting back and forth over this most intimate area of her body. Embarrassed to continue further with the examination, she let her gown fall against her thighs.

How had this happened? Could someone or something wild have come through the window? It seemed highly unlikely. How could anything have inflicted that kind of injury without awakening her? The only logical conclusion was they had been self-inflicted. Lea must have done it to herself, but why? Good Christian girls were not in the habit of touching their private parts and certainly not in a manner violent enough to cause painful injury.

Lea lifted her hand slowly, gingerly bringing it closer to her face. She examined the nails of each finger, looking for the red-brown residue that would indicate that the attack had been carried out by her own hands. As she feared, the evidence was there.

Lea wondered how this thing had come to pass. Such

behavior was not at all like her. As her mind explored the possible explanations, Lea became acutely aware of discomfort in her breasts. She reached for the deep, scooped neckline, pulling it out and away, allowing her eyes an unobstructed view of the soft, naked body beneath. More flesh had fallen prey to this thing. Although scratches were prevalent all over her breasts, the worst injury seemed to have been inflicted around the nipple. Small semi-circular scabs had formed on either side of the left breast, giving the impression that the tender tissue had been pinched till blood was drawn.

Again, Lea's gaze came to rest on her long, slender fingers. Searching for an answer to why such a thing had occurred was important but not of primary concern. Lea was most fearful of the possibility of infection as the wounds were located in the dirtiest areas of the body.

Taking some tissue, Lea dabbed at her genitals, trying to wipe away all the residue of stinging urine. As she pulled the soft, white paper away from her body, she noticed smears of blood. She needed to wash the afflicted area at once.

She stood up slowly, fully conscious of the pain assaulting that area of her body. Never before had she experienced such torment. She lifted the nightgown over her head and allowed it to drop to the floor. Lea moved to the tub and began running the water, jockeying the faucets to assure that the liquid was neither too hot or too cold. When she was satisfied that it would be soothing, she stepped in, pulled the curtain, and flipped the handle for the shower.

The water gently massaged her body as the tiny droplets pelted her flesh. They stung the wounds at first, but after a moment the initial pain vanished.

Lea searched the tub for a wash cloth, but had forgotten to set one out the previous evening. Unwilling to get out of the tub and retrieve the one on the sink, she determined that she could wash herself with just her hands. Mother had always insisted that Lea use a wash cloth, saying that there was something sinful in running slick, soapy hands across naked skin. As Mama wasn't here and since soap on wounds could not in any way, shape, or form be construed as pleasurable, Lea lifted the fragrant square from its holder and began to rub it between her palms.

Strange, massaging the lather gently over her breasts and between her thighs did not cause pain. Instead, she found the experience rather calming. Lea couldn't comprehend why the soap wasn't irritating the cuts and scratches, but she was grateful to God that such was the case.

When Lea was sure that all the injured areas had been thoroughly cleaned, she shut off the faucet and carefully stepped out of the enclosure. She worked the fluffy towel over her body, gently patting the injured flesh. As her hands touched the exterior shell of her being, her mind whirred within. Lea had managed to maintain her calm during this ordeal by assuring herself, at the outset, that there was a logical explanation as to how the marks had come to be. Now she was attempting to reason the whole thing out. She had inflicted these injuries on herself, but why?

There was one possible cause that she could immediately rule out, that being that she had somehow engaged in the sin of self abuse. Lea knew that masturbation was a damnable act. She didn't engage in such self lust while awake, so it was unthinkable that she would do such a loathsome thing in her sleep.

Lea examined the scratches on her breasts a bit more carefully. Surrounding her nipples were slightly raised, red blotches. For a moment, Lea was unsure as to whether they were hives or insect bites; but it really didn't matter what they were, only that they were there. When something itches, one scratches it. Something had probably bitten her while she slept, bed bugs perhaps. That would make sense. After all, the cabin had had years and years to accumulate a population of vermin. It was simply coincidence that the bugs had seen fit to attack both breasts and genitalia at the same time.

A smile crossed her lips. Everything had a logical explanation that would reveal itself when allowed sufficient time.

Lea continued to pat the droplets of moisture from her body, her face radiating a calm, serene aura. As the towel swiftly rubbed over her flesh, Lea planned her day's activities. First, there would be a leisurely breakfast where she could linger over the tantalizingly bitter taste of strong, black coffee. Then, after straightening the kitchen, she would strip the bed, attempting to ascertain the origin of the midnight pestilence. Following that, she'd hop in the car and make the drive to town. That way, she'd have a Bible to read for evening devotions. Mulling it over in her mind, she decided that the chores wouldn't take long. If she worked it right, she'd still have the major portion of the day free to take a long, leisurely, thoughtful stroll through the vast greenness of God's creation.

Lea smiled to herself. For once in her life, she was

going to react like a normal, civilized, non-neurotic, human being. Lea was changing. She could sense it.

CHAPTER VII

Lea lay still on the bed. Her heart was pounding, vibrating the muscles in her neck; pulsating, with sickening regularity, the pit of her stomach. She was drenched in sweat, the drops of perspiration forming small pearls of liquid on her forehead and trickling in rivulets from her arms, breasts, and back. She was much too frightened to cry, not that it would have done her any good. Tears could not wash away the horror. Like so many times before, she had let the panic overtake her, but this time the magnitude of her private hell had grown and multiplied till it threatened to overwhelm her.

She could feel her limbs quiver as the last nervous twinges of the anxiety attack seized them. Was she going crazy? Was that it then? Lea had always believed that only a sane person could think himself a lunatic. The mad person, on the other hand, being so far removed from reality and logical thought, was convinced of his sanity. She now saw the error in such a conclusion. Lea thought herself mad, and her actions of late seemed to uphold her view. She had fought against it long enough; the battle was intensifying and her side was losing.

Her mind momentarily envisioned a scene of war, a bloodied battlefield. At the forefront, sword in hand, stood Lea, calling her forces to follow. Through a clouded mist, she could hear the hated enemy approaching. The monster that wished to seize her mind and devour it was coming. The sword was raised to strike the mortal blow as the mist parted, revealing the identify of her foe. The enemy was known; she was one and the same with it, for it was herself.

As quickly as it had materialized, the scene melted into undulating clouds of color, leaving her more confused than she had been before. Was there no peace? Every thought, every action of late, led Lea to the conclusion that she belonged in a place where she could be cared for, a quiet institution where she'd be protected from her fearsome self. The events of this day could foster no belief other than this.

Rays of sunshine were streaming through the window, forming strange abstract patterns on the floor, as they danced down through the slowly swaying leaves. It was late afternoon, yet she had no desire to stir from the bed. Instead, like a stiff, wooden, lifeless figure she lingered, staring blankly at the ceiling, trying vainly to gather her thoughts. Inside her mind, fear and anger stirred. A cauldron of opposite yet like emotions were waiting to boil forth, to explode. She was fearful of her pounding heart, of the pain it caused in her chest, of her strange behavior, of the spectre of insanity hovering in the background, of the constant torment that it caused her; but most of all, of her seeming inability to maintain control over her own mind or body. It was almost as if something was trying to gain possession of her being.

At the same time, while the weak Lea, the tiny bent creature of the mind, was scurrying amid each cell of the brain looking for a hiding place, seeking refuge, there existed, or rather coexisted with it, an angry, brazen creature of rage. She shook not from fear, but rather from violent fury. How dare the weak one allow herself to lose control, to give in to panic! Insanity could never come to reside in this brain, for the raging Lea would drive it out. This was a part of her that she had long ago repressed. Anger was wrong, against the law of God. This was the badness, the incorrigible bitch, that Mama had tried so hard to beat out of her. Most times this facet of her stayed hidden, unwilling to reveal itself; but now it stormed forward, taking possession.

As the anger stirred with increased intensity, fear began its steady retreat into the unconscious. Her face contorted in a scowl, the eyes glowering at the room around her. There was nothing mentally wrong with her, this entity repeated over and over again in the confines of Lea's brain. What had happened to her today, the succession of frightening experiences, of new and foreign feelings, was nothing supernatural, nothing unexplainable; it was simply the torrid flight of fantasy of a frigid old maid. The thought lingered, and as it did, a sudden feeling of calm washed over her, soothing her body, relaxing the nerves. Just as the fear had fled, the anger now dissipated in the face of rational thought.

The idea made sense. Being a virtuous woman was no easy task. Celibacy, although God's desire, was difficult. Perhaps the occurrences of early morning had served to make her acutely aware of her sexuality. Lea pursed her lips, attempting to put together evidence for her seemingly lucid theory. The locations of the scratches might have caused her to focus attention on her sexual apparatus. In addition, the fact that the marks were self-inflicted might have spurred the mind to conjure visions of impure acts, of furtive masturbation and clandestine acts of coitus.

Lea mulled it over in her mind for a moment, trying to determine if she were on the right track. There had been a great disparity in time between the discovery of the marks on her body and the events of late afternoon; which, up until a few moments ago, seemed capable of poising her on the brink of breakdown.

In her first act of voluntary movement in more than fifteen minutes, Lea raised her arm and let it fall gently across her forehead. Perhaps if she could reconstruct the earlier events of the day she could determine the catalyst, the thing which had begun her swift descent into the realms of Hell. Lea breathed in deeply, allowing the air to linger a moment in her lungs. Somewhere in her remembrances of this day was the key to why everything had occurred as it had; she only need find it, and the knowledge would set her free.

Morning had been a time of anger, a time of frustration. If Lea were something less than a godly, Christian woman, she would probably have spent all of the early hours of the day cursing and haranguing against how miserably her plans had gone. She had been thwarted at every turn, almost as if some invisible prankster, a mischievious troll, had been lying in wait to irritate and confuse her.

After breakfast, she'd spent over an hour trying to discover the identity and nesting place of the vermin which she suspected had attacked her the previous evening. Like a detective, she searched the area, stripping the bed, moving furniture, scanning woodwork, floors, and walls, yet the source of the infestation eluded her. Lea could find nothing. Her search had been fruitless. Not so much as one tiny spider could be found.

Convinced that the culprits existed within the bedroom, yet unable to find a crawling insect to blame, she turned her attention to the possibility that mosquitoes, gnats, or some other winged creature might have ventured through the screen. There was, however, no evidence that such were present in the room. All her attention, the focus of her consciousness, was drawn to solving the puzzle.

After deciding that a further search of the bedroom was futile, she had readied herself for a trip into town, hoping that the local minister could provide her with a copy of the Holy Scriptures and that perhaps the proprietor of the hardware store might be able to enlighten her on the nature and identity of the invisible vermin that plagued her. The man might even recommend some method of elimination or extermination.

Her mood was one of somber irritation as she slid behind the wheel of her car and prepared to begin her journey; but within a few moments, it changed to frustrated fury. The car would not start. Lea turned the key, only to be greeted by silence. She kept pumping the pedal and flicking the key harder and harder; but still the vehicle did not respond to her command. Blind with rage, she lifted her foot away from the accelerator and kicked with all her might into the dash, about a foot from the wheel. Her hostile action proved nothing, except that she had the strength to destroy the radio. Her mood turned from anger to black despair. She was not only despondent over her car's sudden inability to function but also her own stupidity and futile destructiveness. If possible, she had made matters worse.

Lea got out of the car and headed back into the cabin; but not before she had leveled another forceful kick, this time at the left front tire. It had occurred to her that it might be useful to lift the hood and look underneath; however, with her small knowledge of mechanics, she decided against it. When one can't distinguish the carburetor from the radiator or air filter, it is the best form of discretion to call in an expert, which Lea did, or rather attempted to do.

Diverted but not yet defeated, Lea searched the living room for the local telephone directory, but in vain. Whoever had installed the phone had neglected to leave one for her. She'd simply have to call her real estate agent friend and ask him to recommend a good garage.

Lea wandered through the cabin till she found the piece of paper on which she had written Ronald's number. She had felt some little relief at holding the paper between her fingers, but that calm was soon shattered.

Her angry glumness was beginning to dissipate as she lifted the receiver to her ear. At that point the breath caught in her throat. There was no sound to be heard, no dial tone, no hum, nothing. The phone was dead.

It was not just the temporary inconvenience that disturbed her, but the very real danger she was in.

Should something, God forbid, happen to her, she had no way to call for help, no way to flee. She wouldn't starve—at least the likelihood of such a thing happening seemed rather remote; but nevertheless, the situation was not what one would call ideal.

As was her habit when the world seemed to conspire against her, when frustration and anger mingled to shake her body, Lea began to cry. She was a captive in this dark, green, wild place. Like the survivor of a shipwreck, she was isolated on a terrifying island, only hers was not of sand, but rather lush pines and underbrush.

Lea despised the cabin, the forest, all that had suddenly become her prison. She did not want to be here, had not wanted to come. She needed a place, a person, a thing, on which she could blame this and the host of other bizarre and disheartening occurrences which had taken place since her arrival. The recipient was her aunt. If it hadn't been for the interfering old biddy, none of her torment would have come about. If the woman had been in Lea's presence, she wouldn't have survived. The young, mild-mannered woman had several less than charitable visions of herself strangling her aging aunt.

As her anger began to abate somewhat, and Lea's thinking returned to logical paths, she decided that the only person to blame for this whole abomination was herself. Lea was the one who allowed people to direct her life, rather than taking charge and acting as the helmsman of her own ship. She decided then, that once she got out of this momentary bind, if that was all it was, she would be less of an obedient child, and more of an independent woman.

But all the lectures, all the pep talks in the world, could not completely eradicate the fear she felt. She was in danger. No phone, no way out of the cabin; that was a frightening reality. As visions of murder and mayhem flew through her consciousness, Lea attempted to push them out. She tried to assess the actuality of things with an unemotional eye. There was enough food for several days. She could remain in the cabin and wait till help arrived. She was sure her aunt would try to call. When she couldn't reach her niece, she'd call Ronald. He, in turn, would ride out to the cabin to check on things. He would act as Lea's St. George, rescuing her from the dragon forest. The thought was romantic and enchanting, but, in true fact, might not mirror reality. Perhaps her aunt would assume that the phone was temporarily out of order and that Lea was arranging for its repair. After all, how was Evelyn to know that the car was inoperable too? It could take a week or more before her aunt's concern would reach the level where she'd contact the real estate agent to see what the matter was.

Calmly and rationally, Lea determined that the best way out of her predicament was to make the long trek, either into town or to the closest inhabited roadside camp. Try as she might, she couldn't remember passing any place that appeared occupied. Perhaps it was her imagination, but it seemed as if she were the only living being existing in this place of desolation. She had passed many dirt side roads, much like the one her cabin was on, as she drove along the main road. There was a chance, perhaps, that one of those places might have people in residence; but it was too much of a chance to take, leaving the road and heading into the forest. Who could tell what might be lying in wait for her in the towering, green wilds?

Walking in ever expanding circles around the living room, Lea came up with a suitable plan of action. The following day she would arise before dawn and pack a small bundle of food. At the first sign of light, after she was convinced that all the nocturnal wanderers, the bears and skunks, had sought hiding places, she would embark on her journey, walking toward town. She couldn't be sure how far away it was. If she walked all day, she'd either make it into town, encounter an inhabited summer home, or perhaps flag down a passing motorist. Regardless of the method, she was sure that by tomorrow evening she would be out of this mess. After all, sixteen hours of daylight certainly seemed sufficient time to seek out and find another living, breathing human being.

Satisfied with her plan of action, Lea found herself bored with nothing to do but wait for tomorrow. She momentarily thought of taking a walk down to the main road, but then thought better of it. Why tire herself out today? It was better to conserve her strength until the dawn, when she'd have need of it. Lacking her Holy Book, she didn't particularly care to read. Lea had some paperbacks, but they could not offer the spiritual comfort of the Bible, which she required during times of trial and emotional upheaval.

For lack of something else to do, Lea turned on the radio, seeking either a gospel program which would lift her spirits or some soothing, restful melodies which might relax her.

She could remember little of what transpired next. She had vague recollections of continually rotating the dial trying to find a station that possessed a clear signal and was devoid of earsplitting static. Only one was coming in well enough to be heard. It was a station that played only rock music. Normally, Lea could not be bothered listening to such trash, preferring instead classical music or show tunes. But anything was better then the silence of the cabin. She fiddled with the dial, adjusting the tuning, until each note was clearly audible.

Mother had forbidden such music in their home, saying that the melodies and lyrics of such compositions were inspired by Mephistopheles himself. The recurring sounds of bass and drum were like opiates to the body, burrowing into the nerves and muscles, making them twitch, contract and finally sway to the beat. As the sensual movements of the body continued, the brain focused on them, turning from thoughts of morality and holiness to the sinful concerns of the physical, the base desire for carnal pleasure. Mother had always tended to exaggerate the dangers inherent in such worldly pleasures.

Recently, Lea had come to realize that she had become very critical of the way her mother had conducted her life. As time increased the distance between her living and the present, Lea found herself wondering how some of her mother's ludicrous beliefs had been given credence by her aging, yet naive, daughter.

It was not that Lea was abandoning her faith, her adherence to Christian doctrine or the veracity of the Bible. It was simply that the myriad of sins and transgressions against God that had existed in her mother's mind now seemed more like heresy than Christian dogma. Everything, even the very act of living, paved a pathway to Hell. Only by existing in a shell of holy solitude, without any joy or happiness, thinking of nothing but the Lord, could one, according to Mama, assure his place in Paradise.

Lea questioned if the Almighty actually required such sacrifice from man. It was the Lord, after all, who had created man a frail and sinful creature, a being totally lacking his Creator's perfection. If man was conceived in the Deity's eye to be less than a paragon of virtue, flawed from the moment of birth, the indiscretions and minor failings that humanity was prone to could and would be forgiven. Did it seem logical that a loving, paternal Creator would damn a soul for enjoying a bit of music? It seemed unlikely.

Lea decided to lie down and let the music soothe her mind and perhaps lull her to sleep. She could vaguely remember walking into the bedroom and loosening her clothing. At that point the memories faded; but for how long a period of time, she was unsure. It was almost as if she had entered another dimension, been lost in a trance.

The only recollection that permeated her mind was heat, all-encompassing and oppressive; sweat dripped down her body.

As if being suddenly awakened in the middle of a nightmare, Lea found herself kneeling and writhing, naked in front of the wall hanging in the bedroom, unable to gain control of herself or explain her actions. As the little figures depicted in the scene became animated, dancing sensually around the five-pointed star, so had she. It was as if another being had usurped her body and assumed control of it. She rolled on the floor, hips and chest moving, swaying in rhapsodic ecstasy. Drums were beating loudly, coming from somewhere in the room—the picture? The sounds of the radio were being drowned out. In a clouded mist came words, a chant, repeated and repeated. The words were difficult to distinguish. Only one could be clearly discerned. They were calling out for her to worship, to pay homage to the pentagram. At that moment in time, nothing existed for Lea but the picture and the strange beings therein. She became one with them. With perspiration dripping from forehead, breasts, and back, she had continued following the dictates of the thing that had assumed control. A part of her conscious, rational self witnessed this bizarre ceremony as an observer, aghast at her sensual movements and the mesmerized gaze.

She could remember strange, new feelings taking hold; an unexplainable passion, desires that quivered the muscles of her thighs. Something in the picture beckoned her. It was as if an invisible force, the spirit of the star, had reached out and seized her, trying to draw her into the throes of the strange, primitive rite. Its touch was like that of hot wind, blowing over her arms, legs, breasts, massaging and arousing her body, bidding her to follow.

Blinded by the newness of the feelings, the promised pleasure, Lea moved to the wall hanging. Standing on the mattress, reaching for the figures and the star, she began to claw at the picture in a vain and feeble effort to crawl inside it, to be one with it. She wanted to exist forever in this land of song, dance, and pleasure.

Whatever rational being still existed within her had called out into the blackness, breaking the spell cast by the star. *"I am the Lord thy God. Thou shalt not have strange gods before me."* She was violating God's own revealed law by allowing herself to continue with the madness.

Her mind cleared and Lea became acutely aware of her nakedness and her aberrant actions. The reverberations of the drums and the repetitious chanting ceased, leaving only a commercial jingle from the radio in her ears. She stood naked before the picture, unsure of what to do next, confused at how she had come to behave so. After much anguish and tears, she came up with only two plausible explanations. Either she had been engaged in a nightmare and had, while still in a deep sleep, begun to act it out. Or, as Mother had said, the sinful music had attempted to steal her soul. Being an adult, intelligent woman, she rationalized that the only logical explanation was that she was dreaming. With all the emotional upheavals she had endured of late, it was not impossible to assume that they had brought on the strange dreams. The sexual creature who danced with wild abandon was an inhabitant of her own repressed subconscious, the flagrant whore she sometimes longed to be. It all seemed plausible and even possible, except for one minor point—that Lea couldn't remember lying down to go to sleep.

She thought it over for a few moments, finally deciding that anyone as neurotic as herself might have wiped the memory from her brain. Perhaps it was a form of self-hate, self-punishment, making herself believe that she was going crazy, extracting retribution for allowing herself the freedom of sexual fantasies. No matter how much the logical Lea rejected Mama's concept of sin, identified it as being stupidity and lunacy, deep inside, in the inner recesses of her mind, in her childlike conscience, there existed the last vestige of the living Mama.

Like a fly caught in a spider's web, Lea viewed the onslaught of insanity, of breakdown. She was perched on a thin precipice of emotional stability, leaning dangerously close to the edge, about to fall into the abyss of madness. Lea felt that she couldn't stand any more. One more bizarre experience, unexplained erratic act, eerie occurrence, and she'd crack. Her mind would snap like a dead, dry twig. Looking back on it now, however, that had not been the case; more was to come. Sometimes she truly surprised herself with her internal fortitude. There was more substance to Lea than she realized. The events of the afternoon, including the most recent, had frightened her, panicked her, yet her metal had not cracked; she had survived.

After having calmed and once more gaining control of herself, Lea had dressed quickly. She was tired, even more so than before, yet hesitated to lie down for fear that the strange nightmarish rite would again impose itself upon her dreams.

Lea wandered around the house for a while, finally deciding that she was being foolish and childish about the whole thing. If she was tired, she belonged in bed.

Lea could remember closing her eyes and letting her mind drift. It was after the sleep came that the true battle, the zenith of the day's agony, took place.

Within her floating world of gentle darkness the visions came. A naked Lea lay upon a bed of black satin, eyes wide and yearning. With one hand she was reaching out into the shadows, trying to grasp something, while the other was moving in a slow circular motion over her breasts, its long thin fingers gently caressing the rising nipples. From somewhere in the

120

darkness, a voice came. It called out to Lea, giving her name the whispered sound of soft, stroked velvet and the sensuality of satin.

"Lea, child, come. Come to me." It was a voice more tempting and persuasive than she had ever known. "Come let me teach you the ways of darkness, the rites of the evening. Lea, kneel at the altar of stars and moon and sky. Come worship with me the creator of passion, the force that exists in the gossamer mists of cool black evening air, on the fragrance of exotic nocturnal winds, in the shimmering, sensual glow of twilight, in the rapturous cascade of moonbeams. The night is a wondrous, gentle, loving thing, a source of joy. Worship the night, Lea; pay homage to it! Become a slave to its mastery, for it shall be your God, the powerful and jealous Deity whose child you are!" The voice spoke in measured tones, instructing her in a voice firm, yet gentle.

There was something familiar about the sounds this phantom being made. Even though dreaming, she was startled by the voice. Somewhere in the past, in the realm of remembrances, she had heard it before, but where?

"The night enshrouds and protects you. It engulfs you in the pleasures of the mind and spirit. It caresses you and embraces you in ecstasy. For those who are its apostles, who are the true believers, life is devoid of pain, devoid of emptiness. Love the night, child, and it will care for you." The sound of the voice was changing, getting lower and lower, becoming an almost inaudible whisper.

In her dreamlike state, Lea had concentrated harder to hear the words.

"Don't be afraid," it gently chided her. "There is nothing to fear in the darkness, nothing at all. The night is a good thing, a time of pleasure, of joy."

In the dream, a warm wind swept across her body, like fingertips barely grazing the surface of her flesh. It aroused her and made her desirous of more. Its silken touch pleased her. Her body had spent the totality of its existence in ignorance of carnal pleasures. Contradictory feelings collided within her mind. The body was to be a pure temple to the Lord. That's what the Bible taught—and yet, there were such longings inside her, desires long concealed and repressed that now demanded satisfaction. Her body in the dream had yielded to temptation and began to writhe about as the wind increased its intensity and commenced kneading the flesh of her breasts and thighs. Moving, rocking, hands reaching out, fingers caressing the hidden crevices of her body, the Lea of dreams allowed her carnal desires to overcome her. The phantom voice made sounds of pleasure, moaning low as she twisted back and forth. Her long thin fingers explored the satin-soft skin, rubbing and massaging, until with one sudden tensing of muscle, what seemed like an electrical current pulsed through her, and Lea began experiencing the waves of undulating relaxation and contraction that heralded the commencement of her first orgasm. The primal desire which had long laid dormant exploded in sobs of pleasure. Tears formed in the eyes of the dreaming Lea. So this was it, the epitome of pleasure, the height of sin! Such wondrous feelings could not be wrong. The communion of body and spirit, the pleasure-filled sensuality was not the painful degradation she had perceived it to be.

A part of her spoke words of chastisement. This thing she had done, this base and carnal crime, had set her on the downward path to Hades, enslaved her soul to perdition; but there was another part of her that gloried in the new found feelings and screamed out for the puritanical, self-righteous facets of her being to keep silent. There was joy in pleasure and pleasure in joy, that was all she knew and all she needed to know. New unexplored realms were now before her, carnal secrets to be revealed, physical joy to be experienced, pleasures in which to revel. As if having undergone some magical transformation, the Lea of the dream was reborn into a child of the night.

As she awakened from this strange illusion, the phantom called out again, "Worship the night, child. Worship the night! Let it warm you. Let it care for you. Consecrate your being to the God of darkness, the time of pleasure. Love the night, Lea. Take it to your bed. Worship the spectres, the pleasures, be one with them."

The experience was vivid in her mind. It shouldn't have frightened her so badly; after all, everyone has dreams. There was nothing unusual in having erotic, sexual fantasies. Others, purer in heart then she, did. That, however, was not what disturbed her. Lea could get down on her knees and pray to God for forgiveness, beg for help to forever banish the carnal lustings from her heart and mind; but that would not wipe away its words.

As she awakened from her dreamlike stupor, eyes flickering open, the voice again spoke. Only this time its call reverberated loudly through the room, admonishing her to "Worship the night!"

It wasn't part of the dream. She was awake and fully

123

conscious. The sound hadn't come from her mind. It had, in fact, come from the interior of the house, moving from the corner of her room, colliding in the center, echoing in her very being. Something without form or substance occupied space here with her. A creature invisible to the eye, yet a presence that could be felt, sensed. It was this realization, this terror, that caused her to lose control, to abandon rational thought in favor of blind, undirected panic.

Mulling over the day's events, identifying the episodes which were the prelude to this attack of anxiety and fear, did not help to calm her. It was like living a nightmare. Were all these things figments of her sick subconscious, nothing more than illusions, hallucinations? If that were true, she required immediate treatment. Saying that the emotional strain she'd been under of late was responsible for all the bizarre and eerie aberrations was ludicrous. A simple case of nerves did not manifest itself in this fashion. Delusions, seeing things not there, indicated that something was seriously wrong. Was she a hopeless paranoid, a schizophrenic who looked upon her body with alternating feelings of desire and disdain? It could all be so easily explained away, if only Lea believed that she was, in fact, ill. Then she could get help, take medication, be well again. It seemed the only logical conclusion; yet she wasn't totally convinced.

The voice had been real, of this world, as real as the vibration of her own vocal chords. Her eyes didn't deceive or play tricks, for scratches and gouge marks did, in fact, cover her breasts and genitals. The car and telephone had both malfunctioned, that was no illusion. Her Bible had been ripped to shreds and lay in ashes in the back yard. She hadn't imagined that either. Could *she* be the unknown culprit?

The marks that covered her body were self-inflicted, true, but what was it that had caused her to do such a thing? More so, how in the Lord's name could she have been responsible for any of the rest of it? There was an aura about this place that boded ill. All had begun here, the horror, the terror. She had been nervous and overwrought before arriving, true, but that was negligible compared to her present condition.

All the crying in the world couldn't change her situation. Horror surrounded her, and she was powerless to escape.

Lea rose from the bed and gingerly approached the window. Looking out amid the green expanse, she pondered what lay ahead. In four hours or so, the sun would set and all around her would be plunged into blackness. Night would come. She could not stave it off. In a little while, all would be in shadows.

Once more her heart pounded with fear. The spectres of night filled her with hopeless terror and yet something, a tiny voice deep inside her, softly repeated the words, "Worship the night," and that small portion of her being rejoiced in the approach of the darkness.

CHAPTER VIII

Once again as in times past, tears descended the thin, pale cheeks. Lea's eyes surveyed the thick green snare that enveloped and held her captive. The world was gray, covered by shadows. The sun was slowly slipping behind the western slopes. The last rays of its warmth were dancing among the tree tops. Below, on the silent forest floor, the darkness was descending. Night was coming, and with it something terrifying; yet she could do nothing to prevent it. Here she would remain, succumbing to whatever horrid nightmare awaited her.

Should she run, try to escape? Could she make it to safety in time, or would she become lost or be devoured by the things that walk in the darkness of night?

Lea went outside, fearing to remain in the confines of the cabin. It was there that the despicable evil lurked. It was there that her mind took paths of sin, that the carnal beast had evidenced itself. To pass its threshold unleashed the spectered cacodemon that hunched in wait, slobbering in the squalid confines of her brain.

She was unclean, a damnable slut of Satan, allowing reveries of impure, debased acts. She had enraged God and He would rain His vengeance down upon her. Of that, she was sure. She had estranged and alienated the Lord, her only hope of salvation. Somewhere deep within, Lea's soul was festering. Even now its fetid, malignant odor assaulted her nostrils. Her pure Christian soul was decaying, turning black with the continual onslaught of sin. Lea perceived herself damned, condemned to eternal agony, no longer a disciple of the Lord; now the handmaiden of Satan.

Lea's body trembled as she collapsed to her knees in the soft pine needles thickly covering the ground. "Jesus, my Lord, my God, forgive this thing I've done! Through your strength and love, wash this pestilence from my mind. Make me clean, worthy of your care. Allow me to be your well-loved child once more!" With that she began sobbing loudly.

As the shadows cast increased, heralding the coming of night, so did her fear. Lea wrapped her fingers tightly over her shoulders, crossing her arms protectively over her breasts. She rocked back and forth, wailing loudly. The darker it became, the more feverish her movement, the louder her laments, the more ominous the terror appeared.

"Jesus, You who died for my sins on Calvary, take me once again to Your fold. I love You. You are my savior, my Lord. My heart is a temple to Your grace, to Your power, to Your love. Help me gain control of my thoughts, Jesus. Let me, once more, dedicate my mind to You, so that I may worship You to the everlasting glory of Your holy name!"

Her eyes caught glimpses of darkening sky through

the wind tossed tree tops. She needed a miracle, the return of light, the reawakening of the sun so that she might, with God's assistance, excape the clutches of the dark evil that stalked her.

Lea's hair whipped against the pale skin of her face. A wind of storm force had risen up, howling through the trees, making their branches bend and sway. This was the precursor of night, its emissary, who had come to claim her.

With shaking limbs, Lea clasped her hands together to pray. "The Lord is my shepherd, I shall not want. He . . ." She stopped abruptly. Her words were drowned out by the resonating sounds of organ music.

The notes thundered, echoing loudly off the trees. It was a dirge-like piece, reminiscent of the sacred music of which she was so fond. The style was that of a Bach fugue. The sound filled the darkened forest. Never before had she experienced such sensations. The music didn't just surround her, it permeated her skin and moved through her mind, heart, and soul. The physical sensation was akin, she imagined, to being inside a giant pipe organ. As each key was struck and held, the reverberation tingled her flesh. When higher notes were played, the vibration became like tiny fingers gently massaging her trembling body. There was no way that she could ignore the sounds, nor the feelings they engendered in her. Lea couldn't fight against the melodious caresses, the tonal strokings. She allowed the euphoria of the moment to sweep her away as the sounds increased their intensity, rising to a symphonic crescendo.

Her muscles tightened as she began to move rythmically to the organ's eerie composition. She stepped slowly, as if engaged in some ancient dance, swaying gently from side to side, lifting and lowering her arms, fingers outstretched, palms turned upward. She felt as though she were floating, at one with the music. Her measured movement became the fluid, gentle dance of one awaiting a miraculous happening.

For a single moment, Lea felt guilt and pain at what was happening to her, at her sudden abandoment of her life-long pursuit of salvation. This contemplative remorse, however, was soon to disappear. This thing that lured her in the night promised salvation too, only its paradise was of pleasure, of carnal passion, the most secret desires of the flesh.

The sensual, swaying movements excited her. She imagined herself a vestal virgin, the handmaiden of night, dancing for its pleasure in the magnificent verdant temple that was its shrine, its holy place. All fear, all tension, all the myriad of goblins and ghosts that had sought and found refuge in her mind were taking flight, moving out of her body like some strange exuded aura, a noxious, flowing ectoplasm. Lea was at peace, unafraid of her fate. All she desired was to stay in the midst of the caressing, melodic strains.

Her eyes scanned all that was around her, seeking the source of the music. It was coming from the cabin, but not from the inside, as if some record had been left on the phonograph or the radio turned up too loudly. The cabin was the creator of the music, the log walls its keys, the rafters its sounding board, the roof its bellows, the windows and chimney its pipes. It played the sacred music of night.

This was a place of worship, a place of holy rites. She had been called to partake in the joys of her savior, of her Lord, and this new God was named Night. The darkening shadows called the faithful to their evening worship, to the chants and dances, the rites and sacrifices that the black deity demanded. She was a follower, a disciple, now. The ritual of pleasure, of devotion, of worship was about to begin.

Her eyes stared up toward the peak of the roof. There in the window she saw the golden glints. The eyes of Lord Night watched her and beckoned her to enter his temple and partake of the pleasure of worship. It was time for her to make sacrifice, to show the depth of her devotion to him that was her master.

Her eyes became moist with adoration as she watched the golden orbs of the carnal deity. At last she had become a favored child in the eyes of her Lord, an obedient adherent to the law. What matter if she knew not what either were, nor stood for? Lea had finally attained her dream; to love her deity, and be loved in return. The time of her being found sorely wanting in the face of her God was over forever. This God did not have a set of commandments which was impossible to obey, nor would he deny her pleasure, encouraging abstinence and a sober countenance. This was not a deity who would cause her hands to burn, nor her chest to ache for a moment's lusting, a second's physical desire.

To this god, such were pleasing acts, sacraments of the faith. This was religion without sin, repentance without penance, redemption without Christian salvation. This was a faith where music, and pleasure, and dance were the rites. Lea had come to join the cult.

The whisper, low and throaty, could be heard emanating from the cabin door. "Come, Lea, it is the time of darkness, the time of night. The hour of shadow is upon us. Come, child, kneel at the altar, worship the night. Share in its pleasures, experience its joys. The time of devotion is beginning." It was a man's voice, deep and resonant, yet seemed to be gasping, panting, as if aroused. "Come worship the Night, Lea. Love it! Adore it! Keep holy its rituals and you shall be gifted with the richest and most precious of pleasures!" The voice beckoned her. "Come, child, all you need do is but enter this temple and give yourself freely to the Night!"

She blinked several times, trying to determine if her eyes were playing tricks or if she were dreaming. A red-orange mist enshrouded the cabin. It surrounded the structure, making it appear warm and inviting, like the shades and tones of flames in darkness. Through the windows, she could perceive more color, a bright golden glow, through the glass. Her fearful belief that the cabin was evil and demonic had long ago dissipated, now to be replaced by the feeling that the building was a haven from sorrow and want, a place of comfort and contentment. As if suddenly finding herself in the midst of a powerful force field, she was drawn toward the cabin, lured there by something she couldn't identify nor comprehend.

The rites of Night were beginning. Rituals of pleasure, joy, and orgasmic delight would be revealed to her. Ecstasy could be hers if only she would yield to this presence.

Like a participant in a long processional march, Lea began walking slowly, head held high, face reflecting pure contentment and joy. The closer she came to the cabin's entrance, the more peaceful and beatific her expression. She was to be a communicant here in this temple, a sacrifice to her shadowed deity.

The intensity of the music was increasing as with each passing step she drew closer and closer to the door. The vibration shook the ground and caused the trees to tremble. With childlike reverence, she stepped up onto the porch, eyes aglow with awe.

Lea crossed the planking and placed her fingers gently on the knob. It was pleasantly warm, feeling as if something luxuriantly steamy dwelt behind it, a sultry glowing entity. Her fingers remained there for only a second, before the door burst open of its own volition. For a moment Lea stood unmoving, basking in what felt like a gust of hot tropical wind. She was light-headed, her body not yet accustomed to the sudden shift in temperature. It was similar, she assumed, to how a person felt when he took drugs and got the initial rush of euphoria.

Lea stepped over the threshold and into the floating golden mist. There was perfume in the air, the lingering smell of musk. It hung heavy in the streamy confines of the cabin, like clouds of incense rising from an altar. With each breath drawn, Lea felt herself becoming more and more aroused. Perhaps it was a mixture of heat, the smells, even her own sweat, that was causing this sudden rise of passion within her. All the sights, sounds, smells, and sensations acted as aphrodisiacs, releasing her body and soul from their puritan bondage.

Lea could barely perceive the sound of the door clicking behind her. She was being locked in, a prisoner of Night, yet she did not care, was not afraid.

She could feel rivulets of moisture dripping from her body. The sleeves of her blouse were saturated with perspiration, as was its front and back. Lea removed the baggy, cotton vest and began to unbutton the printed blouse beneath it. As the opening widened, Lea peered down at the supple flesh of her breasts. What a waste it had been that, for years, these things of beauty, these sources of sensual pleasure had remained hidden, been denied their purpose. Lea breathed in deeply, watching her chest rise, observing her breasts closely, as a small drop of perspiration descended the cleavage and disappeared from sight. With her index finger, Lea traced its path and found that she liked the sensation. There was something erotic in stroking sweat-damp flesh, even if it were one's own.

Lea removed the blouse and threw it on the floor along with her vest. This temple of Night had become stifling. Her clothing was sticking to her, making her feel confined and uncomfortable. She was taken with an overwhelming desire to kneel nude before Lord Night, to dance naked through the shimmering golden clouds. She reached behind her back and searched the hooks out that kept her bra firmly in place. She tugged for a moment, finally releasing her breasts from their shackles, watching as the nipples peeked out, erect, from under the stiff white cotton. She kneaded them gently, giggling to herself as they grew hard under her caressing fingertips. How nice it was to be so aware of one's own body!

It took but a few moments for Lea to completely disrobe. When the last of the clothing, her white underpants, joined the rest, she kicked the pile away with contempt. She had inhabited this body for years, but had always kept it covered, afraid to look, to see, fearing that it was sinful. Lea surveyed the smooth, taut, flesh. Staring down at her breasts, she determined that they were no better nor worse, in shape and structure, than anyone else's. Lea was amply endowed, with large prominent nipples. As she'd gotten older, her breasts had begun to sag slightly, not much, not enough to make her unattractive. Strange, when she was younger and her curves more pronounced, her breasts and buttocks higher, she had allowed no one to view them, caress them tenderly, to appreciate the full scope of the being that comprised Lea. What a waste she had made of her youth!

Her eyes moved further down her body, this time coming to rest on the thick mound of pubic hair and the rounded form of her thighs. They were heavier than they had once been, dimpled slightly, but still appealing. Lea moved her hands downward and gently rubbed them over the flesh, feeling the silken smoothness. Slowly, her hands moved upward against her body, finally pausing to nestle amid the thick brown thatch. How wonderful it must be, she thought, for a man to gently rub his fingers where hers were now, to slip them in and out of her. If these small physical pleasures be sin, then let damnation be hers.

The musical din increased, drowning out even the thoughts which floated within her brain. Her mind felt empty of will. She desired to do only what the music bid her. As if locked in some hypnotic fantasy, she began moving slowly through the house.

Night was falling as Lea wandered the living room, switching off the lamps and closing the curtains. She paused for a moment at a window, drawing the drapery fabric over her nipples, allowing the nubby fiber to excite her. She caressed the cloth panel, pulling it close, rubbing her pelvis against it. The feelings and sensations caused a quickened heartbeat, deepened breathing, and a permeating feeling of anticipation—but for what, she was unsure.

The fragrance of perfume mingled with the odor of her own sweat, making the air heavy. There was, however, another smell that could be discerned; the acrid stench of charring, burning meat. The golden smoke that had once filled the cabin's interior was lessening in intensity, reduced to a barely detectable glow. All things now meeting her gaze became shades of grey and black—figures, shapes, forms, melding together, inseparable in the darkness. For a moment, the breath caught in her throat. She was, for the first time, aware of the eerie beauty of the darkness. What had once served to frighten and terrify her, now appeared a rare treasure, something to be observed and appreciated. Night was truly a thing of beauty.

She moved through each room, turning off lights, drawing curtains, entombing herself alone in the cabin. Her head spun, her feet felt light as air, her limbs relaxed to the point of exhaustion. Her lips were numb, her eyes unable to focus, her mind swirling in a void of nothingness, her mouth unable to speak a single comprehensible utterance.

Lea was standing in the hallway, just outside the bedroom, when all light faded away. The golden glow vanished, plunging the structure into total darkness. Lea stood motionless, unwilling to move, fearing that she would stumble into hidden danger.

Seeming very far away, drums could be heard. The primitive beat, the rhythmic pulsations, made her blood race. As she concentrated, trying hard to hear the drums over the organ's din, Lea became aware of voices, chanting. They were calling out to the Night to hasten its coming, to reach out and embrace them, to teach them the pleasures of darkness. She swayed, keeping time with the constant, unrelenting beat. With numbed lips, she attempted to echo the refrain; but no matter how hard she tried, the sounds were incoherent, garbled.

The heat intensified. The air was scorching and oppressive. It was becoming difficult to breathe. Lea felt faint, as if she might swoon at any moment. Her legs became jelly-like, unable to hold her weight. She staggered, falling to her knees.

As she struck the floor, all around her became silent. The organ stopped its throbbing, ominous chords, the drums ceased their clamor, even the voiced chants quieted.

Once again, Lea was aware of the strange odor wafting into her consciousness. It was the smell of fire and smoke; of seared meat, blistering, pushed into dancing flame.

Her pupils contracted in an attempt to shut out the sudden flash of light. In the blink of an eye, the darkness had been shattered by flickering, crimson light. Just inside the bedroom, a thick cloud of red hung heavy, like opaque fog. The intensity of the color varied, appearing like the reflection of raging fire. She felt as though she were standing in the flaming midst of an inferno, her flesh hot and tingling. It warmed her, yet did not cause pain. Lea breathed in deeply, forcing her lungs to take in the hot air. She didn't understand what it was that was happening, only that this night was to be the most beautiful and exciting of her life.

From somewhere inside the room, amid the scarlet shaded cloud, a voice called out to her the now familiar words, "Lea child, come. Come to me. Let me teach you the ways of darkness, the rites of eventide. Kneel at the altar of stars and moon and sky. Come worship the creator of passion, for night is a wondrous, gentle, loving thing; a source of pleasure. Worship the night, Lea! Worship the night! Pay it homage. It will protect and keep you. The night enshrouds and holds you safe in its warmth. There is nothing to fear in the dark, little one. The black of night is pleasure. The shadows are joy. Be one with it, Lea. Love the night! Worship it! Adore it! The time of stars and shadows is here and the hour is right for prayer. Pray to Lord Night, give yourself freely, and you shall know a joy which others can only dream of. Come now, worship, child, worship the night!"

All seemed a silken reverie, a fantasy. Could this really be happening? She had no time to ponder the question, for Night had called to her. It desired her, and she could not refuse.

"Night," her voice whispered softly, "You are my Lord, my joy. I am yours!"

She stood up, her body trembling slightly, and began moving into the doorway. The rubescent mist grew thicker, appearing as a wall blocking her path. Lea reached out her right hand and thrust it into the fiery cloud.

A voice beckoned her to come forward. As she moved over the threshold, a small hand with long thin fingers came out of the fog and lightly scratched at her breast. It didn't appear to be that of a man, but rather belonged to a female of small frame, not unlike herself. The hand

140

grasped at her left breast, taking it fully and encasing it within the vise-like grip of the fingers. It was pulling her in, into the fire, into the smoke, into the heat, into the place of Night. Upon the soft, springed, altar within, her body would become the sacrificial offering of the evening's rites. Soon, she would be consecrated, forever, to the Lord of Night.

She stepped, unafraid, into the hellish mist, disappearing into the realm of shadow, lust, and madness.

CHAPTER IX

Lea swayed back and forth, admiring the slim figure reflected in the glass. The face that stared back was not the same one whose eyes had greeted her every day of her life—or rather, the mundane existence she had previously referred to as life. She was different, reborn, alive. Lifelong friends and acquaintances would not recognize her, unable to believe that this strange, smiling being bore any resemblance to the cardboard facade that had been before.

Lea arched her back, bringing her hands forward, then back, in one rhythmic, fluid, motion, until she looked like a bird about to take wing. She lifted her right leg and pointed her toe, tapping it lightly, in time to some phantom melody. Like a prima ballerina, she leapt, rebounded, then vaulted into the air once more; pausing briefly to pirouette and watch as the gossamer fabric billowed into puffs of translucent blackness. She had driven all the way to Lowville, a distance of some thirty-five miles, to purchase this feminine finery, so that it might please Lord Night.

She awoke this morning, a child of Night. As the last shadows of darkness were greeted by the dawn, Lea arose to do her Lord's bidding. Never before in her life, not even in the most remote reaches of her brain, in her most secret fantasies, could she have imagined the rites of pleasure to which she had been initiated. She was a celebrant of the joyous, carnal ritual.

The exact nature of the experience was unclear, foggy, as if recollected or seen through smoked glass. She remembered that there had been some pain, but it was momentary, followed by the most sublime of ecstasy.

Lea had lain on the bed, still with fear, waiting for Lord Night to accept her sacrifice. Her God was a cloud of red smoke, that crawled and slitered up from one's ankles, separating the legs, forcing them wide apart, until it strained the bones and muscles. With flesh of burning fire and red hot sword he had cut her, bled her, and finally become one with her. Lea had smelled the acrid perfume of his being, felt the vise-like pain of his embrace, moaned as his searing flesh throbbed within her; yet she had not seen him. Lord Night had neither substance or form. His was transcendent flesh, hidden amid clouds of wind-blown mist. Her body had experienced his pleasure, exploding in wave after wave of pulsating orgasm. She had been pinned to the bed by the sheer force of his weight. His breath had blown softly against her face. Lea did not doubt the truth of his existence, for she knew and had proof of his reality. The teeth marks on her shoulders, the long thin scratches on her thighs, the bloody discharge which, this morning, had oozed from inside her; all attested to the fact that

Lord Night had made his presence known to her.

Elated as she was with new found passion and carnal joys, Lea had need of something more. She was unable to contain the happiness she felt at what had already transpired, yet in the deepest recess of her soul, a small voice cried out, "If only he were made of flesh and blood and could abide with me always, in the hours of light as well as darkness. Then all the realms of ecstasy would be mine!"

Lea wanted to embrace strong, smooth, flesh. She wanted her lips to strain against his, to look deep into his eyes, to run her fingers through his hair, stroke his loins, gently lick his silken skin. To engage in such endearing intimacy, however, required a lover created of living matter—a man, not a cosmic phantom. Still, if the rest of her life were to be lived in this manner, loving not a man, but rather a formless night visitor, would that be so bad? An honor had been bestowed upon her. She, a mere mortal woman, was the deity's consort, the mistress of Night. If all her life was to be spent anticipating sundown, waiting breathlessly for the star's appearance, clutching at the night wind in a vain attempt to pull the apparition nearer, then so be it. He, Lord Night, had taken her from the depths of despair, of loneliness, of want, and raised her up. Her spirit soared to him, free at last from years of bondage. Her mind, her body, was his; existing for him, through him, one and the same with him. For the first time in her life, she felt sated. He had come in the winds and clouds of night, answering her prayers, laying waste to years of want, fulfilling the needs of body and soul. What more wondrous messiah than he?

The black chiffon lingerie appeared almost transparent as it clung to the curves beneath. This was to be her evening vestment, her robe of prayer, her habit of faith. Lea's fingers gently rubbed across the fabric. She had never before owned such a garment. It was scandalous, low-cut, and lacy. It felt good against her body, arousing feelings of unrestrained sensuality. She was, now, truly a female animal, a knowledgeable, worldly woman.

Lea moved her head from side to side and up and down, admiring her reflection. The being that stared back at her was someone else. The old Lea had died sometime during the night. From the top of her head to the tip of her toes, the image was new. The haircut flattered the small, fragile, features. Her cheekbones appeared more prominent, as the thin wisps of hair curved forward, hugging the rose-tinged flesh. The blue of her eyes was more noticeable, thanks to the wealth of shadow that rested upon her lids and the thick black mascara that had been layered on the lashes. Her lips appeared pouty and full. They were creamed red with soft, glowing color. Her breasts, barely concealed, had had their nipples rouged, to make them more attractive and appealing. The nails of her fingers and toes had been lacquered with several coats of bright crimson polish. Lea's body was soft and pink. She had soaked in a tub of fragrant water, shaving the unwanted hair from her legs, thighs, and underarms. Then, after creaming her body with unguents and dabbing perfume on her wrists, breasts, hair, thighs, and genitals, she settled back to await the coming shadows.

How full this day had been! After her morning coffee, she had gone out to the car, ready to embark on her day's adventure. As she had suspected, as if by magic, it started on the very first click of the ignition key. With the coming of morning, the things that had held her captive the night before suddenly ceased their hold, setting her free. The phone worked. The car performed like a fine-tuned machine. Nothing stood in the way of her escape. Lea could leave anytime she wanted; but such an action would no longer please the once prudish librarian. This was her new home; a place of contentment, happiness, and love. The feeling of peace and calm which comforted her was born here in this place, brought to life in the high, green, mountain glades. It existed nowhere else. If Lea wished the feeling to endure, desired that the virile spectre come nightly to her bed, she had to remain here, within this lonely wilderness. Lea had succumbed to the beauty, joys, and pleasures of this place. She could never leave it, or him; not now, not ever.

Lea blasted the radio all the way to Lowville, a tiny metropolis nestled on the other side of the mountains. She took the dirt road that ran along the reservoir until it veered away and became paved near the village of Number Four.

The first five miles or so of the roadway could have been plucked from an eerie science fiction movie, or so it first appeared. It looked so desolate and unpopulated as to make one think that all human inhabitants had been wiped from the face of the earth. Even the animals appeared to be in hiding. Further on, however, as the road moved closer to the banks of the reservoir, Lea saw cars pulled onto the shoulders and colorful tents nestled amid the greenery. The wilderness campers were out in force, at least twenty vehicles strong. It was comforting that if she ever needed help in an emergency or just wanted the companionship of another human being, she'd know where to go.

Once in Lowville, Lea went first to a beauty salon. There began the make-over, which would transform her from the plain, homely girl she had once been, into a woman worthy of a God's love. She treated herself to the works—haircut, facial, manicure, pedicure, ending the visit by having her eyebrows shaped and plucked. She'd been to beauty parlors before, receiving austere, unsophisticated haircuts and unattractive trims; but this was the first time in her life that she had spent money on such vanity, on unnecessary, frivolous luxuries. Having always been frugal with her money, at first she felt the fifty dollars charged her a bit too steep; but after drawing the admiring glances of several male passersby, she decided that it had been money well spent.

Today was the first day Lea could remember, in all the myriad of sunrises and sunsets that had comprised her life, that she had drawn lusting looks, been thought pretty. It was a nice feeling, both gratifying and ego-inflating, to have a man's eyes follow you, to know that you're desirable. She watched the men's eyes and reveled in the knowledge that she excited them, that they wanted her. How empty her life had been, till this day!

From Gilda's Glamour Emporium, she proceeded into the local chic boutique. St. Ives, she believed it was called. Lea spent twenty minutes picking her way through the lingerie rack, looking for something suitable with which to please the Night. Egged on by the saleslady's encouragement, she tried on several of the sheer garments. Strangely, she, normally modest beyond reproach, had been brazen about undressing and standing naked in front of the store's employees.

Lea ran through the gamut of colors; the pretty feminine, pastels, the deep reds and royal blues. All flattered her, but somehow didn't seem quite appropriate. As black was the color of night, the shade of pleasure, that too should be the hue of the vestments of worship. The store had a large selection. Many were thrown aside immediately because of their length. A short gown seemed somehow inappropriate. There was something sensual about soft fabric brushing against the ankles, blowing gently as one walked across the floor.

Lea selected eight gowns, but quickly discarded five as being too demure, or ill fitting, or constructed of the wrong fabric. She had struggled over the decision as to which of the remaining three to choose. One was made of silk, a Grecian design with shirred shoulders, plunging neckline, and softly gathered waist. The second was of shiny satin, resembling the sexy lingerie that Jean Harlow made famous. The last was structured of yards and yards of sheer transparent nylon, edged in lace. It hid nothing from view, making the naked flesh beneath appear as if it were being viewed through a billowy cloud of blackness.

All three appealed to her, became her, and would please the evening deity; so the decision was a difficult one. Lea mulled over which it should be, racking her brain with indecision, until finally she made the only choice possible. She bought all three. The years of miserly existence had now been put behind her. Lea wasn't poor, never had been. There was no reason why she should deny herself material pleasures. She made a good salary, had no debts, so why play pauper? Money

was for spending, to buy things which brought pleasure. If buying three gave her more pleasure than
making a single purchase, why the hell not do it?

Her mother had inveighed against people who spent
money like drunken sailors. "Excess is a sin," she
always used to say. If Mama was someplace where she
could monitor Lea's actions, she'd be having a fit for
sure. She'd think her only child damned, traveling
quickly down the road to hell. Lea didn't care anymore
about Mama or her silly rules, or her multitude of sins.
The old prude had lived her life without enjoying it or,
for that matter, ever experiencing it fully. She had died
a bitter, moralizing, vindictive old bitch and had tried
in earnest to make Lea a carbon copy; but her daughter
had no intention of denying or suppressing her desires
the way her mother had. Pleasure was a good thing, it
was Lord Night's gift to man, and Lea was damn sure
that she was going to get her fill.

She had wandered aimlessly through the shopping
area until coming to a large pharmacy which had the
word "Cosmetics" written in bold, black letters across
its front window. Lea peered in and saw that they had a
large selection, overseen by a rather attractive looking
saleswoman. The soft tones of makeup that the beauti-
cian had applied would disappear with the first touch
of soap and water, so Lea knew that if she wanted to
maintain the alluring aura, she'd need her own stock.

The woman had been very helpful assisting Lea in
choosing an entire range of beauty care needs. There
was moisturizer, base, blush, liner, mascara, shadows,
and pencil; so many things to purchase and be knowledgeable about.

Painting one's face was always considered sinful in

Mama's eyes. The use of makeup was a sign, held up to men, indicating that the wearer was a loose, immoral wench, prime for the taking. Thank God Mama was dead, because if she wasn't, seeing Lea now would certainly bring about her prompt demise.

There was so much to learn about being a woman, about projecting a sensual, provocative appearance. The art of stroking on liner, of separating each and every lash with color, of patting on soft, pink, hues were skills that females normally acquired early, while still teenagers. Unfortunately, as in all other things, Lea was a late bloomer. She was trying her wings, attempting to reclaim her youth, while other women her age were beginning to feel themselves old, maturing into middle age.

She listened carefully as the woman explained the use of each and every product and the sequence of their application. At first the woman had a difficult time restraining laughter at some of Lea's questions, they seemed so naive; but when she realized that the ignorance was real and not a ruse, her explanations and hints became detailed. Within a half-hour's time, Lea had acquired enough knowledge on the subject to do a decent job of accentuating her good points and diminishing her bad ones, so that the overall effect would be considered pretty.

In addition to all the facial supplies, the woman also convinced her to buy a collection of bath salts and oils, body powders, creams, after-bath splashes, and a wealth of perfumes, which would have aroused the envy of any ancient princess. She had enough feminine ammunition in her possession to encounter, do battle with, and overpower any man who happened within her web of alluring wiles. The only object of maleness she desired, however, was the heart of Lord Night. Being a *femme fatale* was new to her. Never in her wildest imaginings had she conceived herself to be anything but Godly pure, awkward, and, quite frankly, homely.

She had often wondered why Mama's God demanded that His followers be unattractive. It seemed strange that a loving God would decree all his most beautiful creations to be consecrated to Satan. Why should an accident of birth arouse the disdain of a deity and forever damn a soul? Lord Night, whoever, whatever he was, admired beauty in human creatures. By this appreciative, loving, god, Lea's efforts would be looked upon with favor.

Having finished her dealings at the pharmacy, Lea left, weighted down with clumsy packages and considerably poorer. At first, she hustled along in the direction of her car, anxious to unload her burden; but then, remembering the true purpose of her trip, she slowed her pace, pausing to look in all the windows she passed. Her morning's efforts at self improvement and beautification, although important, were secondary to the matter at hand. She had come to Lowville primarily to purchase materials with which she could fashion an altar to Lord Night.

Her phantom lover required that objects be offered up to him in sacrifice. She was directed to build an altar beside her bed. Upon it, in the center, Lea was to place a small bowl in which to burn incense. Two candelabra, containing the darkest color candles available, were to be placed at its sides. At the center front, a small metal goblet, a chalice, was to rest. Their use and purpose, however, remained a mystery.

154

Lea had almost reached the car when she noticed that, directly across the street from it, in the window of an antique shop, was displayed the perfect altar for her god. After depositing everything in the Pinto, she hastened to the shop. As she approached the window, she could see the object more clearly. The legs were dark—cherry wood she thought, carved with an intricate pattern that vaguely resembled tiny, clawing gargoyles. It was higher than a normal table, standing about three and a half feet off the floor. From its unusual design, Lea surmised that it had probably been used as a display console in a foyer. Its unusual height and ornate wood, however, were not what attracted her eye. It was the shiny, thin, black stone top. From across the street, it had appeared to be obsidian; but, on drawing closer, she realized that it was a delicate slab of thin, veined marble. The color, form, and structure were perfect for her needs. What better altar could there be, upon which to worship Lord Night, than one made of gleaming black? No matter what the price, Lea knew that she had to have it.

She didn't haggle with the owner. He named his price, one hundred and fifty dollars, and she paid it without argument. If she had searched the world over, she couldn't have found a more befitting altar.

As the bill of sale was being written, Lea's eyes scanned the interior of the shop for the other items which she required. As if he, the holy one, had led her to that place, all the objects he had charged her to find came into view. She spied a pair of delicate pewter candleholders, each designed to hold two thin tapers. They would look beautiful reflected in the glowing black marble. On a shelf beyond, she noticed a little

155

grey metal incense burner. Its tiny bowl sat on four steel balls. Engraved around the outside edge were dragons, no bigger than her thumbnail.

Lea grabbed the items up, bringing them back to the cash register, where the man was trying to compute the sales tax. Behind him, in a glass-enclosed case, were valuable objects of art, among them a deep silver goblet, whose base and edge were decorated with intricate black etchings of vined flowers. On the outside center of one side, a piece of ornate, hammered silver formed a frame for a small, highly polished piece of black onyx. Its fragile beauty was exquisite. Lea stared at it in awe, as one does a holy communion chalice. It looked as if it had been created to sanctify her sacrifice. How lovely it would look placed upon the altar of Night, flickering candlelight reflecting off the contrasting silver and black, glowing warmly through a cloud of incense!

Lea could remember the man's smile as she indicated to him that she wanted to buy the silver chalice, too. Every merchant in the town of Lowville must have adored her, and why shouldn't they? She had spent a veritable fortune. Conspicuous consumption had suddenly become her credo. The owner of the shop packed the car for her, insisting, much against her protestations, that she would need help carrying the table from the car to the cabin. She knew without hesitation that he was wrong. Lord Night would give her the strength needed. He had led her to that place so that she might fashion her altar from things that pleased him. He would not have gone to all the trouble to achieve perfection, to expedite her search, only to give her difficulty later on.

Lea looked away from her reflection in the glass, to

the place where the altar now stood. A smile came to her lips. It looked precisely as she had envisioned it would. She knew, instinctively, that her endeavors would please Night. Her obedient devotion would be much favored in his eyes. She had followed his desire, in not only the purchase of the items, but their placement as well. It had all been accomplished as he had directed.

All was ready for the evening's rites, the incense and candles in place. The tapers were midnight blue in color, the darkest she could find, the incense a fragrant jasmine.

Lea had purchased them at a little tourist trap she had passed on the way home. The woman behind the counter had stared at her strangely when Lea requested black candles, probably thinking them needed for a satanic mass. She giggled as she remembered the look of disapproval and disbelief. If only the old woman knew to what use they'd be put! Suddenly she was convulsed by laughter, as she imagined the woman standing by her bed, scandalized as the rituals of night transpired.

The laughter stopped as she stared out the window into the daylight. Lord Night would not come to rest with her yet.

She moved to the bed and lay down upon it gently. What a beautiful place this had become for her! Lea moved her hand, sliding it over the satin coverlet. Her mind was functioning, yet at the same time, it was dwelling in a fog, afraid to think of what the future might bring. Her vacation was to be a short one. In this state of happy pleasure, the days would pass by fast and then it would be time to go home. Could she leave this haven of joy? Would Lord Night follow her, or was this green wilderness the only place where he could reside?

Having experienced ecstasy, would she be willing to do without? Never! She would follow the rites of night to wherever they would lead. Her days of self-denial were over. She had found fulfillment in this dark, sensual deity. Now that her body ached for the soft night wind's touch, she would not, could not, ever give him up, ever return to being what she once had been, a frigid, frustrated old maid. Wither goest Lord Night, she too would follow. To move here would mean leaving her job, selling her house, and living like a hermit; but, if need be, she'd do it. At this point, she'd do anything; lie, cheat, steal, even kill so that her passionate, formless lover would continue his nightly pilgrimage to her bed. She'd prostrate herself before his altar, humbled and degraded, debased and demeaned; yet it would not matter. She had no pride, no desires other than the alleviation of want, the satisfaction of the flesh, an end to her groin's aching. Night's touch was addictive; once experienced it became an ongoing need.

She could feel her heart race as thoughts of warm embraces and rhythmic movements flashed through her brain. It was torture, this waiting for darkness. She had to occupy herself with other thoughts, but what? Her mind seemed unwilling to contemplate anything other than the sweaty meshings of naked bodies.

Like the pulsations of a strobe light, scenes of her day's activities once again moved to the forefront of thought. A smile came to her lips as she recalled the phone conversation with Aunt Evelyn. The old woman had called in a dither, saying that she had been worried sick because of her inability to contact her niece. Lea calmed her, explaining that the telephone had been temporarily out of order. She spoke of how much she was enjoying the mountains, emphasizing how beneficial the solitude was. Everytime Evelyn hinted at coming up for a long weekend stay, Lea would go on about how being alone was great therapy, helping one to get in touch with the root causes of problems, allowing them to be worked out and overcome. Her aunt, so worried about Lea's mental condition, was not about to interfere with anything that might be serving to calm the girl's frayed nerves. After four attempts to wangle an invitation to the cabin failed to obtain the desired results, the old woman gave up, hoping that, at some later time, before the end of her vacation, her niece would have need of her companionship and would extend her the offer of hospitality.

In a way, Lea felt bad about putting her off, but there was nothing else she could do. How could the rites of Night be performed with a third party present? True, Aunt Evelyn had conducted her life quite differently than Mama, being quite a libertine; but still, she would not understand the presence of an altar in the bedroom, nor the rituals of devotion, nor the sounds of pleasured moaning emitted from within the cloud of red fog. Evelyn would think her mad. It would take several conversations just to prepare her for the shocking change in Lea's demeanor and physical appearance; the make-up, hair-do, and self-confidence. All other aspects of her life in the mountain cabin had to be kept a well-guarded secret. The only way to accomplish that was to keep people away, especially Aunt Evelyn.

Lea hoped that she could continue sidestepping the issue of having the old woman visit, at least until she could come up with a feasible plan of action. The only real problem would occur if Evelyn took it upon herself to come unannounced. That would spell disaster. Lea didn't even want to think about such a thing happening. With a nosy relative wandering around, there could be no evening ritual and without it, no pleasure. Aunt Evelyn was the type who thought a little harmless masturbation good for body and soul; but she'd be unable to understand or cope with sexual rituals of this magnitude. However possible, at whatever expense, no matter whom she hurt, Lea's seclusion from the outside world must be maintained.

Her eyes wandered to the altar and then to the window. Light was still streaming over the sash. She wanted darkness, desired shadows. If only sunlight could forever be washed from the earth and she could dwell in night for eternity, then she would find paradise, the salvation for which she had spent a lifetime searching.

Lea closed her eyes and let her mind drift; to dreams of evening rites, to the warm wind and hot touch that was her mate, to all the pleasured fare that was the gift of Lord Night, and finally to the restful blackness that was sleep.

CHAPTER X

As if trying to tear flesh from bone, she rubbed her hands, attempting to wash away the fast congealing blood. Tears streamed down her face as she remembered the look on the tiny animal's face. Small, barely perceivable sobs bubbled to the surface from her tortured insides. What she was experiencing was a mixture of sorrow and disgust at what she had done, the bestial carnage of the act, mingled with disconsolate rage at her seeming inability to achieve the desired results. Lea had done something wrong somehow, misinterpreted her deity's desires.

She watched as tiny rivulets of crimsoned water descended the sides of the sink and disappeared down the drain. Gore covered her clothes, her skin, and was splattered in her hair; but that was not the worst of it. Lea had run from the bedroom in terror, seeking escape from the carnage that was within. Blood and tissue had spewed over the altar, the bed, the floor, the walls, and even spattered the ceiling. She could remedy the situation somewhat, scrub the room down, bathe and purify herself; yet how would she ever expunge the vision of that poor suffering animal from her brain?

Her hands moved feverishly, atempting to destroy all vestige of what had transpired. As her fingers worked the soap into a frothy lather, her eyes strained to focus on the upper portion of her forearm, where a large glob of coagulated blood had come to rest. At the center of the appalling, grisly, mass, a small quantity of soft white fur could be seen. It and the blood-drained, crimson-covered carcass were all that now remained of what had once been a living thing. That knowledge turned her stomach, making her retch.

She collapsed over the toilet bowl, allowing the acrid smelling, sour tasting fluid to gush from her lips, all the while wondering why she had committed such a heinous act. Her only answer was that she had done it for him, out of devotion for Lord Night. It was at his command that such a gruesome sacrifice be made.

As the first rays of yesterday's dawn lit the sky, her phantom lover stirred from his place upon the bed. Unlike the previous mornings' partings, he spoke to her. In a deep resonant voice, thick and smooth as velvet, he told her of his desire to be with her always, to remain with her even as the sun rose high into the heavens. Lea had listened intently as he spoke of the necessity of ceremony and sacrifice to make such a thing possible. He could come alive, be man, created of flesh, blood, and bone, if only she would be obedient to him and perform the rites as he directed. Such was the epitome of her desire, the fabric of her need, the very essence of all that would pleasure her. Nothing was as important as this. It was to her that he had entrusted the task of giving him form and structure. She, Lea, was to create a living, breathing, being. The deity would come to life for her. Once flesh, he would provide her with pleasure and joy beyond imagining, far surpassing her wildest expectations. There was nothing, no matter how vile or perverse, that she wouldn't do to grant him life.

He had told her to offer the most sacred of life's liquids upon his altar, to fill the silver chalice with a crimson sacrifice. It was so simple, she wondered why she hadn't thought of it before. Life was blood and blood was life; it seemed a simple enough conclusion.

She had spent the early morning hours wakeful, ruminating as to how this holy offering should be made. At first she'd thought that she'd purchase the blood from a local butcher, under the pretext of making blood pudding. According to Mama, her grandmother on her father's side used to prepare such a dish. That idea was quickly discounted, however. Meat was slaughtered in packing houses nowadays. Even if she could find a butcher shop up here in this wilderness, her chances of finding flesh blood would be almost non-existent.

Next, Lea concluded that perhaps by buying a very bloody roast, she could solve her dilemma; but her peace of mind was transitory. To fill the chalice, would require at least one and a half cups of fluid, perhaps more. She'd need six large cuts of meat, maybe more to provide her with enough to fill the goblet. Even if she could do it, Lea realized that her efforts would be avoiding the basic issue at hand. The blood had to be fresh, life-giving.

In order to imbue her spirit lover with humanity, it

was necessary to sacrifice something alive, to kill one breathing entity in order that Night might live. She had to take a life in order to give one. As repulsive as that had first sounded, she determined that that was as it had to be. What was a life, any life, worth when compared to the creation of a flesh and blood entity? Nothing mattered any more except the realization of that dream. God would become man by her hand. She would not cease her quest until this goal had been attained, until dream became reality.

It had taken time for Lea to accept the fact that her hand would be the one which would take life. She would become the dreaded Angel of Death. She had felt sorrow at this knowledge, yet it would be done with studied swiftness, without pain, without suffering. In one moment there would be life, in the next, none. Surely a quick, merciful death of this kind, for this purpose, was not an act of sadness, but of profound joy. To be chosen to provide life to a god was an honor most high.

Her first decision dealt with what life form should be sacrificed. Initially, her faintheartedness led her to consider insects. She couldn't feel guilt-ridden about eradicating flies and spiders, or worms and beetles. Lea dwelt on that idea for a while, finally abandoning it. It would take her an entire day of digging dirt, overturning rocks, and the like to get enough little beasties to do the job. Even so, how was she to know when she'd found enough? How many mashed spiders would produce enough blood to fill the cup? And then was insect blood red, like the human type? She wasn't sure, but felt that the color was an important ingredient in making the whole endeavor succeed.

Her easy access to the sacrificial creature was all important; after all, how can one conduct a rite of this kind without first having a victim? Using simple logic, she examined her ready options.

She was in a forest filled with all types of animal life—rabbits, squirrels, woodchucks, deer and others; but without a weapon or traps, she'd be unable to snare something suitable.

Living near a large body of water as she did, with its tributary streams and small marsh areas, would provide her with a wealth of fish and frogs. The idea had at first, appealed to her. They were easy to catch and keep, assuring their viability at the time of sacrifice, and she could slaughter as many as need be, to fill the goblet. Their extermination wouldn't make her feel particularly guilty, either. She viewed them as being at about the same level of development in life's scale as the insects; a functioning spinal chord that ate, defecated, and procreated, nothing more. At first, Lea made plans to follow through with the seemingly simple scheme, preparing to buy fishing tackle and bait, determining where, of the areas she had explored, would be most likely to contain a large number of bullfrogs, planning an agenda for the day which would provide ample time both to purchase the necessary equipment and to accomplish the task of capture.

It was while Lea was readying herself for the drive to Big Moose that she had become uneasy. Something about her strategy disturbed her. The plan was too simple, too impetuous. She was trying to avoid the unpleasantness of guilt, taking the easy way out. If she had acted on anything other than impulse, she would have realized it earlier.

Somewhere in the faint corners of her mind, pulsations of thought had occurred. The phrase "sympathetic magic" kept echoing in her brain, and with it, recollections of its meaning. Like produces like. Although not clear, it seemed to her that this philosophy was the basis of voodoo. If you wanted to harm someone, you simply create a doll which resembled them. The hostile acts to which the doll is subjected will occur in reality to the hated person.

Lea had tried to extrapolate some sense from the example to apply to her own situation. The meaning was simple. If it was her intention to create a warm-blooded creature, if that was the goal, then the offering, the catalyst which began the fabrication of life should be the same. In this case, that meant offering crimson, liquid, fresh blood, still warm from the body from which it had been taken. This new logic disrupted all her plans for a simple solution and did away with her hope for a guilt-free sacrificial rite.

Lea couldn't determine in advance what type of warm-blooded creature she'd use. It all depended on availability. Since it had been clear from the first that capturing an animal was not a viable alternative, her only means of obtaining a likely victim was through purchase—but how? The geography of the area would hamper her search, she was sure. How many pet shops could there be in the middle of the Adirondack wilderness? Without a phone book, Lea had no way of knowing. She had decided that for expediency's sake, all further planning would be done behind the wheel of her car. Lea reasoned that since it might take her half a day to locate a pet shop and another half day to drive to it, she had no time to waste.

As fate would have it, all the rushing and worry was quite unnecessary. It was on the way to Big Moose that it suddenly dawned on Lea that somewhere within the county there had to be an animal shelter or pound. Since she was unsure of whether it would be listed in the tiny local phone directory or, for that matter, how she'd ever manage to locate it in the maze of snakelike, winding mountain roads, Lea decided to stop by Ronald's office and enlist his aid. As it turned out, it was a smart move on her part, saving her time and many miles of traveling.

At first he didn't recognize her, with the makeup and new hairdo; but when he finally made the connection, the look on his face was one of utter shock. Ronald was friendly, wasting several minutes making insipid small talk. As at their previous meeting, he invited her to his home for dinner, although this time he seemed some-what less enthusiastic than he had the first time. Perhaps it was because she didn't look quite as lone-some or pitiful as she had on their first encounter. All during the exchange of pleasantries, when he didn't think Lea was paying attention, he stared at her, lest there be some mistake in identity, eyes exploring her softly painted face and her body's fluid, sensual, movements. Lea no longer bore any resemblance to the prematurely middle aged woman who had entered his office but a few days before.

She tried to appear nonchalant and untroubled while he rambled on and on, but her fidgeting betrayed her. She was in a rush and had no time to waste whiling away the morning in such a boring fashion. Lea had things to do. She attempted to interrupt his meander-ings on several occasions, finally succeeding.

With a broad smile, Lea explained to him the purpose of her visit. Her eyes did not betray her, as she fabricated a story of loneliness and the deep need she felt for some type of companionship. She'd gone on about how enjoyable it would be to have a warm, affectionate little creature waiting for her at the end of her day's labors, how it would add purpose and enjoyment to her life.

Ronald accepted her words as truth, commiserating with her on the sad burden of loneliness, bringing up several examples of how pets could fill the void caused by the death of a loved one.

Lea listened patiently for a moment or two and then, feeling pressed for time, she again guided the topic of conversation back to the matter at hand, that being the location of the closest animal shelter. To Ronald's knowledge, there wasn't a county operated facility, each town and village having the autonomy to set up one. The closest one he knew of was in the town of Boonville, a relatively short distance away as the crow flies, but some fifty miles over the twisting curves of the mountain roads. He went on to say that most people in the area tried to find homes for unwanted or stray pets themselves, through word of mouth or signs in local stores. Desperate to save time, Lea asked if he knew of anyone who was offering pets for adoption.

A big grin crossed his face, "Yes, as a matter of fact I know someone just like that. You're fond of cats, are you, playful little kittens?"

"Very much so," she said. "I think they're just adorable and so clean, hardly any trouble at all." Her face was frozen in a look of affected earnestness and interest.

170

Ronald nodded his head in agreement and began to explain, "My next door neighbor, Mrs. Coopersmith, took in a stray a few months back, a pretty little Persian mix. It must have been dropped because it was expecting. Anyway, it threw a litter of five kittens. Jenny managed to get rid of all of them except one little white female. It's eight weeks old and real cute. It's got long hair like the mother and big green eyes. It's all white 'cept for a spot on the nose, a front paw, and a mark on the hind end. Do you think you'd be interested?"

Her lips turned up in a smile, eyes staring straight ahead, fixed not on him, but on the smokey illusions of the coming night rituals. "It sounds just perfect. Exactly what I've been looking for." The smile turned into a large toothsome grin as she came to realize that her search was ended. "It sounds like she'll serve my needs beautifully."

He looked at her strangely for a moment. Perhaps it was the way Lea had uttered the phrase, but when she smiled at him again reassuringly, his unsettling feeling disappeared.

"Ronald, I just can't thank you enough! This is so wonderful," she gushed, watching his reaction. Right about then, Lea would have done anything to get her hands on a sacrificial offering. If necessary, she'd even have screwed him to obtain something alive, filled to capacity with warm, red blood.

He smiled innocently at her, unaware of what was going on behind the facade of sweet purity. "I'll call Jenny to make sure that the kitten is still there and see if you can go pick it up now, OK?"

"Fine, fine," Lea stated enthusiastically. She could remember thinking to herself how he'd pale, perhaps regurgitate, if he knew for what purpose she had enlisted his aid. For some strange reason, this charade pleased her. It was fun to dupe the ignorant, to make them participate, however innocently in, to their way of thinking, such a wholly base and despicable act.

He called the cat's owner and arranged for Lea to pick it up, giving her directions so that she might find the Coopersmith residence.

When all had been accomplished, Lea said her thanks and goodbyes and moved to leave. As her hand was poised on the doorknob, Ronald called after her, "Hey, by the way, what are you going to name the little bundle of fur?"

Lea thought for a moment, and then a thin, cruel smile came to her lips. "I think I'll name her Beatrice," she said thoughtfully.

"Beatrice?" he questioned, "Isn't that a rather strange name for a cat?"

She smiled sweetly, the picture of wholesome piety. "That was my mother's name," she said, all the while imagining the sacrificial rite, the blood pouring forth into the waiting cup—Mama's blood draining, dripping, drop by drop, into the chalice. What divine justice that would be! Giving up her life so that the thing which lay upon her daughter's bed, who slipped gently in and out of her hidden places, might have real life, might become man. Perhaps her blood could make up for the years of denial, the hours of guilty longing. The thought much pleased her.

Once again, that strange, questioning glance crossed his face. Perhaps it was the look in her eyes or the set of her jaw; but something about her, that frail, smiling form, suddenly seemed menacing.

Lea sensed his feelings and, unwilling to engage in a discussion or be scrutinized further, she raised her hand high and waved goodbye.

Mrs. Coopersmith appeared to be cut from the same cloth as Ronald; country innocence, old fashioned values, and totally boring. Within fifteen minutes of their meeting, Lea knew all there was to know about the gaunt housewife; how her mother had succumbed to cancer of the colon, how her husband was plagued by piles, how she worried that sinful, citified views of premarital sex would become the norm for innocent mountain youth; and on and on, ad nauseum.

Lea listened with seeeming interest, but barely hidden contempt on the inside. Thank goodness she hadn't been in any rush. The woman's mouth just kept moving, words and sounds droning on and on without end, nonsensical phrases, inane thoughts; but Lea escaped it all, her mind floating in the future, to the evening, to the rituals of shadow, to the time when a god, a lover without substance, without form, would become man, would become hers.

Jenny asked probing questions about her past; how she came to find herself in the wilderness, how she supported herself, and what her interests were. Lea resented this assault on her privacy, but she dared not show it. While her insides seethed, she smiled sweetly and answered the questions; most assuredly she'd get the kitten the necessary immunizations, certainly she'd have it spayed, why of course, the house she lived in was large enough so that the cat could remain indoors rather than being allowed to roam the woods. There seemed to be some unwillingness on Mrs. Coopersmith's part to give up the animal without first thoroughly investigating its new adoptive home, if not an onsight inspection, then one of words.

Lea grew increasingly uneasy as the barrage of questions continued. The interrogation went on punctuated only by periods of pregnant pause, when Mrs. Coopersmith would stare at her with accusing eyes, trying to decipher her real motivation. In the end, Lea won her over and the fuzzy white kitten became hers. If only the nosy bitch knew the fate to which she had consigned the creature!

On the way home, Beatrice cuddled against Lea's thigh, curling up safe, secure, and happy. Lea could remember feeling vaguely saddened then at what she had to do, but that soon passed. What price was this to pay, she convinced herself, to achieve her end?

The little kitten spent a goodly part of the afternoon scampering behind Lea, making vain attempts to use the cabin's furniture as scratching posts. Actually it had been rather pleasant, relieving the loneliness of the day. It was fun to frolic on the floor with the animal, playing tug-of-war with a hankie or batting a string.

As the time of evening approached, Lea was again overcome with remorse. She wished there was another way to accomplish her task without sacrificing the poor innocent animal; but try as she did to come up with a last minute alternative, she could not. The sacrificial rite had to be performed as planned. Her only consolation was that she would make the act as quick and painless as possible for the kitten. The most humane approach, Lea determined, was to take a razor blade and slit Beatrice's throat with one swift stroke. She assumed that, by exerting enough pressure while slashing, the cut would be so deep as to kill the animal almost instantaneously.

Lea trembled as she remembered the kitten playfully batting at the hem of her black satin gown, romping along behind as she walked from the bathroom to the bedroom holding the razor blade carefully between her fingers. The white ball of fluff had watched with curious interest from her vantage point on the bed, as Lea arranged the objects on the altar; first lighting the candles, then the incense, and finally centering the chalice with the blade beside it.

Beatrice followed close on her heels as Lea moved through the house, closing doors and windows, drawing shades and drapes, in preparation for the evening ritual. When all was as it should be, Lea looked around, finding much to her dismay that the animal had suddenly disappeared. Frantic that it had escaped or was nestled in an unfindable hiding place, she ran through the cabin searching, praying to Lord Night that nothing occur which would prevent her sacrificial rite.

Her worry had been for naught. She found Beatrice on a living room window sill, playfully batting at a lowered shade pull.

"Here kitty, kitty," Lea had called out, getting the animal's attention. "Come on, kitty. Be a good kitty," she cajoled and encouraged. "Come on baby kitty, kitty. Come with Mommy."

Like a lamb to the slaughter, the little green eyes looked up at her and then, in total innocence of what was to transpire, followed. Lea toyed with the idea of providing Beatrice wiht a special last meal, a bowl of warmed milk, but then thought better of it. It would only serve to prolong the agony and indecision over what she had to do. Better to do it now, she had thought, and get it over and done with, once and for all. Besides, she'd have a flesh and blood companion to console her and help deal with the guilt.

As she approached the altar, Lea picked Beatrice up and cuddled her for the last time; then grabbing her tightly by the scruff of the neck, she dangled the animal above the chalice. Breathing in deeply, Lea reached for the razor and brought it up on a level with the kitten's throat. With a lightning quick stroke, she drew it across the tender flesh. It would have worked as planned, if only Beatrice hadn't begun to squirm. The razor cut a huge gash on the left side, but didn't even scratch the right. Beatrice began squalling in pain, baring her claws, flailing her limbs, trying to dig and scratch Lea's flesh. The kitten was in agony, writhing in torment, while Lea stood motionless unable to determine what to do next; how to put the animal out of its misery. She tried holding Beatrice securely over the goblet, so the blood would drip down into it; but without success. The animal's movements served to loosen Lea's tenuous hold on it, finally causing Beatrice to fall onto the altar, tipping over the silver chalice. As she reached down to reclaim her victim, the sharp claws lashed out at her again and again, trying in a vain attempt to ward off a resumption of the torture. After struggling a moment to regain hold, Lea again lifted the animal, only this time the neck was not so well exposed. Lea slashed at it time and again as the tiny feline shrieked out in pain, unwilling or unable to die. As the razor repeatedly struck out at its target, Lea cried out begging Lord Night that this thing be over and done, that the carnage end. Tears descended her cheeks as the creature's body vibrated in what appeared to be convulsions. Lea stared on in horror as the fuzzy coat changed color, from white to red.

"Die, damn it, die!" she screamed, madly slashing at her defenseless victim.

Blood was everywhere, spewing out as fountains from the wounds that now covered the tiny body. It splattered the wall, covering the altar, dripping like tiny rivers to the floor, clinging like glue to her own body, yet the tiny beast continued to thrash about in agony. Lea was so terrified at the carnage that, although she continued to strike out at the kitten, the force of her blows was not sufficient to cut deeply and kill. Her ineptitude only served to prolong the horrored torment.

Unable to withstand anymore, Lea dropped the razor and grabbed the animal, holding it tightly; one hand on the head, the other on the breast. With all the strength she could call forth, Lea snapped both hands downward until she heard the sickening crunch indicating that she had broken the kitten's neck. The writhing stopped. At last it was free of pain, death had finally come.

Tears etched Lea's cheeks as she remembered the torment the poor thing had endured. She hadn't meant it to be that way. It was supposed to have been so simple, so easy—painless, not agonizing.

Lea held the carcass over the chalice, allowing the crimson liquid to flow into the cup. When the goblet was filled to overflowing, Lea lay the corpse in front of it. Still covered with blood, she had stretched herself out upon the bed, to await the coming of Lord Night.

Red mist covered the room as he came to taste of the sacrifice. The night wind moved upon the bed, caressing, stroking, bringing her pleasure; but the thing she desired most was denied. He was still a formless shadow, a phantom lover. When dawn came and darkness disappeared, so did the object of her desire; melting into the soft light of sunshine, leaving only an overturned chalice, a sacrifice deemed unacceptable.

Standing over the sink now, watching the red tinged water, her tears cascading, Lea tried to make sense of what occurred. Had she done something wrong? Why was Night displeased with her sacrifice? A sudden chill ran through her, as she recalled the phrase, "Like produces like." Perhaps she shouldn't expect a kitten's blood to produce anything but another cat. To create a man might require a sacrifice of human blood. To offer the death of one man in exchange for the life for another. She trembled in fear. Even the thought of such a thing sickened her; yet what other answer could there be? Lea breathed in deeply, calming herself, setting her jaw. Just how far would she go to realize her dream, to obtain her desires?

CHAPTER XI

Lea turned back to look at the car, pleased at her thoroughness. It was well hidden amid the lush greenery, inconspicuous, obscured to passersby. If she were to complete her evening's work, it was necessary that her anonymity be maintained, that no one make the connection between the shoreline campsite and her.

Evening was fast approaching. The sun had already settled behind the mountain tops and the woodlands were being cloaked in ever darkening shades of grey. Against this backdrop of changing shadows Lea's movements were almost imperceivable. Resembling a black-garbed goddess, she hastened down the narrow, rocky pathway which led to the shore. Lea had traveled this way earlier in the day. It was here that her quest had come to an end. Clutched firmly to her breast, protected from possible harm, was a small bundle formed of kitchen towels, containing a pocket knife, a candle, a flashlight, and an empty quart jar. She moved swiftly along, attempting to maintain her footing on the craggy, rutted path. Her gown brushed against the rocks, occasionally hooking itself on the dense underbrush. The hem was being destroyed by a series of tiny rips and tears. At first she had hesitated wearing it, for fear that it would be ruined; but it was the required vestment of evening. It didn't really matter what happened to it. In a few hours, there would be no need for it or the sacred rituals of night. Evenings spent conjuring a formless mate would be a thing of the past.

Her sandaled feet were becoming bruised and scratched by the stones and twigs that covered the trail. As the going became more difficult, Lea slowed her pace, worried that she'd slip and fall, dropping the precious bundle and destroying the treasures within it.

Her mind floated, imagining scenes from the coming hours. She smiled to herself as she visualized Tony's reaction to her sudden unannounced appearance at his campsite, especially his response to the filmy black negligée she was wearing. She could see it all now. He'd look up from his campsite, giving her one of his sexy, crooked smiles, eyes opened wide, straining as they examined the form that lay hidden beneath her gown. He'd laugh, not loudly, but rather contemptuously, under his breath; all the while thinking that she had come to him overwhelmed with desire, ripe for the bedding. How wrong he would be!

She'd met him this morning, while out surveying the number of single occupant campsites near her cabin. Lea had walked a mile, without seeing any sign of human habitation, when she noticed something, a dot of orange, down the hill by the bank. She left the road and walked the quarter mile through the woods to investigate.

What she had found was a low tangerine colored mountaineering tent nestled under a large tree near the bank. Beside it was a crudely put together wooden platform, on which a single burner camp stove and some aluminum cookware sat. Suspended from an overhanging branch was a large orange and blue backpack which seemed full and heavy. Between two nearby trees, a rope had been strung and over it had been thrown a single sleeping bag to air. Not far from the tent, Lea saw that a large fire pit had been dug and encircled with a ring of stones. Next to it was placed a thick log to be used as a chair. It took little deductive reasoning on her part to realize that the campsite was occupied by a single person, probably one man. Her theory was to be proved fact, shortly thereafter.

She wandered around the site looking for signs of life—warm coals on the fire, the crackling of twigs and leaves, the driving rhythm of music from an unseen radio—but all was strangely silent. Lea stood for several minutes surveying the shoreline, thinking perhaps that the owner was fishing nearby. Unable to locate anyone on shore, she returned her attention to the immediate area of the campsite, making several slow turns around the area before finally giving up the search and returning to the path.

Lea had only gone five paces, when she was overcome by feelings of dread, of lurking danger. Frightened, she surveyed the woods that surrounded her. Her heart began pounding when she realized that the thin shadowed figure hidden behind the bush to her left was not part of a tree, but a tall, dark-haired man.

"Looking for something?" a deep voice arrogantly inquired. "Like me, perhaps?"

Her first inclination had been to run away. There was something in the tone of his voice—an element of foreboding, as if he meant her harm. Lea's heart raced and her feet were poised to skitter off like some scared rabbit, when she hesitated a moment to analyze the situation. This was precisely what she had spent the morning searching for. A lonely campsite, occupied by one lone human, isolated from the prying eyes of the world. She forced herself to be calm, thinking that no matter what, no ill could befall her; her god, Night, would not permit it.

He moved out of the shadows and approached her. Naked to the waist, he was quite handsome, with an aura of sexy ruggedness about him. He was tall, perhaps six feet or more, and muscular, with broad shoulders and small hips. His skin was smooth and tanned, his chest and arms covered with a curly black hair. His features were sharp, appearing to have been chiseled from marble; the cheekbones high, the nose thin and aquiline. A day's growth of beard covered his face, adding to the impression of macho maleness. Beneath eyebrows of bushy brown were his most striking feature; large blue-grey eyes, fringed with long, thick, black lashes. His eyes studied her in a fixed gaze, as hers continued their close examination of his virile physique. His features were framed by masses of loose brown waves and curls, which were being gently tossed by the warm mountain wind. The focus of her gaze shifted downward, first along the muscular expanse of chest and bulging biceps, then to the flat, rippled belly, finally coming to rest on his strong thighs. The denims he wore were skin tight, pulling snug against his genitals, accentuating his large, bulging, penis and leaving little to her imagination. Her eyes tarried there for a moment, fixed on the barely hidden testimony to his maleness.

She knew then that if her basic philosophy were right, he, with all his unconcealed attributes, was the perfect candidate.

While Lea had been coyly exploring his body with her eyes, he had done the same, except he did it overtly, making sure that she was aware that he was staring at her breasts and crotch. His gaze was meant to unnerve her, but she was sure that he was relatively harmless, not your everyday, garden variety wilderness rapist. The arrogant attitude, the blatant sexuality in dress, the steamy stares, the well choreographed movements designed to show off his body to best advantage all led her to believe that this fine example of American manhood fancied himself a champion of the sexual revolution, a real super stud, a temple of machismo.

She had been attracted yet repelled by his swaggering attitude. He smiled at her, eyes half closed in what appeared to be his best effort at a bedroom stare, probably thinking that she was beside herself with desire, about to pounce on him, tearing his clothes to shreds. If only he knew what it was that she had planned for him, he wouldn't have been quite so cocky.

After preliminary introductions had been made, Lea learned that his name was Tony Delucia. He was a twenty-three-year-old would-be actor from New York City who worked at odd jobs between roles. In need of a little relaxation from his hectic schedule, said Tony, he was presently taking a two week backpacking trip through the Adirondacks.

It was immediately apparent from the way he spoke

that he thought she should be justifiably impressed and wholly thrilled to be in his presence. He was enamored of himself, in love with his own image, the most conceited bastard she had ever had the misfortune to encounter. He insisted that Lea must recognize him from the commercials and acting jobs he'd done on television, not believing her when she told him she didn't even own a TV, and therefore could never have seen his face before.

Their first encounter consisted of an hour spent in verbal sparring that ran the gamut from mild displeasure to genuine animosity. He kept saying things geared toward making her believe that he was a real swinger, a man about town, a jet setter. He spoke of the famous New York discos he frequented, and how he had shared snorts of coke and tokes with the rich and famous. His eyes searched her face for some evidence of the admiration and awe she must surely feel, but they became angry and cold when he realized that she was not, in even the smallest way, impressed. By his smirks and disgusted looks, Lea could tell that he thought every aspect of her work and life, her very being, boring. To his way of thinking she was a bumpkin, a real hick, a mousey librarian completely out of step with the times; but, what the hell, he was lonely and in need of female companionship. Tony hadn't ripped off a piece of ass since before he left the city, and he didn't have to like her to play in her pants. All she had to do was lie still till he satisfied himself.

He put some moves on her, offering her a beer and sensually patting the ground next to where he sat, bidding her come spread her legs. In a most impudent fashion, he told her how all the girls he'd ever bedded referred to him as the new Don Juan, only better, exceedingly so. The long winded dissertation he gave on his uncanny ability to provide sexual partners with multiple orgasms, although impressive, didn't do anything to arouse her or make Lea want him. Why should it? After all, she had the most consummate lover in the universe and she was faithful to him.

She could remember her thoughts at the time, as he moved his hand downward, attempting to draw her attention there. Lea had been angered by his superior attitude. She had never seen a man who would unashamedly adjust his erect penis while in her presence. The being that stood before her, she convinced herself, was a repulsive pig, a vile purveyor of smut. How dare he behave so in full view of the consort of Lord Night? He was trying to lure her into an adulterous liaison; but she would not succumb to his throbbing bulge, the smooth texture of his skin. She would be strong and true to her Lord.

He had pressed the matter by grabbing her arm and pulling her down upon the soft pine needles and grass, rolling over on top of her tiny frame and suggestively rubbing himself against her. His soft full lips had forcefully moved across hers, trying to convince Lea that more such pleasure awaited her if only she'd agree to make love with him.

For a few terrifying seconds, she was afraid of him and the situation, but it was unclear to her whether she feared rape, or her own weak willed nature.

Lea pushed him off her with all the strength she could muster, explaining that regardless of what he was used to, she was less liberal in her sexual mores and liked to get to know someone before she jumped into bed with him. Lea almost giggled when she said it, remembering how until a few short days ago, she had been a shriveled virgin prune. Lea wondered whether Tony sensed her inexperience or whether he just decided that she wasn't worth putting up a fight for. Regardless of the reason, he released his hold of her and let her up. After that, Tony was inhospitable and unfriendly, acting as if he couldn't wait until she left.

She obliged him, returning immediately to the path that would lead her back to the highway, all the while thinking that what she had to do had suddenly become less repulsive. In fact, it might even be counted as pleasure. If anyone deserved such a fate, begged for it, then it was Tony Delucia. He had sinned exceedingly against Lord Night. How dare he try to seduce the god's woman? Such transgressions had to be punished and Lea was the instrument of the chastisement. Lord Night would have his revenge.

Just a little bit further and she would be there. Ahead, she could see the warm, inviting glow of his campfire. The beat of her heart quickened. The time for action had come.

Lea saw the crouched form rise from beside the fire, standing tall, then turn toward her. He had heard the soft crunch of twigs and leaves under her feet and was straining to find the source of the sound. She lifted her hand and began waving to him. He didn't respond. In the swiftly descending shadows, Lea was unsure of how much of her body was visible to him, amid the trees and brush. Perhaps he had been unable to see or recognize her.

"Tony," she called out to him loudly, "It's Lea.

188

Remember, from this afternoon?"

From the campsite came a loudly echoing hello and an invitation to come forward.

As she neared him, his eyes opened wider and wider, becoming almost saucer-like. He was clearly unprepared for her night's vestments. Tony's glances darted over the shimmery black fabric, lingering a moment to stare at the full breasts and nipples, visible through the almost transparent cloth. His eyes moved downward, focusing on the thick mound of pubic hair that formed a darkened contrast against the pale skin.

Her behavior this evening was markedly different than on their first meeting. She seemed somehow different, transformed. Even the look in her eyes was unfamiliar. This afternoon she had seemed a hopeless prude, cold and distant; now she was sensual, seductive, inviting him to feast on her luxuriant flesh.

For a moment they stood together, neither speaking. His eyes moved over her body, like tiny fingers exploring every aspect of her being. What was she doing here? Why had she come?

His blue eyes searched her face. "I never expected to see you again. I kinda—" he stopped short, a sudden look of suspicion crossing his features, "I got the impression that you didn't like me."

She didn't respond, but simply smiled at him. It was an inscrutable look, one that would have befitted the Mona Lisa, revealing nothing of her motives, needs, or wants.

Lea moved past him, approaching the fire. She stood before it, allowing its warmth to take the night chill from her bones, listening appreciatively to the gentle crackling sounds it made.

The golden glow of the fire flickered behind her. Through the thin fabric, she now appeared naked before him. The soft round smoothness of her buttocks, the muscular expanse of her thigh, the gentle crevice of her nether lips, all were revealed to him. Dressed like that, coming to him as she did, it could only mean one thing; the bitch wanted him. The afternoon had all been a farce, he thought, like some ill conceived play. She'd been acting the part of the scandalized virgin; but now that the loneliness of night was coming, she desired a little male companionship. He had met weirdos before, but she was a bit much—by day Heidi, after dark Mata Hari.

He feasted his eyes for a few minutes more, trying to make sense of her actions. Women—would he ever understand them? They acted like they never thought about it, never craved it, but that was all a big act. Inside they never thought about anything else but sex. It was most evident to him that she had come here to get laid and he planned to oblige.

Tony moved to the tent and dragged the sleeping bag out, moving it near to the fire.

"Thought that maybe you might be getting a little tired," he said smiling. "It's a long walk from the road. You want to lie down?"

A broad grin crossed his face, crinkling his eyes and wrinkling his nose. He was thinking about how good it would feel to spend himself inside her. The way she looked now, it would not be a difficult task.

Her eyes roamed over his body, from his belly, to shoulders, to groin; then, up to his face. Again she didn't respond, preferring instead to curve her lips into a small smile, allowing her eyes, twinkling at the

190

thought of what was to come, to flash back her answer in the affirmative.

As if having suddenly remembered something, Lea looked at him; raising her right hand and moving it out in front of her, palm forward, index finger extended upward. In her language of silence, she was telling him to wait a moment, that she'd forgotten something.

He stared at her quizzically, wondering what in hell she was doing, what kind of tease and run game she was playing?

Sensing his suspicions and irritation, she drew her left hand away from her breast, holding her tiny bundle firmly in her fingers. With a look of sweet allure, she smiled at him again, holding it up to view. With her right hand she pointed to an area behind the tent.

"Oh, I get it," he said knowingly, nodding his head, "Protection, huh?"

She moved her head slowly up and down, grateful that her little charade was working. His assumption that the bundle contained a means of contraception would give her the opportunity she needed to remove the necessary implements.

"You're my kind of woman, ready for anything! Hey Lea," he said, calling out to her as she began walking toward the rear of the tent, "Are you a girl scout?"

She looked at him strangely. "What?" she asked, unable to determine the meaning of his words.

"You know," he laughed, "Be prepared!"

Lea shook her head in annoyance. Eliminating him could be counted as one of life's minor pleasures. "I'll be right back," she called to him, furious by his arrogance.

Once behind the tent, Lea quickly unwrapped the

towels and removed the contents. The jar, candle, and flashlight were placed neatly on the ground where they could be easily retrieved. When things started happening, she'd have need of them. Lea picked up the knife, and with her fingernails pried out the blade, clicking it into place. It was not very big, but would suit her purposes. It was small enough so that she could partially conceal it in her hand, yet large enough to accomplish the task adequately. This time, she promised herself, there would be no slip-ups, no foolish, stupid mistakes. Tonight she had no intention of blundering or panicking. She would muster all her strength to do what was necessary.

Her right hand was held straight down at her side as Lea rounded the corner of the tent and walked into the soft fireglow. Tony was lying on top of the sleeping bag, stripped to the waist, having removed his shoes and socks. How impatient of him, she thought.

He didn't move a muscle as she neared him. The look in his eye was that of a spider waiting to prey upon a poor unsuspecting fly; but in this case appearances were deceiving. Lea dropped to her knees beside him, taking care to place the knife next to the bag and quickly hide it from view.

Her fingers reached out and gently caressed his chest, then moved up over his throat to his face. The muscles of his jaw were taut, his eyes fixed as she bent her head to kiss him. For a few moments they moved against each other, two strangers, each involved with the other for their own selfish needs, without affection, without caring. While his hands caressed her breasts and kneaded her warm thighs, she imagined that this form of flesh and blood was her loving Lord, not some brash bastard of momentary acquaintance. They explored each other's bodies, taking time to linger on occasion when their partner's reaction revealed pleasure.

Tony pulled away from her, desire emanating from his eyes. He would have her now! He unbuckled his belt and then, with one swift stroke, removed pants and underwear together, revealing a large, thick, stiff organ. A strange feeling came over her, as if she were reliving a piece of her life. Lea knew very well that this was the first time she'd ever seen an adult male penis, yet when she touched its soft warmth, it engendered a foggy, gray memory of a previous time, a sexual meeting from the past. For a split second, the eerie feeling lingered; then, directing her mind back to the matter at hand, it slowly slipped away. She'd have to act soon. He was much too aroused. Allowing this thing to proceed would make her unfaithful to her god, prove her sorely wanting, unworthy of the love of Lord Night.

He reached for her gown and began to tug at it, trying to raise it up, revealing the naked thighs beneath. Lea reached out her hand, grasping his, momentarily stopping him.

"You know what I like to do?" she asked softly. Then, not waiting for his response, she answered her own question. "I like to massage a guy's back before sex. It really turns me on, gets me hot, you know?" she stuttered shyly.

No matter how hard she tried, the words of love made her uncomfortable, reddened her face. It was the result of too many years of considering all things carnal as sin. Perhaps under Lord Night's tutelage, she would lose this false shame, finally enabling her to feel free to want, to lust. For now, she just hoped that Tony would not see the scarlet blush of her cheeks. It might cool his ardor, or arouse his anger. Whatever his reaction, she couldn't chance anything ruining this golden opportunity.

He stared at her, eyes growing cold. Now what was she up to? "You want to rub my *back?*" he said with a certain degree of anger and disbelief raising his voice's tonal quality.

"Yes," she responded faintly.

Tony covered his face with his hand. Never before had he encountered a broad as freaky as this one. Mentally he was kicking himself for ever starting up with her. Maybe she imagined herself a wood nymph inhabiting the mountain forests, lying in wait to entice men; teasing yet never delivering. For a fleeting moment, he wondered what she'd do if he forcibly spread her legs and pumped it to her. Tony dropped his hand, staring at her. She looked to be the kind of cunt that would scream rape and go crying to the police. That kind of publicity, he didn't need. Companies frowned on using alleged rapists to sell their margerine or jockey shorts.

Regaining her composure, Lea smiled at him, the promise of sexual delights dancing in her eyes. "You're going to love it. I promise you." With that she reached down and gently stroked his genitals. "I'm a really good masseuse. You'll see. Come on, big boy," Lea cajoled, giving his penis a gentle squeeze. "Turn over and let me have at you."

He looked at her askance and then, resigned to the fact that it was either get his back rubbed or anger her and do without his evening's tail, Tony rolled over on his stomach, leaving the next move of their sexual chess game to Lea.

A satisfied smile crossed her face. The sacrifice had complied with her wishes, assuming the ritual position. Lord Night was with her, assisting her, looking down with pleasure upon her endeavors. Lea lifted her gown and gently crawled up on Tony's back, positioning her naked bottom just above his waist. She squirmed a bit, allowing him the sensation of warm, moist tissue gently moving against firm, muscular flesh. Her fingers reached up and began massaging his shoulders. Then, as a trial run, she grabbed his hair; forcing his head up and back toward her, exposing his throat. He let out a deep growl of annoyance. Acting as though she were a character in a play, Lea moved forward and began voraciously biting his neck and licking his ears. As hoped, he laughed at her antics.

One hand held tightly to the hair, as her mouth continued its assault. Silently, Lea's right hand sought out the hiding place of the knife. Her fingers touched cold metal. The sacrifice could begin. The holy instrument of extermination had been found. Tony laughed louder, yelling to her that it tickled, but she didn't stop, didn't cease the action.

In an inaudible whisper, Lea began to pray, "Lord Night, master of my being, object of my desire, giver of pleasure, satisfier of all my wants and needs, look with pleasure upon this thing I do for you. To you, I consecrate this sacrifice." Lea breathed in deeply then poised her hand to strike.

The newly sharpened knife cut through the pale flesh as if through butter. It stopped the laughter, replacing it instead with gasping, gurgling sounds. He writhed under her, trying to pull away; yet her weight and the

195

agonizing pain he felt prohibited such an action. Lea moved the knife back and forth across his throat, cutting deeper and deeper. Tonight the victim would not get away, would not suffer needlessly. This sacrifice was to be, relatively, pain free.

As more and more blood flowed from the wound, the gasps and thrashings became weaker. Moments passed like hours, as she continued the repetitive gesture; until it appeared that she would completely sever the head. His body convulsed, muscles vibrating; then a strange calm washed over him. He lay perfectly still, unmoving.

Lea had done well. He was dead. The knife dropped from her hand and her fingers released their grasp of his curls. Slowly she rose to her feet, staring down at the motionless form that lay beside the flickering fire.

Darkness had descended and her task was almost done. She raised her hands in thanks to the blackened, star-dotted sky. A warm night wind fluttered her gown as she began praying. "Welcome, Lord Night! The time of evening has come and I, your servant, await your presence. You that have delivered me from the land of want, shall be made of flesh, made man, by my hand. To you I give my sacrifice, my gift. Let this be proof of my devotion and love for you, given so that I might abide by your side always."

She reached down, grabbed the knife, and then began twirling around, faster and faster. The gown billowed, climbing higher and higher on her legs as she undulated wildly before the corpse. There was music playing. Somewhere in the inner recesses of her brain, the drums had begun their rhythmic rhapsody. She circled the fire, frantically dancing out her primitive rite, finally falling to her knees in exhaustion.

She lifted the knife to her lips and began to slowly kiss the blood from the blade. "Praises be to the God of Night, to his blood which is my life and salvation, and to this crimson sacrifice which shall form his creation. Oh most holy lord of blackness, reside within my heart always!"

Once again the knife fell from her hands, as she licked her lips and ran behind the tent to retrieve the other objects necessary to complete the ritual of death.

With treasures in hand, she returned. Kneeling beside the still remains, Lea first lit the candle from the fire, then drove it into the soft earth, so that it might shed more light upon the sacrificial offering. Her hand searched the ground to retrieve the knife and when she found it, she positioned the jar so that it might be filled to overflowing with the precious liquid. Lifting his arm, she cut deeply through the large veins on the inner side of the elbow, watching as the blood flowed forth to fill the glass.

"This be the holy candle of life, that symbolizes the journey of man," she whispered softly, watching the jar slowly fill with crimson. "It will light your way from the land of shadows into the glow of day. With shining candle to guide you and warm blood to give sustenance, you shall become a creation of flesh, with form and structure like that of man. This offering of blood shall make you strong. It is my hope and salvation, washing me free of longing, fulfilling my needs. Red be the color of life, the hue of warmth and pleasure. These things I shall provide for you, my Lord, so that you will know of my love and faith. To you, Lord Night, my god, my master, I give this gift of blood to be spread upon your

197

altar, to course through your veins, so that you might be made whole!"

The blood was dripping too slowly, the jar remained unfilled. Lea rose moving to the other side, repeating the procedure, hoping that there would be sufficient liquid to meet her needs.

The container was two-thirds full and the crimson flow seemed to be arresting. Unsure of where to cut next, Lea pushed Tony's head to the side and with cupped hands began scooping up the semicongealed fluid. It was lucky that the sleeping bag had been water repellent; otherwise all this wealth of blood, this life giving solution, might have soaked in, making her task more difficult. Four handfuls did it. The jar was filled to over flowing.

Lea capped the jar quickly and then began searching for something with which to dry her blood-covered hands. The kitchen towels she had brought would suffice.

When finished, Lea wiped the knife, then threw it into the fire, purifying and destroying it. Now her work was almost at an end; there was but one thing left to do.

She looked down at Tony's back. It was smeared with fresh blood which had spurted when the arteries in his neck were severed. Lea took the towel and began to wipe, then suddenly stopped. This was not the way. The sign should be placed over his heart, so that all might know that he was dedicated to Lord Night.

Utilizing all her strength, Lea attempted to turn the body over. It was difficult work for one so physically weak; but she knew that her Lord would imbue her with the necessary strength. The head, attached to the trunk by only the vertabrae, hardly moved when she rolled the

198

corpse. As best she could, Lea centered it, positioning the skull so that it seemed to be searching the heavens. His eyes were open, but appeared as vacant black pits. Not liking the look of it, she closed them, giving the body the guise of peaceful tranquility. When she had satisfied herself that all was as it should be, Lea began wiping his chest, assuring that all the spatters of crimson had vanished from view. That accomplished, she took her right index finger and dipped it into the torn, oozing flesh of the wound. Then, pulling it back, she began to draw the sign of the five pointed star over his heart. Lea had to repeat the process several times, in order to get a sufficient quantity of blood to make the symbol clear and easily visible. She wanted all to see it, so that they might know he hadn't died in vain. Tony was a holy sacrifice, an offering of devotion. He had been consecrated to the night, had become a chosen child. Blessed with salvation, he would exist forever in the grandeur that was Night.

Again she dipped her finger in the wound, but this time, to draw the symbol on her own breast. She too was holy, a priestess. Lea had sanctified the mere mortal before her. She had given him everlasting life. A chosen child, a keeper of the holy rites; Lea was one with Night and wore his mark proudly. She belonged to him; of that, there could be no mistake.

Rising slowly, she extended her arms upward in a gesture of worship, as stars twinkled above. "All for you," she whispered up to him. "All for you!"

She had to get home. The rites and rituals of night awaited her there. Upon the altar, she would light the candles, burn the incense, and offer the blood; then he, like a soft night wind, would come to her, would dwell within her. This time, when her muscles quivered in orgasmic delight, the thing which moved inside her would be made of flesh, to reside with her always, through eternity.

She wrapped a single towel securely around the jar, ensuring that it would be protected from damage. The rest she threw into the fire, watching to see that they were wholly consumed in the flames, leaving no evidence as to their owner's identity.

Next the candle was discarded, melting amid the sounds of sputters and high-leaping tongues of fire. She was strangely excited, exhilarated. She felt as if she could fly, sail up to the stars, carried on the arms of the night wind.

It was done. The holy rites had been observed, the sacrifice made. All was well. She gathered up the jar and flashlight, moving in the direction of the path.

As she neared it, Lea turned to look at the flickering glow of the campfire and what lay still beside it. In a way she was saddened that the rites of night required the letting of blood. The ending of life, no matter what the purpose, was always a cause for mourning. Lea was weak, she knew that; but thank God, Night was strong enough to show her the way, to direct her devotions so that his work might be accomplished. Tonight, upon her bed, his promise of eternal love and salvation would cease being just words and would become her reality.

She turned toward the dark forest, lighting the path before her, hastening to the warmth of home and what awaited her there. In soft whispers, she repeated her simple prayer of praise; "Glory be to him that walks the realms of darkness."

CHAPTER XII

Flesh of one flesh, blood of one blood, kindred souls embattled in a whirlwind of love and hate. All to each other, friend, companion, sole relation; yet now nothing, separated for a time, through death. Was this a reality or part of some devastating terror-filled nightmare that had suddenly taken control of her mind?

A flood of tears cascaded downward as the shovel scraped away yet another layer of sandy soil. Lea glanced at the still form, its empty eye sockets glaring at her accusingly. She looked away, turning her attention back to her work.

Was the hole large enough to accommodate the waiting body? She truly hoped so, not knowing how much more she could take. Her head was floating. She was feeling faint, ready to be engulfed by the murky sea of restful blackness. The temperature was up in the high nineties, a rare occurrence for the area. It was hardly a fit day to engage in any form of physical labor, let alone the type that had consumed her late morning and early afternoon. Dragging the body here had been difficult. The plump old woman wasn't what one would refer to as fat, but when lifeless—dead weight, so to speak—she seemed to weigh a ton.

Although she really wasn't sure how it had been accomplished, utilizing all her strength, with frequent stops to cover her trail she had brought the body a half mile into the woods. The bones would rest here for eternity amid the shelter of pines. Their tall, bending branches would provide her cathedral, the whistling wind her sacred music, the sun and stars her light. Was this peaceful tranquility such a horrid fate? Lea wanted to believe that it wasn't but couldn't truly comprehend the sense of nothingness, the cessation of being, that was death. Strangely, throughout her life, she had either feared it, awaiting the pains of Hell, or longed for it, desiring the sweet rapture that existed in the realms of Heaven; but that was long ago, when she had viewed life and death through the eyes of superstitious, unbending dogma. Now, things were wholly and entirely different. The once mysterious rites of religion had assumed startling new dimensions.

Was the cold flesh that lay before her merely a shell? Had its soul made the journey to whatever lay beyond this life? If that were true, then Lea had committed no sin, had not transgressed. She had simply hastened the old woman on her voyage to another dimension. But—the thought chilled her heart—what if there was nothing beyond this planet, this time, this realm of existence? Then the letting of blood was unholy, sinful even to the eyes of Night. No, such thinking didn't make sense! There was no sin, no trespass, nothing villainous in the act. It was but a simple rite of consecration. The old woman should have rejoiced that Lea had chosen her to be a celebrant of the ritual. It was an honor.

The wicked imp who occupied the darkest part of her being questioned the value of the old woman's life. It had meant nothing. Who, after all, would mourn her passing? The sad answer echoed loudly in her head; she alone would miss the old woman, her gentle kindness, the tender caring.

The sweat poured down her forehead, dripping in rivulets from her temples, mixing with her tears. Lea felt nauseous, overcome with pained emotions, with deep feelings of fear. Perhaps the heat or maybe the act itself engendered in her overwhelming panic.

Lea stepped up and out of the grave, unable to remain there one moment longer. She had worried about its depth; but whatever its measure now, it would just have to suffice. She couldn't continue. The place of interment would have to be a shallow one.

She didn't think Aunt Evelyn cared where she came to rest. After all, she'd never been much concerned with the hereafter during her lifetime. It seemed strange to stare down at the once animate and vivacious form, lying there so still. Lea honestly wished that the whole horrid turn of events could have been avoided, but the onus was not hers. Why couldn't her aunt have ceased her meddling, left Lea alone? Why had she descended on the cabin, interfered with the rites of Night?

Lea sat down beside her Aunt's stiffened corpse, trying to understand why things had occurred as they had. Her mind, her heart, the very essence of her being was racked by guilt, by profound sorrow. Strange, but three days ago when she had, for lack of a better word,

205

exterminated Tony, Lea had felt no remorse. She had done him great service by shedding his blood for the holy one. Yet this time, her emotions followed a different course. She was repulsed by this sacrifice. Perhaps before, she hadn't felt guilt because she viewed Tony as being a much needed object. She neither loved nor cared for him the way she did for Aunt Evelyn. In the deepest recess of her soul, Lea wished that some other female could be lying there instead of Evelyn. Anyone else would do. A wealth of questions assaulted her. Why had Lord Night seen fit to bring the woman to Lea at that precise time, when she had been searching so hard for a suitable offering? Was this a punishment for her previous failings? Was taking a loved one his chastisement? No! Night had brought this sacrifice, a lamb to the slaughter, to make her endeavor easier. It was his gift so they might be one. His love, their life together, would serve to lessen the pain of her loss.

Lea tried to remember the sequence of events that had preceded this tragic state of affairs. It was hard to recollect all the occurrences. During the previous three days, most of her time had been spent in a fearful fog, running like some captive rat, consigned to a horror-filled maze, bumping into walls, terrified of each turn, waiting for the opportunity to escape.

It had begun, of course, with Tony. Lea had carried out her grisly duty with utmost precision and attention to detail. She had performed the ritual as required; but apparently the sacrifice, the victim was not pleasing to her Lord.

That night, she had spread human blood upon the altar, then retired to wait naked on the bed. The transformation from spirit to flesh that she had risked all for had not materialized. The warm night wind pulsated her groin and blew gently across her body, but it did not become man.

Night was not pleased by her gift of male blood. What he desired was the crimson outpourings of a female. Lea had had great difficulty conceiving of and accepting this reality. It not only crumbled her theory of sympathetic magic, but also meant that she had, in fact, committed a murder, taken a life, for nothing. Tony had died in vain. At first she was burdened with guilt; but that quickly subsided as her focus turned once again to the matter at hand. The only thing which held any import for her was the harvesting of blood with which she could create a living Lord. She had set her mind to that purpose, only to find that her endeavors and her very world were being invaded by unwanted trespassers.

At ten a.m. on the morning following Tony's death, before she could begin scouting for a suitable female sacrifice, the county sheriff and several state troopers descended on the cabin. Their faces were set in expressions of gravity, their tones ominous. They told her of the existence of danger in the woods, of a monstrous, maniacal presence who had mutilated a young man. Lea had listened intently, eyes wide. They assumed her look to be one of fright, but that was not it, not it at all. The look was one of awe at their total misunderstanding of what had transpired. The psychopath, the crazed pervert to which they constantly referred, was she— none other than the innocuous-appearing Lea.

At several points in the conversation, she had wanted to scream out to them that they were wrong, that their eyes had deceived them. She wanted to explain about the holy rite of sacrifice, the consecration of the offering; but she dared not. They would never understand. They were too wrapped up in the mundane to comprehend the spirituality of her act. Being uninitiated into the ceremonies of Night, they would think her mad.

They tried to persuade her to leave, to go back home until the case was closed and the culprit caught; but Lea resisted, saying that she had nothing to fear and was able to protect herself. If only they'd known how foolish they appeared to her! What idiots, imbeciles, to be so concerned for her welfare! They had no inkling of what thoughts flew through her mind, how she secretly laughed at their stupidity. They were in the presence of the ritual executioner, the bloody priestess of Night; yet, like innocents, they were unaware, allowing themselves to be duped by her fragile frame and innocent looks.

Unable to convince her to go, they vociferously demanded that she exercise a greater degree of caution in all her actions, locking herself into the cabin at sundown, confining her walks to the highway and not the woods, being wary of strangers, and most importantly, reporting any unusual happenings.

After much pleading and cajoling, she agreed to follow their directives. Satisfied, they had turned to leave. It was then that they gave the bad news. Until the murderer was apprehended, they would maintain a constant twenty-four hour a day surveillance on the western shore of the reservoir. With an audible gasp, Lea had breathed in deeply. They wrongly assumed that it was a sigh of relief, but in fact it was a moan of dread. Now that they were on their guard and looking, it would be difficult for her to identify and seize an appropriate victim.

After they'd gone, Lea tried to figure out ways of accomplishing her task without risking discovery. The search for a new offering would be simple enough. No one would suspect her on her daily walks of having any involvement in the bizarre rites nor the carnage that had taken place on the shore. Problems had developed, however, when she began to ponder how she was going to find a single female camper who had not been scared out of the woods by the previous day's folly. Perhaps no such creature existed. To seek out a female that was a member of a larger party was more than dangerous, it was downright stupid. To assure her anonymity and a scarcity of witnesses, she'd have to silence anyone with whom she came in contact. That was risky. To hold a group at bay so that she might systematically do away with one of them, would require something more threatening than an agressive stance and a knife; a gun perhaps, or maybe experience in the art of guerilla warfare and the ability to kill victims one by one in absolute silence. Since she possessed neither a weapon nor the training of a terrorist, she was facing a seemingly insurmountable problem.

In the end, after having spent hours pondering her prospects, all bleak, Lea decided that she'd have to resort to kidnapping. Of necessity, she'd be required to stake out likely sites containing not one, but a group of campers. She'd watch and wait for a time when a female member of the party was alone, while others fished or swam out of sight, then menace her victim with a knife, forcing her into the dense, shadowy forest. Once secure in the knowledge that no one could see, Lea planned to do what had to be done, taking the blood and making her way home through the woods.

Her plan might have worked if it weren't for the constant interference of the damn police. They patrolled the road every ten minutes, waving at her, getting a fix on her location, assuring her continued safety. If they were to discover a body anywhere along the way, she knew they'd tie her into it, knowing that she'd been walking in the area at an hour which would coincide with the time of death.

She wasn't even at peace in her own home. The bastards sent patrol cars by her cabin at least every two hours to assure that no harm had come to her.

Aside from meddling police, other problems existed. There had been a sudden exodus of campers from the woods. The campers, not renowned for bravery, were packing up and deserting the mountains for the safety of hotels and home.

After two days of searching, she abandoned her plan, deciding that perhaps the deed would have to be done in some other town or hamlet away from this area, a place not alerted to her presence, not wary of strangers. Perhaps then she'd be able to bring this nightmare to a conclusion. There she would find the crimson fluid which would create her lover, thus bringing her bloody rampage to an end.

It was, however, unnecessary for her to have planned anything or to have worried so. Lea should have realized that Lord Night would provide for her. He had already selected a victim to fulfill her needs and would lure her to the holy place of sacrifice when the time was right. All Lea needed to do was wait.

If only she'd taken more notice of the phone calls, been less preoccupied with the rite of consecration, then all this might not have happened and the old woman might still be alive.

Aunt Evelyn, always the busybody, called often, making sure that Lea was well, getting enough rest, eating properly; but, most of all, the conversations assured her that Lea was learning to cope with her grief, able to come out of the experience with emotions and sanity intact.

From the first, although Lea tried to hide it, there had been a marked change in her nature. It was noticeable, even across the miles, in the tone of her speech. Her meek and mild-mannered propriety had somehow given way to a brusque and arrogant demeanor. Lea no longer spoke of Bible study, nor going to church, nor chastised her aunt for using saucy language. The person who answered the phone in the evening was someone new and unknown to Evelyn. All their conversations had been kept short at her niece's behest. Evelyn was talkative, inquiring about the north country's weather and people, all manner of things; but Lea was tightlipped, especially concerning the manner in which she spent her days and nights.

This unexpected change made Evelyn fearful for Lea's wellbeing. What did the innocent young woman know about life or the dangers that could await her in the world of reality? Being sheltered for so long, her existence so sternly dominated by her mother, Evelyn felt Lea ill equipped to survive.

From their later conversation, it appeared that last night's call was the magnet which drew Evelyn here. Lea, unable to find a suitable sacrifice, frustrated at every turn, wildy impatient for a human lover, insane with desire, was less then pleased to hear her aunt's voice at the other end of the line. She usually disguised her displeasure, trying to tactfully sidestep the prying questions; but that evening, with her dreams falling apart, she did not. It was controlled anger that poured from her—not loud, but wounding, nevertheless. She accused her aunt of spying and trying to run her life, just as her mother had. Perhaps her aunt wouldn't have been so shocked if it hadn't been for her constant use of profanity to punctuate phrases and drive home points. It was grossly out of character for Lea to behave in such a manner.

Lea regretted her words immediately, not only because they alerted Evelyn to the sudden overwhelming change in her personality, but also because she knew it hurt the old lady, who, regardless of her meddling and other numerous faults, had always treated Lea with much concern and kindness. In an attempt to smooth things over, she had apologized profusely. The call had ended on an amicable note, but Lea should have realized that Evelyn's curiosity, once stimulated, would not rest.

Truly worried about what was happening to her shy, quiet niece, unable to comprehend the change in her personality, Evelyn immediately redialed the phone; only this time, the party at the other end was Ronald Penn. Making small talk, Evelyn tried to glean as much information as she could from the real estate broker. She was relieved to hear that he had recently seen Lea and that she was looking well, although a mite different than the first time he had met her. The news of Lea's altered appearance disturbed her. The more she talked to the man about how dramatic the make over had been, the more frightened she became. If her worst fears were true, then the girl had become so emotionally distraught that she had succumbed to a nervous breakdown. Ronald had described the transformation as being from caterpillar to butterfly. It seemed strange that a personality so well fixed and stable could shatter and reform into something so foreign, so different.

As it turned out, Evelyn didn't determine her plan of action until Ronald, in passing, inquired as to whether the Albany papers were covering the local murder story. Evelyn was taken aback by the news. Lea had never mentioned it. Ronald, evidently taking great delight in relaying all the grisly details of the slaughter, frightened Evelyn out of her wits, when, after a long pause, he informed her that the maniac who had done the bloody deed was still wandering through the mountain woodlands.

As would be expected, Evelyn panicked, fearing for Lea's life. After quickly thanking Ronald for his help, she hung up the phone and ran to pack a bag. To her way of thinking, the ritual murder could be blamed for Lea's strange unexplained behavior. How could the poor girl hope to get well, attempt to overcome her nervousness, depression, and emotional upheavals, when she was in mortal fear of her life? If she had taken time to stop and think, Evelyn would have realized that the change in Lea predated the murder; but refusing to view the evidence objectively, she came to the wrong conclusion.

It had taken her but a second to decide definitely that she would go to the cabin. The trip would serve a dual purpose; it would provide Lea with a modicum of safety and security—no murderer in his right mind would attempt to harm her with the hefty old woman for protection—and it would enable her to see for herself this curious personality turnabout which had suddenly afflicted her niece. Wasting no time about it, after only the most minimal of preparations, Evelyn left the comfort and safety of her home and drove through the night to the cabin, to Lea, and the fate that had been decreed for her.

Unaware of what had transpired earlier in the evening, at four a.m. Lea was roused to wakefulness by intense pounding on the door. Startled by the sound, yet still half asleep after hours of lascivious lechery, she switched on the light, stumbled to the door, and without questioning the name of the visitor, pulled it open. Stunned by the face that stared back at her, Lea stood speechless in the presence of her aunt. The old woman's face was a study in shock and disbelief. Her staid, prudish niece was dressed in a lowcut, slinky, black satin gown. The pillow hadn't rubbed the rouge from Lea's cheeks, nor smeared the shadow and mascara from her eyes. Evelyn had never seen her looking better. As Ronald said, Lea had turned into a truly beautiful butterfly. The once dowdy woman was lovely, fragile, with the most exquisite of features. Startling what a bit of paint and a new hairdo could accomplish. Only a mere handful of days had gone by since they'd last been together, but to Evelyn it seemed like the passage of centuries. What had once been a plain and unattractive woman was now an ethereal, blossoming, flower.

They stood for a moment staring at one another, neither speaking, both faces revealing the shock of the encounter. Embarrassed by her garb, Lea raised her hand up to cover the deep cleavage of her breasts and motioned for her aunt to cross the threshold and enter.

Passing the doorway, her aunt began surveying the room and sniffing the air with obvious interest. The sweet smell of incense wafted to her nostrils and she began searching out its origin. There was a disconcerting look on Evelyn's face, a strange mixture of shock and curiosity, of pleasure and delight, but most of all the eyes had reflected internal churnings of fear. She sensed that something was wrong, very wrong. The woman who answered the door, who walked like Lea, looked like Lea, was not, in reality, her niece. She knew it instinctively. It was someone else, living like a parasite on the bones and flesh, a creature whose intentions were not known.

The amenities were observed, with the women exchanging nervous greetings, and then sitting down to trade banter over cups of coffee. Angered as she was at the imposition and blatant interference in the wee hours of the morning, Lea managed to conceal her displeasure, setting her mouth in the most saccharine of smiles. It took but a minute for Evelyn to tire of the game of avoiding the issue at hand, that being Lea's strange behavior and her own sudden appearance here. Not known for her tactfulness, Auntie jumped right in, looking Lea in the eye and asking what in hell had been going on. She followed up with an inquiry as to why her niece was dressed like she was in the business of entertaining males for profit. She had always imagined Lea to be the high-necked flannel type. It was not that Evelyn viewed a friendly bang as immoral, it was just that she had a hard time visualizing Lea crawling into bed with a guy who was hell bent on screwing her. Frankly, Evelyn had thought that getting laid would be of enormous benefit to Lea, loosen the girl up a bit; it was just going to take her considerable time to get used to the idea that Lea did such things of her own volition. For years she had assumed that Lea would die a virgin, never having uncrossed her legs; now the young woman appeared to be moving in quite the opposite direction.

Ire aroused, Lea announced to her aunt that what she wore to bed was her business. She wore such things simply because *she* liked them. As for her behavior, it was alarming only to those who were trying to maintain control over her. In no uncertain terms, she informed her aunt that she had, at this late date, finally grown up and was intending to be her own person; independent, liberated from confining rules and regulations, free of family interference.

Evelyn listened quietly as her niece's speech continued, intimating that her youth had been wrecked because she had allowed others to run her life. Loudly, Lea declared that those times had come to an end. The words, pouring from her mouth, were true enough. It was Lea's right to be left alone; but something struck the old woman as being amiss. For years Evelyn had waited, hoping that the girl would free herself from her mother's domination, wanting her to be young and free and enjoying life. No one wanted Lea to be happy more than she; but this sudden rash of independence had too swift an onslaught. Something had triggered it and Evelyn wanted to know what.

For a half hour they argued back and forth. Lea accused her aunt of coming to the cabin to snoop. Evelyn was upset and hurt by Lea's accusations, informing her niece that she had been frightened for her safety because of the horrid happenings. It was at that point that an alarm had gone off in Lea's head. She'd never mentioned the murder because she had feared that her aunt would do just what she did; it was immediately apparent that Evelyn had been in contact with someone for the sole purpose of keeping tabs on her niece's whereabouts. The only person it could be was the chatty real estate broker. Lea was incensed that her aunt would have the gall to involve Ronald, to pump him for information. But as adamantly as Lea accused her, Evelyn denied the charges, saying that she was simply attempting to look out for Lea's welfare, not meaning at all to pry. If there was a sin, it was that Auntie was just being a mite over-protective. Regardless, it had not been done out of malice as Lea seemed to feel, but rather out of love.

The issue was not settled to anyone's satisfaction, least of all Lea's. Tiring of what she felt were weak excuses for meddling, she reiterated that she wanted to be left alone and pointedly asked her aunt to leave.

To describe Evelyn's reaction as shock would be like calling a typhoon a spring rain. Never in her wildest imaginings could she envision her niece treating her so. In the old days, Beatrice used to order her out regularly; but that was due to her "moral outrage" at Evelyn's lifestyle. Lea doing something like this while holding a Bible and preaching about damnation, hellfire and brimstone—now *that* she could identify with, could understand; but this was not the same thing. Lea's outrage seemed directed just as much at Beatrice as at herself. Quite a turn-around for a girl who used to think that her mother represented the epitome of Christian womanhood. The last time they were together, and for all the times she could remember previous to that, Lea had always interspersed her conversations with scriptual phrases and moral parables, but that was no longer the case. Since Evelyn arrived, not once had God's name entered the conversation, except when used in vain. The words "damn" and "hell" were no longer used to describe the fate of lost souls, but were instead cursed at the old woman. The gentle piety that had once been Lea's trademark vanished, leaving instead a seething, vicious-tongued harpy. Although she seemed rational enough, Evelyn was convinced that Lea's mind had snapped. How else could such an overwhelming departure from her old self be explained?

Just as adamantly as Lea had demanded that she go, Evelyn insisted that she was staying. It was at that point that her sad fate became fixed. Seeing that the more she yelled, the more intractable Evelyn became, Lea began to calm herself, trying to convince her Aunt that nothing was wrong, that she really just wanted to be alone. But Evelyn was buying none of it. The more she refused to listen to reason, the closer she drew to her own doom.

From the very moment Lea had opened the door and seen her, she knew that this thing had not come to pass by chance. Lord Night had summoned the old woman here. Bright enough to recognize the immediate possibilities of the situation, the sudden appearance of a suitable female offering, Lea struggled to push the thought from her mind. Evelyn was a much loved, but unfortunately meddling, relative. Regardless of their past differences, there was a bond of caring between the two. She viewed sacrificing her aunt in much the same way as she would have her own mother—a form of convoluted, guilt-inspiring matricide. She hadn't realized at the time the degree of anger and hatred that raged within her.

Words would not sway the old biddy, and try as she might, Lea was unable to convince her to leave. Evelyn didn't understand the tears that appeared in Lea's eyes when she unequivocally told the young woman that she was staying regardless of what she said or did. There was no use fighting it. The die was cast. Her fate was sealed. Once again, blood would drench the altar.

Evelyn was no genius, but once she stepped into the bedroom and saw the black altar and other appurtenances of the new religion, the faith of the flesh, she began to put two and two together, thinking her niece mad. Evelyn would try to take action; even, perhaps, involving the police. Lea dared chance none of it. At her own stupid insistence, her aunt would view the altar; but sadly for her, she would never live to tell anyone about it.

Looking back on it now, Lea remembered that that was the moment she decided to do away with Aunt Evelyn; but not the moment she came up with a suitable plan. That came later.

Evelyn began looking around the kitchen, babbling to Lea about the fond memories she had of the place in the years before her parents had separated. From there, she had moved to the living room. A peculiar look crossed her aunt's face as her eyes scanned the contents.

"You know," Evelyn commented in disbelief, "This looks almost exactly as I remembered it. Nothing seems to have aged here but me. Almost thirty years and it's as if I was never away!"

Shaking her head, she moved out into the hall. At first she appeared to be heading toward the bedroom;

then, as if something had seized her attention, she moved past the doorway, coming to a halt in front of the wall. Lea took immediate notice, for it was at that precise place, at what appeared to be a walled up doorway, that Lea always felt chilled, fearful of some unnamed, unknown horror. Since her arrival, Lea had dreaded passing it. Invariably her breathing would quicken, her heart pound, muscles tighten, sweat drip profusely; yet she couldn't understand why. She had often chided herself about allowing the wall to discomfit her so, yet the strange apprehension, the nerve-induced malady, continued.

"Did you do this?" her aunt queried, staring at the flat surface before her.

"Do what?" Lea inquired in little more than a whisper.

"Block the doorway," her aunt answered, still staring straight ahead.

"No," Lea responded. "It was like that when I got here." She paused for a moment, then turned to her aunt. "Do you know where it led?" she asked.

"Sure, upstairs to your room," the old woman replied. "Didn't you remember that?" she questioned gently. "When you were a little girl you used to sleep up there in the loft."

For one split second a scene flashed across the screen of Lea's brain. A tiny child with soft brown curls lay frightened and crying in a large wooden bed. Amid the dark shadows that surrounded her, a figure approached, reaching out. As it loomed nearer, the vision had suddenly melted into oblivion, leaving Lea to ponder its significance. Was it a real memory or simply a flight of fantasy? She wasn't sure. The only thing of which she was positive, however, was that her skin began to crawl when she neared the wall, and the chill that ensued moved through her bones with such rapidity as to make her body convulse with tremendous spasms.

All that she could muster, in response to her aunt's inquiry, had been a weak shake of the head. Lea could remember nothing of those early times.

"Guess you were too young," her aunt reasoned. "It's really lovely up there, quite spacious, and there's a beautiful view of the reservoir from the window."

The breath caught in Lea's lungs. From a place deep in her forgotten past, she could visualize something; large, deep blue in color, with diamonds dancing on its surface, shimmering in a field of green. Above it, the clear blue was dotted by puffs of soft white. This was the panorama that had long troubled her. It hadn't been a fantasy, this expanse of blue and green, but rather a vague recollection from a long ago childhood. Lea tried hard to force other memories out, but they would not come. She didn't possess the key which would unlock her elusive past.

"I wonder why anyone would have walled this up?" Evelyn asked aloud.

At that precise moment, Lea was thinking the very same thing. The cabin was certainly not spacious by any stretch of the imagination. Why would anyone try to further cut down on the usable living space by closing off a serviceable area, especially the only room that commanded a view of the massive Stillwater Reservoir? It made no sense, no sense at all.

Evelyn hesitated, jaw set, pondering the stupidity of such a remodeling, wondering who it was who had carried out the labor. Then, as if drawn by some force more powerful than herself, she turned and began slowly walking toward the bedroom.

The room had been cloaked in darkness; but from memories long ago thought forgotten, she reached out, flicking the switch bathing the cubicle in light. Evelyn stared at the coverlet in disbelief. How unlike Lea, she thought, to possess such extravagant and frankly flamboyant items! The bright crimson satin had been strewn about, as if reclined upon by two forms, giving fuel to the contention that Lea had a lover. Black clinging nightgowns and rumpled satin sheets could lead to no other conclusion.

Next to catch her attention was the strange wall decoration that hung above the bed. Evelyn's eyes opened wide as she viewed the tiny naked worshippers bowing in homage to the five-pointed star.

"Where did you get this? she cross-examined, voice rising in a crescendo of abhorrence. There was something vile about the scene depicted that chilled her soul. Evelyn knew little about theology, caring not for the mutterings of ministers; but she did recognize the symbol. In ancient times, the five-pointed star, the pentagram as it was called, was symbolic of evil, representing the overlord of Hell, Satan himself. It took little intelligence to realize that the hanging represented an act of devil worship, some form of demonic ritual; but what, she wondered, was it doing here? Of all people, Lea, with her strict Biblical morality, did not seem the type to possess such a profane and diabolic representation.

It was apparent that Evelyn was deeply troubled by what she had seen. Her eyes darted back and forth between the unmade bed and the wall hanging, growing wider with each passing moment. It appeared that she was struggling to come to some sort of decision as to what was going on, what it was that she was seeing.

"It was here when I arrived. Kind of interesting, don't you think?" Lea volunteered, peering out of the corner of her eye at Evelyn, an impudent smile curling her lips.

It wasn't often that she was able to startle someone, to shock them by her conduct or possessions, so Lea truly relished the encounter, secretly giggling at her aunt's look of consternation.

Auntie had looked at her coldly, eyes fixed and unmoving. "I know *one* damn thing for sure," she snapped at her smirking niece. "This wasn't here when your mother was! You call it interesting, I call it damn weird," she stated emphatically. "It looks like a frigging black mass!"

Never really having thought about it before nor given it a name, Lea pondered the possibility that her aunt was right, that it was in fact a picture of a black mass. While she remained engrossed in contemplation, the focus of Evelyn's attention turned to other items in the room.

Lea had been standing, still staring at the picture, when she suddenly became aware that her aunt was no longer by her side. Her concentration broken, Lea looked over her shoulder, startled at what she saw. Evelyn's eyes were wide with fright as her fingers moved across the shiny black marble. She eyed the various items on the table, set out as if upon an altar of worship, examining them, analyzing their purpose for being. It was not the candle holders, or the incense burner that disturbed her, nor held her unswaying attention; but rather the silver and black goblet.

Lea watched, becoming fearful that the old woman was beginning to fit the pieces of the puzzle together. Evelyn glowered at the chalice with such revulsion and disgust, that it seemed as if she knew its ritual purpose; knew that, but days before, it had held the warm blood of human sacrifice.

"Yours?" her voice began its interrogation.

"Yes," Lea rejoined, staring defiantly at Evelyn. "They're mine."

"I see," Evelyn snapped, eyes beginning to mist over, her worst fears confirmed. "Is this an altar of some sort," she grilled, voice cracking. "Lea?"

Evelyn knew that it wasn't unusual for fanatically religious individuals to set aside areas of their home in which to pray; but this was wholly and decidedly different. Lea's clothing, the picture, the strange black altar with its implements of ritual—all led her to wonder what strange rites her niece was party to. She wouldn't have been quite so alarmed except for the fact that the Bible, which had previously served as Lea's constant companion, was nowhere in evidence and neither was a crucifix.

Lea didn't respond. Her smile was broad and toothy, eyes twinkling, as she stared at Aunt Evelyn, amazed at how perceptive the old woman was.

"Lea, what in God's name is the matter with you? What is all this? What is it that you do here?" The words poured from her mouth like a dam breaking, and with each syllable, a storm of emotion rose. Her hands were shaking as she held them outstretched, imploring Lea to answer. *What is it that you do here?* she repeated. There was a long pause as she waited for the reply. When it was apparent that no response was forthcoming, she clenched her fist, shaking it at Lea, screaming, "Answer me damn it, answer me!"

Since the scenario for the coming hours had already been decreed, Lea saw no need of keeping the truth of her faith a secret any longer. Aunt Evelyn would not be leaving the cabin, so who might she tell—the worms?

Eyes wide and shining in a hypnotic stare, Lea smiled as she began. "This, dear Aunt Evelyn, is the temple. My place of worship." She paused to see what reaction it would elicit.

It was evident that the old woman was afraid. She first moved away from the altar toward Lea; but then, shrinking from her niece, she began backing slowly toward the doorway.

It was obvious that Evelyn was trying to leave, to get away. Such behavior could not be tolerated. She had been brought here by the one that was most holy. Evelyn should have been grateful and obedient to his wishes, but she wasn't. Like a frightened rabbit, she was trying to run, attempting to flee her destiny. Lea could not permit that. Chosen by the god to do his will, Lea had moved quickly, blocking the path of escape.

"With the coming of the sundown, I am transformed," Lea began again in a whisper, looking at her near hysterical aunt with eyes that reflected the innocence and joy of devout belief. "I am a priestess of shadows, a consecrator."

Evelyn, shaking, with tears streaming down her face, half mad with fear, questioned Lea in quiet tones. The young woman appeared menacing, ready to do harm, but Evelyn reasoned that perhaps with calming conversation, she might be persuaded to allow her to leave in peace. "Who is it, dear, that you worship? Whose

225

priestess are you?"

Lea's eyes revealed astonishment. How could her aunt be so naive? "I am consecrated to Night. He is my master, my Lord!" Lea then paused for a minute as her aunt began sobbing loudly, once again backing away from her, only this time moving toward the bed. Lea shook her head at the stupidity of her aunt's reaction. Those who were not initiates at the altar of night were like frightened children when confronted with the presence of the holy one. "Don't cry!" Lea implored. "He is a wonderful God, a deity of pleasure." She moved toward the old woman, forcing Evelyn back onto the bed. "He's freed me. I'm saved. All I need do is bring him the offering, place the holy blood before him, and I shall be forever free of want." Her eyes were saucerlike, searching Evelyn's face. There was no understanding there, no comprehension, only blind fear.

Evelyn shook, flailing around on the satin coverlet, trying to move away from Lea. She was sure that the girl was insane, to a degree far surpassing her worst nightmares.

Lea kept coming, eyes opened wide, as if begging for understanding.

Evelyn, struggling to get up, pushed aside the comforter, revealing brown blood stains. When she realized what they were, she screamed out in terror. With one swift burst of strength, she raised herself up from the bed, only to be intercepted by Lea's strong right arm grabbing out at her. She resisted, only to find her neck caught in the ever-tightening grip of her niece's fingers. They rolled on the bed, finally tumbling off onto the floor.

It was here, at this point, at this precise moment, that the memory became unclear. Lea was unsure of whether the rest of her recollections were fact or fantasy.

She had vague visions of straddling her aunt's body, then lifting and slamming the old woman's skull onto the floor repeatedly, until the body lay motionless. From there, Lea had run to the kitchen. She'd found a thin bladed butcher knife in the drawer and returned to the bedroom to begin the sacrifice.

She dragged the unconscious form near the altar, reaching up to grasp the chalice, and set it down beside her on the floor. This was the moment for which she had been waiting, the time when he would become flesh; but all was not ready. Once again she ran to the kitchen, only this time it was to obtain fresh candles and incense for the sacred altar. She needn't have rushed. The sacrifice could not begin. Lea had tarried too long. The sky had already begun to lighten with the first glow of morning. The shadowed time of ritual had passed, she'd have to wait yet another day before he could come to her.

Angered at the delay, she resumed her place above the body; only this time, held securely in her hands, was the thin, shiny blade of salvation.

"To you my Lord," she whispered softly, "I give this gift!"

With that phrase, the blade began its rapid descent downward. When it was but an inch above the chest, the eyes of the sacrifice opened wide in terror, the mouth screamed out. As the knife plunged into the waiting breast, the body lurched upward, practically knocking Lea off. As the agonized form thrashed about, emitting piercing screams, the face of the sacrifice began to change before Lea's eyes. No longer was the offering the aging Evelyn; but instead, a strange face, one that Lea at first did not recognize. With each second that passed, the screams grew louder, the writhing more intense. As if made from some malleable substance, the features of the face began to distort. The brow became etched with scowling furrows. The eyes became piercing and narrow. The cheeks were wrinkled and colorless. An internal chord had been struck—Lea knew the face. It was so familiar, yet she had been unable to give it a name. Not until the mouth was transformed, evidencing the thin, cruel, lips and the yellowing teeth within, had she realized the identity. The body before her had become Mama.

Lea remembered little of that moment, except the sudden rage that had swept over her. She had lifted the knife and repeatedly plunged it into the chest, belly, and finally the face. All life's denials, the loneliness, the want, the fear, the beatings, the punishments; all could be blamed on Beatrice. During her lifetime, Lea hadn't had the strength to fight her, to repay the cruelties, right the injustices, to free herself of the woman's crushing, smothering control; but now—now it was different. This was Lea's world, Beatrice no longer belonged. If she were trying to come back, trying once again to gain power over Lea, then her daughter, acting in defense of her new and wondrous life, was justified in trying to send her back to the realm of death from whence she'd come.

Lea could remember vividly how the knife had turned from silver to red, going up and down, repeatedly. Into the eyes, the nose, the mouth; stabbing harder and harder, in an attempt to remove the hated face from view.

How long the carnage continued, she had no idea; but by the time the knife finally dropped from her hand, the thing beneath her was a featureless mass of oozing flesh. The blood was everywhere, puddled and congealed as if the bedroom had became a slaughterhouse.

Strangely, when she'd stood up, leaving the room to cleanse herself of the gore that had splattered over her, Lea began laughing hysterically. The morbid cacophony continued through her shower, subsiding only after all the blood had been washed down the drain.

The bedroom resembled visions from a nightmare, imaginings of hell. After collecting enough blood to fill the cup, Lea mopped up the mess, cleaning the floor, walls, and furniture with every available piece of cloth. She wrapped the corpse in the blood spattered satin bed linens, securely tying the ghastly remains with string.

Lea dragged the body through the house to the back door, abandoning it there until she could determine her next move. An eerie feeling manifested itself, as she tugged the body past the hidden threshold. Not only did the usual chill pass through Lea's frame, but an unnerving sensation of having endured it all before washed over her. How could that be? Perhaps in a dream that she couldn't recollect or in a moment of hatred, Lea had imagined such murderous activity; yet the feeling had been strong, making her feel that she'd previously lived through such an ordeal. It frightened her so completely as to shake the depths of her soul.

Among the myriad of terrors which had pursued her following the act was the profound fear of being found out, apprehended, punished for her crimes. The world was incapable of understanding that she had acted at the direction of the Night god and therefore was blameless. If Lea were caught and arrested, there could be no sacrifice, no altar, no night ritual; her lord would never become flesh.

Suppressing her fears, she rummaged through her aunt's purse, got the car keys out, and left the cabin to dispose of the most obvious piece of evidence. Without tangible proof, no one could attest to the fact that Evelyn had ever been here. Lea had been unsure as to whether Auntie had told Ronald, or anyone else for that matter, that she was coming up to the cabin. If her disappearance should be discovered, Lea would have to insist that she knew nothing, that to her knowledge her aunt had never arrived at her north country destination.

Her daily walks in search of likely campers had been worthwhile. Not far from her cabin, no further than two miles away, was an overgrown, abandoned logging road that ended abruptly above the reservoir. It was a fifty foot drop from the edge into what appeared to be fairly deep water. Lea had decided to dispose of the car there.

For a change, her endeavors were successful. The ground was hilly and aptly suited for the task. When Lea placed a stone on the gas pedal and put the gear shift into the drive position, the automobile began rolling forward, picking up momentum, finally sailing over the small cliff, landing a distance away. It hit with a resounding splash, slowly sinking from sight, finally disappearing beneath the ominous, gray-blue water. From the look of the road, it was evident that few people knew of the spot or used it. There was no easy access to the water, so campers could neither fish nor swim there. In this environment of solitude, it would take years before anyone would chance upon the auto's hulk. By then, it would be nearly destroyed, too rusted to be identified.

Lea was going to get away with it. She sensed it in her bones. Lord Night would provide for her safety, see that she was protected from retribution.

The walk back to the cabin was made through the woods, assuring that no one could see her. At all costs, suspicion must be averted. It took her longer than expected, as she tried to erase the scars that the car's tires had made in the soft carpet of pine needles covering the road.

Arriving at her cabin after an absense of two and a half hours, she repeated the procedure again. No connection must be made between the cabin and Evelyn's disappearance.

Upon returning, she went through the bedroom and hall again, assuring that no telltale spatters remained. Once satisfied, Lea began the big job, the disposal of the corpse. Filled with trepidation, she waited for the patrol car to make its pass by the cabin. When she heard the sound of an engine approaching, she moved out onto the porch and waved nonchalantly to the approaching officer. As she had hoped, he nodded his head to her in greeting and wheeled his vehicle around, heading back out the way he'd come.

Lea waited ten minutes to assure that he would not return and then set to work at her task. She propped open the back door, pulled the body out, and blindly headed into the woods, hoping that she would come upon a clearing where there would be soft earth, free of large roots, to bury her aunt. It took her a while to locate such a spot. For some strange reason, a large circular area, perhaps fifty feet across, was treeless. It was as if someone had taken the time to plant them, yet she knew that that was impossible.

Promptly determining that this was the perfect spot, Lea retrieved the body, bringing it to this place of rest. Once there, she concealed it in nearby shrubbery, then returned to the cabin to obtain the needed digging tools, a shovel and a large ax.

Her work went slowly. Although the ground was soft, the undersoil was riddled with roots which had to be chopped. The work had proved both exhausting and traumatic.

All during her labor, she experienced the continuing feeling that once before she had stood beside a wood-land grave, only that time the hole was gaping and monstrous, threatening to swallow her up. The rec-tangular cavern had contained a giant; a bloody, black-haired behemoth. She could see the vision clearly in her mind, yet couldn't remember its origin—a story book, a fairytale. Certainly such scenes had no basis in reality.

Lea lifted her hand up to her head; she was tired, yet there was so much to do. She was filled with conflicting emotions. She felt guilty, yet happy; repulsed at her actions, yet satisfied. She was sorry that Aunt Evelyn was dead, yet she was joyful in the knowledge that her desires for a flesh and blood lover would soon be realized. Lea knew that to feel so was selfish. She should be overcome with shame at the barbarous act she had committed, sobbing and mournful by the side of the grave; but the only emotion she could conjure up was relief, that soon the phantom of passion would be man, to dwell with her always. It was a sad commentary on her own humanity. Somewhere, somehow, she had learned to place the needs of self before the welfare of others. A whispered voice, deep within, chided her; but a far stronger voice told of a firm-muscled lover who would soon be hers.

Anxious to end this chapter of her life and begin the new, wanting to return to the cabin in preparation for the night ritual and her lover's strong embrace, Lea rose and approached the body. She positioned it near the edge of the grave, then pushed it in. As luck would have it, it came to rest on its side. There was something about the burial site that gave Lea unspecified feelings of dread. She certainly didn't want to climb down into it again, to lay the body out properly; but she had no choice, the grave was shallow enough already.

Gingerly she stepped down into the pit and positioned the body on its back. Once again that same vision of an enormous grave came to her. In the distance, the soft whimperings of a child could be heard, as a shadowy figure began throwing dirt on the giant's bloodied face.

It scared her so that Lea leaped out of the grave. The vision aroused strange emotions in her. Suddenly she felt like crying, yet didn't know why; for the giant, for herself, for her aunt? She was confused, but didn't want to be. She had to finish the job and go. No time for crying, no time for morbid, nightmarish apparitions.

As fast as she could, Lea began throwing the dirt in the grave. She wanted to get out of here, before she was driven crazy by bizarre hallucinations.

Should she say something, Lea wondered? Was it necessary? Aunt Evelyn was in no position to care, and not having been religious, she wouldn't want some idiot incantation about the glorious hereafter recited over her remains. Still, it seemed somehow disrespectful to keep silent at this time.

After a moment's pause to gather her thoughts, Lea mouthed the only words she could think of. "Rest in peace," she whispered softly.

She stood staring at the corpse, reminiscing about the times she and her aunt had been together, feeling sorrow at the loss. And then, through a thin veil of soil, the face again began to transform itself. From the mutilated flesh, a mass of tissue began to grow, covering the skull, filling the eyes, forming the lips. The features were not Evelyn's, but those of an awakening Beatrice. The spectre's expression was one of anger, of menacing vengeance, of raging hatred.

Lea stepped back in terror. *Why wouldn't Mama die?* She had come back again to take away her lover, just as she had done before; but this time, but this time . . . Lea lifted the shovel high above her head and smashed it down into the grave, over and over again.

"Die, damn you! Die, damn you! Die! Die! *Die!*" she screamed while destroying what remained of the head.

The skull was reduced to pulp. Lea began feverishly shoveling dirt on it. She had to work fast, otherwise Mama'd try to climb out and be alive again. Beatrice was dead and Lea meant to keep her that way.

Sweat dripped down as the grave began to fill. Although it was shallow and small animals might eventually gain access to it, Lea was quite sure that no human would be able to uncover it. Mama would be entombed there forever.

Lea worked harder and harder, limbs aching, head pounding in pain. She wanted to go home, lie down, rest.

234

She didn't understand anything, didn't understand it at all. She'd sacrificed Aunt Evelyn to Lord Night, so why was Mama lying in the grave? It must be a hallucination, caused by the stress and strain of the last few hours. That was natural, explainable. It was only logical that killing her aunt would play havoc with her emotions, would be traumatic enough to make her start seeing things that weren't there.

Still, why was it a zombie in the form of Mama that she had imagined, and why was it that after all these years, Lea suddenly found herself filled with hatred against the woman? She feared that somehow her mother would wreck this love, take away her happiness just as she had done in the past. Yet how could that be? There had been no men in Lea's past. Perhaps she'd cared for someone when she was younger and Mama had destroyed the friendship. Perhaps it had so affected her that she had thrust the painful experience into her subconscious, forgetting names and places, yet secretly harboring an immense resentment all these years. That could be the only explanation.

When the last shovel of dirt was thrown on the grave and the top soil was once again covered with leaves, needles, and twigs, the spot appeared just as sylvan as it had a few hours before, when she'd first seen it. Lea had done her work well. No one would ever know what this vision of woodland paradise concealed. So strange, it was as if Evelyn had never existed; in just a few hours, wiped from the face of the earth, never to exist again, consigned forever to silent darkness.

She rebuked herself for not mourning the woman, for not being the slightest bit repentant at the dastardly act that she had so easily committed, but there was no time for such mental self-flagellation; it was getting late. Lea needed to get some rest before preparing for tonight's ritual. This evening everything had to be perfect, so that he might be pleased with her. If she pleasured him and served his needs well, then he would become man. She must rush home to prepare for this most glorious night.

Lea turned from the gravesite, lifting the tools onto her shoulders, and, without looking back once, began walking swiftly toward the cabin, the coming sundown, and her awaiting Lord.

CHAPTER XIII

Was it madness or Hell, this state to which she had been consigned? Although darkness besieged her, Lea wasn't fearful. Let it come, take her, engulf her, swallow her up, consume her very being. She no longer cared. Ending it might be preferable to continuing this miserable existence. She was a prisoner here, sentenced to a lifetime of unabating desires.

Once more she'd tried, resulting only in failure. Lea was bewildered, confused, incapable of rational thought. She had brought the gift of blood, setting it upon the altar; yet he was displeased. Instead of bestowing youth and vibrancy, she had presented him with an aged offering. He refused it, demanding instead the life-giving blood of a child. Nothing else would appease him. Her ineptitude and incompetence had ruined everything. She had angered him. Tonight there was no joy, no time of pleasure.

Lea had quietly waited for him upon the bed, dreaming of the ecstasy to come. He had approached her, taking the form of a warm night breeze, blowing gently by her; but that soon changed. As Night's shadow passed over the chalice, the wind of his rage began to rise, extinguishing the candles, twisting the curtains, and finally hurling the crimson filled cup onto the floor. With acerbic tongue, he mercilessly chastised Lea. To punish her, the night was spent in solitude, without the companionship of a loving Lord.

If Lea wanted to give him life, to be with Night forever, then she'd have to find another sacrifice, provide for him the most precious offering of all, the blood of a child, an innocent. The next time the chalice was filled, it must contain the life-blood of a little girl. That knowledge consumed her.

Sacrificing the kitten had been a grisly task, leaving her sickened. Offering Tony up to the holy one bothered her less. He was, after all, an asinine braggart bastard. He had behaved so obnoxiously that she couldn't really berate herself for having carried out the task. The world, she convinced herself, was actually better off without him.

Aunt Evelyn was another matter altogether. Although she loved her relative dearly, Lea had acted as necessity dictated and there was no turning back now. She felt a certain degree of remorse concerning the futility of her aunt's death; but no overwhelming sense of guilt preyed upon her conscience. Evelyn had lived a full life and probably didn't have many good years left anyway. Viewed objectively and dispassionately, it might be said that Lea had done her a great service. Her death had been quick and relatively painless. If Auntie had lived on, there was always the possibility that she might contract some dread, debilitating disease. In such an instance, she might have lingered, suffering. It would have saddened Lea greatly if that had occured. This way had been so easy. One moment Auntie was alive, active, and healthy; the next she wasn't. It had been just that simple.

To this point, Lea had been able to cope with the reality of her past actions; but that wouldn't be the case if the next victim were a child. She had always cared for the little ones, spending years involved with the Sunday school program at church. Strangely, Lea didn't perceive the sacrifice of a grown-up to be something despicable. She felt her ceremonial duties unpleasant, yet hardly loathsome. In that fractured entity that was her brain, Lea rationalized that an adult had had a chance to grow to maturity, experience the world; but a child—now that was something entirely different. Life lay before them. All the wondrous times, the joyous phases, the learning, the happiness; how could she deny them that? How could she, with one stroke of the knife, take a blossoming life away? What right did she have? The bloodletting had been initiated to bring Lord Night to life, true; but that was not its sole purpose. Her primary concern, selfish as it might seem, had always centered on the acquisition of a virile mate to satisfy her most primitive needs. The question to be asked now, was at what point her own needs stopped taking precedence. Was the love of self, the continual indulgence in orgasmic pleasures, worth the life of an innocent child? Where was her humanity, her ethics? Had all morality been forgotten in pursuit of carnal pleasure?

No matter how loudly the voice of conscience pleaded, disparaged, accused, one fact remained unchanged;

241

Lea wanted him, desired him so badly, that it oft times felt as if the longing would consume her. She yearned for him to emerge from the shadows, transformed from soft wind to firm, pliant flesh. Before he had come to her, made himself known, life had been nothing—a void of feelings, a series of wants, of passions, without resolution, without satisfaction. Such an existence was little better than death. With him there was excitement, joy; a whirlwind of experiences and emotions that left her breathless, anxiously awaiting the arrival of each new day. Lea couldn't face the possibility of losing him; yet how could she live with herself if she lured an innocent babe to the altar of execution?

Whichever way she turned, however she tried to resolve the dilemma, the outcome could only be tragic. Such ambivalent emotions could only presage disaster.

Perhaps he was testing her, asking that she perform the barbaric butchery to measure the degree of her caring, her love. Like ancient Abraham called by Jehovah to sacrifice his son Isaac, showing proof of his devotion and submission, Lea might find reprieve. There was always the slim chance that Night wouldn't force her to carry out the heinous act. For a moment, she deluded herself, thinking that the tyke might be spared once she'd proved her adoration; but that peaceful fantasy soon melted away, replaced by the glaring horror of reality. There had to be blood, had to be sacrifice; for he, the holy one, required it. Only fresh, crimson liquid, taken from a young one, would meet his needs, would serve to form him. There was no escaping it.

Some manner of decision had to be made. She couldn't continue to live in this limbo of uncertainty;

yet what was she to do? Could she deny herself the strength of his embrace, choosing instead the moral ethics of her humanity; or would she offer up all vestige of the gentle being she had once been, discarding all belief in right, giving herself completely to him? Her mind swirled. What to do? What to do? There was a battle raging within her, a crusade. Forces of good were waging war, attacking that in her nature that was evil. What should she do? How should she proceed? She didn't know, couldn't think any more.

There was sound, organ music, coming from the cabin, droning on and on. Around her, a symphony of evening songs played. Cries of creatures great and small echoed through the night, as the gentle lullaby of rustling leaves and swaying branches formed a low, melodious cadence. The moonlight barely pierced the darkened forest floor. Everything was blackness.

Lea couldn't see a thing beyond the soft, dim glow of the lighted windows. Nothing was discernable, not the trees, not the road; everything melded into and was one with the opaque cloak of night. It was a feeling akin to blindness, this strange state of sensing, yet not seeing, the surroundings. For the life of her, Lea didn't know what she was doing here, why she had left the safety of the cabin to wander outside amid the shadows. There was nothing to see; neither moon nor stars were visible from her vantage point.

She'd had to get out of the cabin, breathe fresh, clean air, get away from the blood-covered floor with all its reminders. A week ago, she would never have ventured outdoors after sundown, fearing bears and other nocturnal predators; but now she didn't care. Let them come, attack; who gave a damn? Her life had suddenly become a shambles. No matter which way she turned, Lea was doomed; sacrifice a child and deal forever with the burden of guilt, or cease the offerings now and live out her days without the lover she so desired. This was Hell, not fantasy; not a nightmare, but horrid reality.

Lea had spent the last hour or so alternating between uncontrolled sobbing and maniacal laughter. She cried for the dead, yet laughed at the folly of it all. Three beings had ceased to be for naught. Here she was, hands bloodied, yet still alone. How had such a state of affairs come to be? She wasn't sure. Lea wanted to forget about the altar, forget about the sacrifices, just concentrate on the holy music, and the peace and calm it could bring. Lea didn't want to think about tomorrow, or the child, or the blood-consuming altar. She needed rest, tranquility; freedom from fear, from horror. Somehow she had to silence the accusing inner voice which repeated the magnitude of her crimes. Was this insanity? Lea wasn't sure, but suspected that it might be so.

She was swaying to the sounds of the funereal music, trying not to think of the most pressing issue at hand, that being where she would find a female child should she decide to go through with the gruesome ritual; when suddenly, above the organ's tones, the high pitched sound of a crying child could be heard. Was it another of her hallucinations or was it real? Lea searched, looking for the source of the commotion, but in the dense shadows, she could see nothing. A million thoughts flooded her brain. There must be campers nearby, a family with small children and one of them, she was sure, was female. Lea could tell by the sound of the voice; no denying it, somewhere in this area a little girl lay frightened in the darkness. He, the deity of shadows, had brought a fitting sacrifice. It was here, close by. All she need do was find it and offer it up to the Lord of Evening. Her head pounded, mind whirling. It was so simple. He had set the stage, now all she need do was act out the hideous drama.

Lea's body was still, riveted to the spot, not knowing what to do. How could she mortally wound a little one, give it pain? Was she capable of such barbarity? Had her morality completely disappeared? The child's crying became louder. The poor little thing sounded terrified.

Unsure of what actions to follow, Lea sought out the origin of the cries. For a split second, her body tensed, muscles quivering. Something was wrong, out of place. The sounds were not emanating from the forest floor, but rather from above.

Lea's attention focused on the cabin. There, in the second floor window, a faint glow appeared. In the dimness, she could see that the window was open. Upon her arrival, several days before, the sash had been securely shut, of that she was sure. As the child's voice grew louder, strange golden orbs of light appeared in the darkness, just as they had on previous occasions. Something was watching her, spying, making its presence known.

Mesmerized, Lea stared up at the window, watching as the hideous golden eyes moved from side to side, as if attempting to study her. It had to be a dream. The door to the attic loft was barricaded. There was no access to whatever lay upstairs. It was not only unlikely, but veritably impossible that a child could have sneaked up there without her knowledge. It was just illusion, Lea thought; her ears and eyes were playing tricks again.

She began to pace, shaking her head with such force

as to rattle and pain her already tortured mind. She couldn't stand much more of this. If the organ music and damned infernal crying didn't cease soon, she'd go stark raving mad. Why was Night doing this? Why was he tormenting her so?

"Daddy," the shaking little voice called out. "Daddy, I'm afraid. It's so dark and I'm alone."

The music subsided to silence. The animals no longer chittered and hooted, creaked and squalled. The only sound heard throughout the forest was the shrill, frightened call of the child.

Its sobbing continued, the small voice begging and pleading for someone to free her from the loneliness of night. She was very little, perhaps four or five, and she was so afraid of the dark.

Lea listened to the fearful creature calling, tears filling her eyes. From a hidden corner of her mind, a scene came to her. She too had always been fearful of the coming night, cried at the darkness. A vision appeared—there was blackness, punctuated only by variation of shadow. The only source of comfort, a light, shone from the stairwell beyond the big bed. The child, Lea, tearful and sobbing, lay huddled near the headboard, fearing attack by the monsters of night who come to steal little children from their beds, the bogey men who devour the young. She could remember the feeling of terror, then the sudden sense of relief when someone came to comfort her, when the room was once again bathed in light.

Her head cocked slightly to the side, mind lost in thought, she tried to recapture the little girl who once lived here.

She was expending great effort, concentrating on her

246

youth; but something was making it difficult, attacking her senses. Lea blinked her eyes, returning to the present, and suddenly realized that the mysterious organ was once again blaring. The dirge shook the ground beneath her feet, making her head throb with pain at the intensity of the notes. There was, however, another sound; piercing, yet unable to be heard through the tonal thunder. Screams, but from where? Was it the cry of the night creatures who wandered the darkness? The sound was one of pain and terror. Perhaps it was the scream of prey, become victim to a more powerful predator. It grew louder and louder, until its volume echoed throughout the forest, rivaling the clamor of the organ. The cries amplified, becoming more strident. Lea's head turned from side to side, seeking the location of this life and death battle.

As her eyes scanned the darkness, she became aware of tiny flecks of golden light peering at her through the night mist. Thousands of little eyes, staring. She cringed, skin turning to goose flesh. The screams grew thunderous; not one now, but two. One cried out in terror, the other in pain, as if enduring the most dreadful of agonies. Her head drummed with sound. Lea's eyes narrowed, as the pinpoints of light moved out of the forest, nearing her. Her body shook. What was happening? What ghastly journey had she suddenly embarked upon?

Louder still, the sounds drew her attention. They were not animal bleatings, nor banshee wails, but the strident utterings of humans. From the darkness came new sounds, crashing, banging, clanging; things colliding together, shattering, hurled about. There was no doubt in her mind as to the location of the din. All sound, even the resonant organ music was now being emitted from the cabin's attic room. Illusion or reality? She wasn't sure. Could her ears perceive such a myriad of tones and pitch, if they weren't really there? And what of the tiny orbs that spied upon her, were they an actuality?

She was ready to concede herself mad, when her eyes again lifted to the attic window. The glow had instensified, forming a strange backdrop to moving, abstract, forms. Two shadows moved across the glass, appearing then vanishing from view, engaged in what seemed mortal combat. Their bodies at first entwined, then separated; limbs lashing out, assaulting the companion form.

Lea lowered her head, refusing to watch. Why should she encourage her own insanity, give credence to these strange delusions from which she suffered? For several minutes, she doubted her senses, attempting, however unsuccessfully, to ignore the sights and sounds that lay siege to her being. She tried to block them out; but it could not be done.

Unable to wipe it away, Lea's eyes again moved upward. What they beheld made her shudder. Clinging to the window sill, as if trying to escape the violence engulfing the room, was a tiny child. She wasn't a shadow, but a creature of flesh and blood. Her hair was dark and wavy, eyes large. Her tiny hands held fast to the wood while her body shook with sob after sob. The little cheeks were covered with tears and the look on that face was one of horror.

Lea couldn't think, didn't want to. A thousand questions flashed within the grey confines of her mind. Whose child was this? What terror had transpired to scare the little one so? How had she gained access to the concealed staircase without Lea's knowing? They whirled like wind inside her head. She had no answers to the myriad of riddles which plagued her. There was a fear in Lea so intense that it clawed her throat and chest, making each breath a trial to overcome. She tried to wipe this insanity from her consciousness; but the questions would not go away. The same six words repeated and repeated like drum beats in her brain. Was this the child of sacrifice? Had Lord Night provided her with a victim of his choosing? She didn't wait for the answer to come, didn't want to know; but instead began running toward the cabin. Lea had to get to the child, save the little girl from the unnamed danger that lay in wait for her in the attic.

The wind rose to a howling gale as she approached the now ominous-looking structure, stepped onto the porch, and then disappeared through the door. Of primary concern was the destruction of the wall. Lea ran through the house till she came to it. There was no way that she could kick in the planking. It had to be chopped down, if she wished to free the little one from her dark bondage.

Lea went to the back door, taking the ax from its resting place and returned to begin her labor. With all the strength she could summon, Lea drew back, then swung forward, allowing the blade to crash into the wood. Over and over again she repeated the process until she heard the sound of cracking lumber as the head broke through a board. Lea continued, opening a hole she perceived to be sufficiently large to squeeze through.

Lea twisted and turned, trying to force her body

through the tiny hole; but she didn't fit. From the other side of the opening, she could hear the child's hysterical screaming. It seemed as if someone were hurting her. Acting on impulse, Lea began frantically pulling at the boards with her bare hands, trying to dislodge enough of them to gain entry. The effort caused great pain, as the slivers of wood rubbed against the soft, sensitive skin of her palms, opening a wealth of small wounds. In the end, however, she finally gained access to that mysterious, stangely foreboding area of the cabin.

Lea gingerly edged her way through the opening, trying to keep her tender flesh clear of the jagged points of broken wood and bent nails. When she was fully into the stairwell, a strange thing happened. As if by magic, all sound ceased and the top landing was plunged into total darkness. Lea stood for a moment, unsure of what her next move should be. She listened intently, waiting for a sound to break the stillness. There was, however, nothing to be heard. All movement from above had stopped.

Was it a dream, a walking trance, that had somehow assumed nightmarish proportions? It seemed the only answer. Once again it appeared that her mind was playing tricks, mixing fantasy and reality, allowing the two realms to overlap, causing Lea to fear for her sanity. What had really happened outside? Had she truly seen a frightened little girl peering down at her from the window, or was it simply a configuration of shadows taking human form by virtue of an active imagination? Lea wasn't sure. Maybe it had just been illusion. That could explain the strange sights; but what about the sounds, the screams, the music? She had heard of eyes playing tricks, but never ears. At first she thought of crawling back through the hole and forgetting the whole experience, but then changed her mind. Since she had gone through much trouble to get to this side of the wall, she might as well explore the area to her satisfaction, assuring beyond a doubt that there was nobody, hobgoblin or otherwise, living in her attic loft. Once she proved that it was simply a wild delusion, she could forget the temporary attack of lunacy and get the rest she so badly needed.

Apprehensive, Lea turned and began ascending the steps, unable to see in the darkness. As her foot touched the second riser, a chill numbed her body. It was much the same as that which she had experienced before, when passing the concealed entrance; only this time, it was more severe. Lea's heart began to pound. She was frightened—no, more than that, terrorized—by what lay at the top of the stairs. She could not, however, imagine what it was that inspired such all-encompassing feelings of dread. Some past experience perhaps that she had seemingly forgotten, yet which lingered in the shadowy confines of her unconscious mind. No harm could come to her, she assured herself, for Lord Night watched; cognizant always of her welfare, keeping her safe from harm. Lea tried to calm herself, to abate the fear; but the effort was useless. She had never known a feeling quite like this before, a terror of such magnitude.

She continued her upward climb, steadying herself by pressing palm to wall as she ascended, going deeper and deeper into the blackness.

Her foot searched for yet another step, but there wasn't one to be found. Lea had arrived at the loft. She could see nothing, save for tiny bits of moonlight

flickering through the surrounding forest. That minis-
cule hint of light was a welcome sight, helping to allay
her fears.

Lea crossed the room, moving ever so slowly, trying
not to fall or trip on some unseen hazard. She approached the window, eyes wide at the view. A mass of
shimmering diamonds, dancing on a sea of blue-black
velvet, greeted her. The reservoir was glinting in the
moonlight, appearing as a vision from a beautiful
fairytale. She stared out over the forest and water,
imagining how it must appear in daylight. Vague
recollections began coming back to her. This was the
place where she'd spent many childhood hours. She
could see herself, peeking out over the sill, gaping at a
scene that seemed so vast and enormous to a child, as to
be the world in its entirety. By closing her eyes she could
behold the reservoir at dawn, with sun coming over the
eastern hills; in the day, with golden light bouncing off
each ripple of deep blue; at sunset, garbed in reds,
oranges, pinks, and purples; and then at its most
beautiful, in the evening. She had been taken with its
magnificence even then. But what of the other things of
childhood, the memories which eluded her—where
were they to be found?

Lea was staring out the window, trying to cull her
brain for more information. Somewhere in the room
was a small cupboard where her toys had been kept.
There came to her a faint recollection that she had used
it as a hiding place to escape sounds that she feared. Lea
concentrated hard on the darkness of the little cubby-
hole, trying to remember what had caused her to
scamper there for safety.

It was the naps. Every day at one, the family would

take a rest. Lea would be sent to her room and the door at the bottom of the stairs would be bolted. She was confined there for several hours at a time and would spend most of the afternoon sitting by the window, staring out at the sunshine which she was denied. It was not being alone nor locked in that frightened her; but rather the fearful sounds. When the noise commenced she would run to the safety of the cupboard, wedging herself in among the stuffed bears and rag dolls. Lea thought back to the origin of the sounds. It came from downstairs, her parents' room. The bed would bump rhythmically against the wall and there'd be gasping breaths, moans, and cries of what Lea, the child, perceived to be pain.

How she hated it when they rocked the bed and laughed! Naps meant you were to be quiet and asleep. If she made noise when she was supposed to be asleep, her mother spanked her; so why wouldn't they be still? It happened almost daily, much to her chagrin.

Lea could envision herself huddled and crying in the darkness; the reaction, however, was not of fear, but rather rage. Lea shut her eyes tightly, wondering why, as a child, she had been upset at her parents intimacies. Slowly it came back to her. Her father had been a big man, a gentle giant, who spent his free time entertaining his little daughter. Lea had resented the closeness he shared with her mother, becoming angered when he showed Beatrice affection, or focused his attention on the mother to the exclusion of his daughter. Even as a young woman, in times of seeming happiness, Beatrice hadn't been particularly kind to her little girl. Lea's arrival had been viewed as an untimely intrusion in her life. She saw to Lea's physical needs, but sorely neglected the child's psychological wants for love and affection. Those needs were satisfied by the tall man who bounced her on his knee and on whose shoulders she rode. Lea now remembered that as a child, closeted with her toys, she had beat her fists in rage, thinking that her daddy should take his naps in the loft, on the soft mattress with his little daughter, instead of the nagging witch that was his companion.

He was tall, very tall, this shining love of her little-girl life; perhaps six-four or five. He had masses of black ringlets covering his head and large, translucent blue eyes, just like hers. Mentally, she was piecing a puzzle together, putting the hair where it belonged, placing the eyes, dislodging a memory about the mouth, hoping that in the end she would get a finished product, that somehow the long ago forgotten face would take form and she could remember its features.

Lea was succeeding, when suddenly another scene superimposed itself on her consciousness. It was the giant's gaping forest grave that she had so horribly imagined this past afternoon. The Goliath in the vision had a similar mane of black hair, with wide shoulders and large hands, just like her father's. Lea tried to shake off the memory, choosing to ignore it, hoping that it would go away. Her father, she assured herself, was no giant. How ridiculous she was to try to confuse past reality with macabre fantasies! Lea tried to clear her mind, have it move on to other thoughts; but it resisted, preferring to return instead to the bloodied colossus lying in a wilderness grave. Something was causing her to feel decidedly uncomfortable. A memory was pending, just out of reach. She sensed that it was pertinent and could shed light on the present matter; but it wouldn't come into focus. The blank spaces in her mind, the missing times, had always bothered Lea; no, more than that, had troubled her deeply. Lea had always known that she loved her daddy deeply, had sensed it; yet was unable to explain why it was that his face was cloaked in such mystery. It was almost as if she had made some sort of concerted effort to blot him out of her mind.

From the times of childhood, she could remember a story, a bedtime tale that was her favorite. The memory was about to emerge, to reveal itself. Jack and the Beanstalk with its angry giant had been an almost daily staple. The person who had told and retold the exciting tale was her father. She could remember the deep, throaty voice calling out, "Fe Fi Fo Fum!" The phrase was used not only in the telling of the story, but also when they played hide and seek or when he caught her doing something she wasn't supposed to. He was the giant, stamping his feet in mock anger, causing the floor boards of the cabin to shake.

Lea gasped, suddenly aware of the ominous possibilities. If she identified the person of the giant, and the giant was her father, then what was the significance of the grave? Once more she closed her eyes tightly, trying to recall something, anything, that might serve to clear the matter; but nothing would come. Her mind was a blank.

From below the window, she heard the sound of the front door closing, of footsteps on wood. It was distant, yet near, coming to her through a veil of memory.

As if entering the portals of Hades, a blast of heat assailed her, seering her lungs, sucking the breath from them. Her chest began to heave as it attempted to pull in

255

needed air. Her head pulsated with pain. She could remember now, recall it all—every ghastly, lurid, detail. Lea was dizzy, feeling as if she were about to swoon. She had tried so hard to retrieve her past, but now wished that the memories would sink once again into her subconscious, dwelling there with the other monsters that populated her nightmares. Once the demons were free, they would not go away. This was the hour of truth, the time to confront her madness.

There was sound coming from across the room, the motion of bed springs, the soft patter of little feet.

Within her a voice echoed, resounded. "Turn, Lea," it ordered, "Turn and witness your past." The voice was that of the devil dwelling within her. He was laughing, shrieking. "Look Lea, cast your eyes upon the place. Come, child, let us join the nightmare!"

As if in hypnotic trance, she obeyed, turning to relive the hell, the agony, the slaughter, that had once occurred here. The scene was about to unfold before her. She was being called upon to relive the torture. Her eyes opened wide as the memories came rushing in.

It was the hour of secrets. A time of darkness when only two remained within the confines of the cabin. The brown-haired child had risen fearfully from her bed and gone to the window to look out. All was shrouded in darkness, in shadows that concealed night monsters. The little girl watched as the grey figure moved away from the cabin and vanished into the forest. Mama had gone for a walk. Now was the time that the monster came and hurt inside her. The tiny Lea ran back to bed, pulling the covers up over her head, and began to cry in fear of the night. As had happened many times before, she heard footsteps moving around below her that night. They had come to a halt outside the stairwell door. The giant was coming to get her. By day the gentle playmate, but in the evening a dealer of pain. Lea began to sob as she heard the latch click. He would soon be upon her and the torment would begin. The door opened slowly, allowing the light to seep upward and soon the stairs began to creak under the weight of the approaching antagonist. The child's weeping continued, gaining momentum as hysteria and fear increased. With tear-filled eyes, she looked up to see the shadowy figure standing at the top of the stair, hands held on hips, framed in the dim glow from beneath.

"Child," the voice chided her, "You mustn't fear the darkness. The night is a wonderful thing! It wraps you in warmth. Keeps you safe. It'll make you feel good, if only you'll let it." The tone softened, became gentle, "Don't be afraid, Lea. Don't be afraid. The night won't ever hurt you."

She continued whimpering as the giant neared her bed and pulled back the covers. The large hands tugged at the flimsy cotton nightgown, until it bunched around her chest; then forced the little legs apart. With that the child cried out louder, body shaking, trying to restrain screams of fear.

"You want me to give you a good spanking?" the voice asked sternly. "Do you want that?"

"No," the little voice answered meekly.

"Then lie still like a good girl. You hear me?" the voice asked, pausing momentarily for her response.

Lea continued sobbing, with no words passing her lips.

"Lea," the voice said menacingly, "Are you going to

be good and lie still or am I going to have to take my strap, welt your bottom, and make you be good?''

The tiny being sniffled, fearful of what was to happen; yet more afraid of the possible consequences. "I'll be good," the little voice promised.

"That's my girl," the voice said gently, bending over the tiny shaking form. "It's not going to hurt, honey," he assured. "Just relax, and it'll be over in a very little while."

She'd whimpered, almost silently, as his finger probed her, moving in and out to some unheard diabolic rhythm.

After a few minutes of tormenting the tiny victim, the giant, hulking, form backed off, straightening up to his full height. It was then that she had heard the sickeningly familiar sound of the zipper coming down. The giant always made her touch that snake-like thing, rub it until it became erect. She hated it. It frightened her, this night serpent, with its evil-smelling hood of skin. The Goliath forced her to wrap her hands around his organ's girth, massaging it until it spewed the sticky excretion, amid body-convulsing moans.

This, the giant had told her long and often, was the time of secret night games, which Lea was not allowed to divulge to anyone. If she so much as breathed a word of it to her mother, the giant promised that he would seek revenge. He'd make the ghosts and bears and assorted bogey men descend on her darkened bedroom, then let them eat her up. To a four-year-old, no fate could be worse.

Lea couldn't remember when the giant had begun his nightly visits, but as far back as she could recall there had always been calloused fingers and erect flesh.

258

Fearful of retribution, afraid of the possible consequences, she had never told a living soul about the nocturnal visits at either the cabin nor the small frame house. It was a terror that she had learned to keep concealed, abuse that she had come to think of as a normal part of living. In her mind she accepted the fact, assuming that every little girl had a bad giant who came to her in the darkness and caused her pain.

Tears poured down her cheeks as she visualized the poor little thing desperately trying to get the whole revolting encounter over with as quickly as possible. The giant had been so engaged in the act that he hadn't heard the creaking footsteps that night. Lea had heard but didn't signal to warn him or let him know. She feared that by speaking or stopping the hand movements, he might become so irritated that he would punish her. Lea was more terrified of his ire than of the thing on the stairs.

The sticky liquid was spraying forth, as the shadowed figure reached the top of the stair. It stood there, barely a moment, watching; then ran toward them, brandishing a glinting object in its right hand. Goliath screamed as the figure's hand came down squarely on his back. Lea pulled back her hands, retreating against the headboard. She cried out as her eyes absorbed the pure horror of the scene. The giant, having fallen to the floor, was struggling to crawl away from his attacker; but his attempts at evasion and protection were to no avail. The figure struck out again and again, repeatedly slashing at the writhing form. The giant extended his arm, trying to ward off the blows; but such action only seemed to further enrage the figure. It kept up the rain of blood-inducing blows until he lay unmoving on the floor. Once its anger had abated, the figure stood motionless above the giant and began to weep loudly. The long pointed object fell from its hand, landing beside the hulking corpse. When the shadow was at last convinced that Goliath lived no more, it dropped to its knees and began kissing what had once been a living creature.

After the passage of several minutes spent silently shuddering in her bed, terrified of what would happen next, the room suddenly became bathed in light. It was then that Lea learned the identity of the attacker. Beatrice stood covered with blood, staring at the little girl. On the floor nearby lay the large limp carcass of what had once been a man, its features unrecognizable beneath the gaping wounds and jelling blood. Tiny Lea cried out in terror—blood was everywhere, covering the sheets and blankets, the floor, Beatrice and even spraying on her own nightgown. As the child began to whimper, dissolving once more in tears, her mother came nearer, eyeing her with revulsion.

Lea could not, no matter how hard she tried, ever remember a loving look from her mother; but on that night, the eyes that glared at her showed pure hatred. There was no sympathy for the child, no understanding of what horrid encounters she had been made to endure.

"*You*, damn you," Beatrice had shrieked at her, "*You* did this! It's your fault, all your fault! Your doing, damn you!" The voice was that of one who was teetering on the brink of madness. "I never wanted you! Curse the day I had you!" Her words slashed out like cutting knives, meant to wound.

Even at that early age, Lea had understood that something was terribly wrong with her Mommy and that she should be fearful of the woman's possible erratic actions.

"Damn you," her mother again screamed. "Damn you! I wish you were dead. Never been born, you conniving little devil!"

Beatrice walked in circles, wandering in undirected rage, drawing closer to the bed with each pass, unable to comprehend the magnitude of what she had done nor to focus on anything other than Lea. Her speech, thoughts, and actions became more irrational as the seconds ticked by. Somehow, in that convoluted mentality, she perceived the innocent four-year-old as being the seducer, the temptress, who had cast an evil spell upon her much loved husband.

Beatrice's steps were slow and uncertain as she came forward, a look of menacing intent in her cold, steely eyes. Her hand shot out cruelly and grabbed the little girl's arm, twisting, then snatching it toward her, pulling the tiny child off the bed and hurling her onto the floor.

"You're dirty, bad, Satan's imp! You're a filthy little pig. That's what you are, a horrid, dirty child! Lea's bad, sinful! All this, all of it, every last bit, is your doing. I punished him for being bad. I made him bleed!" She screamed. "He was bad and I made him pay!" Saying the words, her body began to convulse and her face took on a maniacal glare. "You touched him, didn't you, you despicable little tease? You let him touch you. You're no good, you're dirty, you're bad; but I'm going to fix you. I'm going to make you good, you godless little beast!"

The avalanche of memories was too much. It was so real, almost as if it were happening now, right here in the loft. Her body shuddered and sobbed in sorrow for that poor little being who had once been. Lea dropped to her knees, then crumpled, pitifully pulling herself into a fetal position. She began rolling on the floor, agonizing over memories of the past, crying for the terrors of her childhood, for the nightmares which had, in fact, been reality.

The spectres disappeared from the room; but inside her brain, Lea was still reliving that night. She remembered how she'd been set upon by her mother's flailing fists, then dragged bodily down the stairs to the kitchen, where her mother took the scrub brush and cleanser and proceeded to scrub the little girl's hands and genitals until they bled. It was Beatrice's idea of fitting retribution for her child's sins.

Later that night, Lea had been forced to assist her mother in mopping the blood from the floor; then had dragged the shovel and held the flashlight as her mother first transported the body, then dug the pit which would forever entomb him.

What Lea had insisted were macabre illusions and hallucinations were in reality her unconscious mind trying to force recall of the horrors which had occurred. For nearly thirty years, the truth had lain hidden in the inner recesses of her brain. There it festered, bringing Lea dangerously close to phobic hysteria. The memory had been so shocking, so traumatic, that she chose to ignore it, denying that it ever occurred.

She knew even then that her father was the dark ogre who visited pain upon her, yet she refused to accept it, believing instead that the shadowy figure was a cruel and base giant. In her own way, Lea had loved the man and the sexual attention he had bestowed upon her. Even

262

after witnessing his death, the child had somehow convinced herself that her mother's lies of his desertion were true. She loved yet hated him; glad that the evening abuse was ended, yet sorrowful that she no longer had an affectionate adult with whom to relate.

Deep inside, Lea hated and despised her mother for taking him away. Thoughts were swirling with unbelievable speed, flickering, exploding, then disappearing. Beatrice's perverse dogma of unyielding virtue had so badly damaged Lea's psyche that she came to fear sex, viewing it as a diabolic act, created by men to degrade and debase women. Even the sanctioned marital union was laden with sin. It was quite apparent that the mother had never pitied the daughter's suffering, but instead blamed the girl. Now from this new perspective of the past, it appeared that Beatrice's all encompassing reliance on this religion of her own creation, with its strict discipline, unmeetable standards, and fanatical doctrine was her only way of coping with the overwhelming guilt and loneliness she felt at the death of her loved one. The austere life of self-denial it imposed was her chosen punishment. It was useless to try to analyze her mother's motives now. It was already too late to matter, the damage had already been done.

Lea shook her head knowingly. The devil that lived in her, to which her mother always referred, was that early loss of innocence, that exposure to the world of primal pleasure. Lea pondered a moment on the veracity of the statement. No, that wasn't possible. She assured herself that she hadn't *liked* what occurred in the loft—in fact, had been afraid of it. That was her truth, but was it really? Like squirming worms, other memories began making their way forward into conscious recognition. She recalled a little girl whimpering with smiling lips, calling out in mock fear of darkness, longing for the warmth and companionship of her night visitor. As quickly as they came, Lea tried to shut the memories out. It wasn't true, simply not true! She hadn't been the instigator of what happened here, but rather its victim. Although rationally Lea knew that she was right, a part of her, so steeped in mother's hellfire and brimstone, called out her name as harlot and demanded punishment.

Lea forced the thoughts out and away, trying to turn her mind to something else. The most pleasant flight of fancy she could conjure was that of Lord Night. She tried to concentrate, focusing only on him; when sudden terror grasped her, refusing to let go. Who was Lord Night? The realization, the answer, convulsed her soul. He spoke in the voice of her father, approached in the darkness like Daddy, provided her with the enticing mixture of pleasure and pain that had become so familiar during childhood; the only possible solution to the question of identity must be that he was a bastardized illusion, a conjured spectre of an incestuous lover brought to life by Lea. Unable to accept the fact of her own sexuality, her biological needs, feeling it sinful and wrong, she had created the phantom in her own mind. She masturbated; but he, the prince of eroticism, was blamed. This godlike lover could give her pleasure; but never her own hands, for that was perverse and sinful. If it had all been illusion, a maddening masquerade, entered into to deny her own self gratification, then to whom had she been offering sacrifice, and why had living forms died? Her eyes closed tightly, contorting her face into a grotesque mask. It was an exercise in futility—the scenes would not go away; blood-covered kittens, attempting to wrest themselves free, slashed, gaping, throats with blood pulsating out, moving in rhythm to a dying heart—breasts, eyes, and belly sliced open like so much red meat, and for what, to whose benefit? It had all been madness, *her* madness. They had died for nothing. The blame could not be laid at the grave of a perverse father, who thought the sexual abuse of his own daughter gratifying, nor upon the shoulders of a cold and heartless mother who spent her life punishing and condemning. Her parentage, her lineage, was less than what one might desire; they were, of course, both mad in their own unique fashion. An incestuous father sired her and a homicidal, abusive mother bore her; but their shortcomings in no way made her blameless for her own actions. Many children suffered sexual abuse, were victims of incestuous attack. Others were raised in loveless homes, subject to the same physical violence as she; yet those children didn't grow up to commit murder as Lea had done. Perhaps insanity was an inheritable trait of the Eaton clan, and Lea was simply following in the pathways of her ancestors. She was truly her mother's child, fruit of her father's loins. Lea wished that she could bring them back: Aunt Evelyn, Tony, and even the tiny kitten; but there was no way to undo the evil she'd done.

She wept, as the tenets of her old childhood religion and visions of a vengeful God of Wrath came back. Lea perceived herself as truly evil, having sinned in a way so perverse that she was sure even a God of mercy and love couldn't forgive. What should she do? How could she rectify the wrong she'd done? Lea knew that she was in need of chastisement. Hadn't Mama always told her that only punishment, hard and unyielding, could cleanse the soul from the blackening ravages of sin?

Lea rose to her feet, shaking her head with such intensity as to almost lose her balance. How was she to pay for taking those innocent lives? She swayed and sobbed, not knowing what to do next. Throughout the cabin, the echo of her wailing could be heard. She moved through the darkened loft, alternating between loud screams and barely audible whimpers. With each passing second, the magnitude of her sin seared itself on her brain. Guilt assaulted her, vanquishing hopes of redemption. The gentle, pious librarian had become the purveyor of evil, the instrument of Lucifer, called upon to mete out deaths of horror.

She held her head as the memories bombarded her. Her mind kept harkening back to years before, to the night of horrors when punishment took the form of blood. Fresh, bright crimson in color, it had been atonement for the misdeeds of mortals. Lea wondered if one life, hers, would be enough? The answer was unimportant. She had to die. Only then would she be cleansed. There was no other way. She didn't deserve to live. Her very presence on earth would contaminate the godly ones. Lea had committed the most heinous of crimes and therefore had to pay the supreme price.

She wasn't bothered by nor afraid of the act of self destruction. Lea realized that she'd be unable to exist, her conscience heavy laden with such a burden. It would drive her mad, far beyond this present state of disorientation and delusion. The Bible, God's inspired word, states that suicide is sin. This, however, was a self inflicted punishment; allowing her to bask, once more, within God's loving grace. To her way of thinking, it

266

was the Lord's verdict, bearing no resemblance to the Hell-paved act of taking one's life.

Lea nodded her head in child-like fashion, attempting to assure herself that this was the only reasonable course of action available. Once convinced, she ran toward the landing and down the stairs.

While trying to wriggle through the opening, it occurred to Lea that, of necessity, she should decide on a method which would bring about her demise in the quickest and most painless fashion. She had no pills, save for a small tin of aspirin which she was sure would be wholly ineffective. Lea gave fleeting thought to jumping from the loft's window; but quickly determined that such a fall would only break a few bones, nothing more. The next possibility was gas; but she quickly cast it aside, suspecting that it would only serve to make her very ill. Stabbing was out, too messy and inaccurate. Poison was unavailable. Blowing her brains out was out of the question, as she didn't possess the necessary weapon. After she had quickly examined all the alternatives, Lea decided that the easiest and best way would be to cut her wrists. It wasn't a particularly quick way to die, but at least it was said to be relatively painless.

After crawling through the hole, Lea headed straight for the bathroom, to search for the required lethal instrument. A razor blade would prove most effective for the task. One lightning quick slash across each wrist, and it would be over. The torments of a lifetime would cease to be. In opened, bleeding gashes, there was rest, in gaping flesh, the sleep of eternity. Soon she would make the most important of journey, crossing over from the dimension of flesh to that of soul. Once done, she would stand before her Maker to plead for salvation, for a place beside Him throughout eternity. Was she worthy? Hardly! Was a murderess, a liar, a self-abusing harlot, the child of God? Lea didn't know! Was she so filled with sin that even a God of forgiveness, if such a one existed, would be unable to wash the blackness from her soul? Was it her fate to endure the everlasting fires of hell, withstand the torment, in payment for transgressions of a lifetime? She was a sorrowful supplicant at the altar of the deity, let Him do as He will. If she were to be welcomed a sad, mad sinner, then angels be joyful; but if she were eternally damned, then so be it, His will be done. She left the decision wholly in His merciful hands.

After switching on the light, Lea opened the medicine chest and searched the contents. It took but a second to locate the silver-colored dispenser. She drew it from its hiding place and carefully removed a single shining blade. Lea examined it closely; holding it up to the light, turning it slowly so that she might watch the glints of brightness bounce off its surface. It seemed rather ludicrous that a thing appearing so simple and innocuous could be an agent of death. After a moment's hesitation, determining that she should dispense with the theorizing and get on with the act, Lea held out her left hand, palm upward. Funny, but she had never, in all her times of trial and tribulation, envisioned that her life would end in such a manner. She was fearful, yet determined that it be done; that this life which God had given her, would be ended by her own hand. It was a just and fitting punishment to which the Lord had directed her.

Lea drew the blade near, and with one swift movement, cut the skin. It was not a deep gash, only a superficial scratch which bled but a little. The tiny cut began to sting, giving her a premonition of what was to come. Lea realized that in order to do the job properly, she had to cut through a vein. Only then would she bleed sufficiently to bring about unconsciousness and death. Resolved to succeed, she once again slashed at her wrist. The pain was excruciating. She'd done it right this time. The crimson fluid was pulsating from the incision, covering the nearby flesh, then falling, in small puddles, to the floor.

With left hand shaking, she grasped the blade in her blood-covered fingers and repeated the procedure on the right wrist.

Lea didn't know how long it would take for the end to come, but felt that it would be some little time. She wasn't feeling even slightly faint nor weakened by the sudden loss of blood. The only thing which disturbed her was the uncomfortable, continual throbbing of her wounds.

She left the bathroom trying to determine how best to spend the last few moments of her life. So many things had happened, all without reason, without logic. None made sense within that mass of confusion in her brain. Why had God allowed her to sink into sin, to flounder in madness? Was it to prove her unworthy for salvation? She knew not the intention of God, yet prayed that He would be merciful. Were lunatics precious in the eyes of the Lord? Could the Lord Jehovah heal her troubled, tortured mind, cleanse her soul of its perverse malady?

Lea moved down the hallway and into the bedroom. In the dimness, she could see the darkened splatters of blood which covered walls and floors. She stood motionless for a moment, remembering to whom the sacrificial offering had been consecrated. How could she have acted in such madness, to do away with the only living being who truly cared for her? Lea began to tremble as visions of Evelyn flashed within her mind. If only she could resurrect the old woman, go back in time to a point before any of this horror occured, prior to the appearance of Lord Night and ritual sacrifice! Her eyes again clouded as tears began.

From her position in the doorway, she could see the hideous altar of her madness, the structured proof of her sinfulness. Through all, it had stood, the shiny blackness an insult to Him who had died upon the cross, an ugly desecration to all things holy.

In the shadowed confines of her mind, she repeated the first commandment given man: "I am the Lord thy God, thou shalt not have strange gods before me."

How could she expect mercy while allowing such an abomination to continue? It must be destroyed so that she might do honor to Jehovah and somehow right the wrongs she'd committed upon its demon surface.

Lea ran to the loft entrance to retrieve the axe. With it in hand, she returned to carry out the destruction of Night's heathen altar. Feeling slightly dizzy, she crossed the room, axe poised to strike. A crimson trail was left in her wake as she moved to the altar's side. Around it, as if storm tossed, were scattered the things which had once been deemed to have sacred significance—the candle holders, the incense burner, and finally the silver chalice.

With one mighty stroke, Lea brought the axe down upon the marble surface, cracking it in two. The altar which had destroyed others, consuming their blood, was no more. In a maddened frenzy, Lea struck blow after blow. In the end, all that was left of the thin marble top were scattered pieces of rock chips flung about the room.

Satisfied that it was wholly and irrevocably destroyed, she dropped the axe and turned her attention to the wall hanging. That, too, offended the Almighty. Lea walked slowly toward it, reached up, and ripped it from its moorings. How had this piece of filth cast such a wicked spell on her? Thinking that in the end God would prevail, she began smashing the frame against the wall until it shattered. Her vicious attack caused the fabric to tear, making it impossible to decipher the meaning of the scene.

The room was silent as Lea neared the chalice. It too must be destroyed if she were to be saved. How innocent and beautiful it appeared! If it weren't for the congealed fluid surrounding it, Lea might have forgotten what purpose it served. How often evil masquerades in a guise of fragile beauty, she thought.

As she stood looking down at it, Lea became aware of strange sounds, reminiscent of hot oil sizzling on a griddle. As she stood contemplating the strange auditory sensations, her nose was assailed by the acrid smell of burning matter. The origin of both smell and sound was near.

At first, her eyes did not perceive the faint curls of smoke moving upward from the chalice, nor the red glow emanating from the floor surrounding it. She stood rooted for a moment; then realized what was happening. *Her* blood was the source of these strange happenings, the causative factor. As it dropped upon the chalice, the fluid began to burn, then vaporized into mist—but how? Lea reached down to touch the goblet, but drew her hand back, sensing its tremendous heat. The more the blood dripped upon it, the larger the cloud of red. Lea tried to turn and run; but her body would not cooperate. It was as if the chalice held her captive, freeing her only when it was sated with her blood.

The glow grew brighter, usurping more space, as Lea stared in horror. Like a cancer, it was growing larger. Whatever it was, was gaining height and breadth. Within the mist, something was forming. Areas of it were opaque, filling with a viscous substance, taking the conformation of a human. The top was expanding to form a head and from the sides of this glowing, crimson embryo, budding limbs grew downward. From the floor, hideous, rod-shaped growths wriggled up to meet the bulbous torso. They appeared as thickened, writhing snakes. Lea had created a being. Within the swirling red gases, the droplets of her blood had fed and nurtured it.

World of fantasy, insanity, what was this thing she now endured? Was this the prophecy of Lord Night, finally come to fruition, or a maddened demon come to claim her soul for Satan? Since Lord Night couldn't exist, it must all be an aberration, a convoluted, hysterical, creation of her demented mind; yet this had been the promise. She had given blood and this thing before her had taken life.

Her mind was swirling with uncertainty. What was real, who was real? Did God exist as supreme being of all the universe, alone? Or was there, perhaps, another, a dark evil, blood-lusting entity, with whom he shared his realm? The Lord of Night, the master of shadows, whom Lea had conceived in darkness was no illusion; he was real!

Lea could see the chest heaving within the crimson fog. It was breathing, coming to life.

"Don't be afraid, child," a familiar voice called out to her. "You mustn't fear the darkness," it admonished. "Night is a beautiful, warm, thing. It brings you pleasure, Lea, all the pleasures of the world, all the love you want, all the affection you've been denied; those things for which you've been searching all your life." The carmine cloud pulsed, undulating with movement, as the voice continued. "You have nothing to fear from the night, it will keep you safe, child."

Lea began weeping. That horrid apparition knew her too well. It had breached the facade of her being, delving into her brain, uncovering the true fabric of her desires. More than treasure or other earthly pleasure, she wanted someone to love who would return her caring. All her life, even in childhood, she'd been denied that dream of dreams. This would be her joy, her rapture, if only the voice spoke the truth! Its tones were recognizable, calling to Lea over a distance of time and space. Perhaps she had been wrong. Maybe there was someone who cared for her after all.

"Daddy?" Lea whispered. "Is that you, Daddy?" she questioned, fighting back tears.

The cloud shook as sinister laughter thundered forth. The sounds rose, melding into maniacal, fearsome shrieks. As the cacophony continued, Lea watched as the transformation began. From within the swiftly dissipating cloud, two golden eyes glared at her. Upon the head, horn-like growths appeared. The legs, massive at the thigh, tapered down to bone, resembling those of beasts. Whatever she had created, it was not the handsome, human lover of her dreams.

"Come Lea, come worship the night! Worship, child, for thou art consecrated to me, one with night through eternity!" The tone was loud and demanding.

Lea tried to step back, but dazed from loss of blood, she stumbled, falling to her knees. Unable to draw strength to stand and run, Lea looked on in terror as the thing moved out from its concealment, away from the glowing mist.

Its eyes were wholly yellow, lacking in pupils or other human attributes. Its nose was long and thin, above the cruel, pale lips. The ashen flesh was pitted, as if diseased. His chin was unduly pointed, as were the large, flaring ears. The hair on his head was greasy black and two gray horns curved upward from his temples. He was truly a fearsome being to behold. The muscles of his body were sinewy. His bare chest and arms were covered with sparse, coarse hair. The creature's abdomen was like to that of a fur covered animal, from which descended two robust legs, ending in cloven hooves. Amid the wooly thatch of its groin, she could see the massive swell of his penis. This thing before her was demon, formed not here but in the bowels of Hell.

"I am Night, lord of shadows," the incubus proclaimed, eyeing Lea with contempt. "And you, bitch, are mine! For all eternity you shall dwell with me as my handmaiden. You shall partake of the rituals and rites and proclaim my glory!"

Lea shrunk from the odious form. Her breasts heaved as she tried, without success, to catch her breath. Lea's vision blurred as weakness overtook her. There was no way to escape this diabolic presence nor to cheat or

274

waylay the fast approach of death. Lea could do nothing but endure, hoping that whatever fate awaited her be swift.

"Don't I pleasure thee, slut?" it questioned with contempt. "We struck a bargain. Thou shalt have thy love and I shall possess thee. With blood we sealed the pact!"

Her head shook furiously from side to side. "No," she screamed out as he approached, "No! Dear, sweet Jesus, save me!" she implored.

His claw-like fingers reached out for her, grasping her hair and pulling her head upright. "Woman, gaze upon thy lover," he hissed at her, parting his lips to reveal rows of sharply pointed teeth.

He snarled, biting down several times, allowing her to hear the sickening sound of gnashing teeth. Her fear greatly pleasured him.

"Come, child," he beckoned. "It is time to worship the night, time to give sacrifice, time to offer blood!" As he finished, his mouth opened wide, showing crimson amid the glinting, razor sharp teeth.

Lea screamed as his vise-like fingers held her fast. She writhed and thrashed around, but to no avail. He was a vile spider and she was his pitiable fly. As his face neared and the putrid smell of his breath assailed her, she shut her eyes tightly, trying to hurl him from her consciousness.

"If it be illusion, then let it pass. Destroy this dream, this nightmare," she prayed. No force, however, came to save her, to ward off the evil which was her companion.

She screamed in agony as the canines ripped through her throat, gnawing at the flesh. She couldn't breathe.

Her body quivered as blood began flowing from her nose and mouth. Lea opened her eyes for a split second only to see the growling beast's blood-drenched lips feasting on her own flesh.

She was suffocating, falling into a pit, into blackness. Pain surrounded her as she gasped for air. All was lost. All was over. There was no one to save her from this fate, this doom, this thing of her creation. She was slipping deeper and deeper into the shadows, into unconsciousness, moving toward the time of endings.

Her mind called out its silent agony. "Mommy? Daddy?" but no answer came.

All was still within the cabin, the blackness hanging heavy. The ritual had been observed and Lea lived no more.

CHAPTER XIV

He lay in bed, naked beneath the sheet; wondering in the darkness, what it might be like to have a woman, to place his hands upon her breasts and in her most secret places. In all his lifetime, no one had loved him, no one had cared. Fat and ungainly, unappealing to the eye, it was his curse to remain forever alone.

There was a gentle breeze, flowing through the open window, flapping the curtains. The night wind was comforting and welcome after the searing heat of the day. There was something about darkness that he found enticing. It was a time when he could dream, could fantasize.

He reached under the sheets and began groping for his organ, so that he might know some small, if lonely, bit of pleasure. As his fingers encircled it, a gust of wind blew through the room. He looked up to find a strange shape poised upon the sill. Embarrassed, his hand withdrew. Lit only by moonlight, it was difficult, at first, to determine what it was. On closer scrutiny, he

279

realized that it was a woman.

As if moving from behind a cloud, the moon's glow suddenly increased its intensity, until it virtually lit the room. He could see her clearly now. She was a tiny thing, with short cropped hair and large blue eyes. The appealing form was perched upon the sill staring at him. She wore a gossamer garment of black, transparent silk. It displayed the comely beauty of her firm, full breasts, her slender thighs, and the triangular thatch of hair which nested between them.

He shook his head, trying to dispel the siren's image. It had to be illusion, a waking dream; certainly she could not be real.

He was conscious of a soft, sweet voice, calling to him. "Come, worship the night with me. It will bring you pleasure, all the joys of existence."

He looked up, meeting her gaze. She smiled innocently, barely parting her lips. Of all the creatures he had ever encountered, she was the most pleasing to him, and he longed to possess her.

With perfect grace, the succubus descended from the ledge and drew near.

Heart pounding, he tried to speak. "Who are you?"

"I," she stated softly, smiling to reveal rows of sharp, white, pointed teeth, "am Night!"

SISTER SATAN

Dana Reed

SHE WAS
THE DEVIL'S SPAWN

Lauren had been blessed – or cursed – with mysterious powers since birth. As a shy, lonely teenager, she longed for a sister to share the joy and pain of growing up, and began hesitantly experimenting with the strange forces within her. And she succeeded only too well, for she found to her horror that she had called into being an exact duplicate of herself who was the personification of pure evil. As Rachel grew stronger and more malevolent with each passing day, Lauren was driven to the brink of insanity. How long would it be before she herself became the victim of her hellish alter ego? Was there any way to destroy the evil creature she had summoned? Would even her own death put an end to its fiendish power?

0-8439-2152-8   Price: $3.75 US/$4.50 CAN

MORE BLOOD-CHILLERS FROM LEISURE BOOKS

2039-4	**LOVE'S UNEARTHLY POWER** Blair Foster	$3.50
2112-9	**SPAWN OF HELL** William Schoell	$3.75 US, $4.50 Can.
2121-8	**UNDERTOW** Drake Douglas	$3.75 US, $4.50 Can.
2152-8	**SISTER SATAN** Dana Reed	$3.75 US, $4.50 Can.
2185-4	**BLOOD OFFERINGS** Robert San Souci	$3.75 US, $4.50 Can.
2195-1	**BRAIN WATCH** Robert W. Walker	$3.50 US, $4.25 Can.
2215-x	**MADONNA** Ed Kelleher and Harriette Vidal	$3.75 US, $4.50 Can.
2220-6	**THE RIVARD HOUSE** Edwin Lambirth	$3.25
2225-7	**UNTO THE ALTAR** John Tigges	$3.75 US, $4.50 Can.
2235-4	**SHIVERS** William Schoell	$3.75 US, $4.50 Can.
2246-X	**DEATHBRINGER** Dana Reed	$3.75 US, $4.50 Can.
2256-7	**CREATURE** Drake Douglas	$3.75 US, $4.50 Can.

EERIE NOVELS
OF
HORROR AND THE OCCULT
BY J. N. WILLIAMSON,
THE MASTER OF DARK FANTASY

1168-9	THE RITUAL	$3.25
2074-2	GHOST	$2.95
2133-1	THE OFFSPRING	$3.25
2176-5	PROFITS	$3.25
2228-1	THE TULPA	$2.95

BLOOD OFFERINGS

Robert San Souci

AN INHUMAN EVIL FEEDS
ON THE
BLOOD OF HUMAN SACRIFICE

Consumed with desire for revenge on the man who had caused
the death of her child, Suzanne sensed an ancient evil invading
her body, seeping into her very soul. It offered her strength, but
at a hideous price – she must shed the blood of one she dearly loved before it would bestow its power upon her. Joining
forces with another woman who sought the destruction of
Suzanne's nemesis, she offered herself to a deity older than
time itself. Sated by the blood of their victims, the great god
Shango drove them to prepare for the final ceremony, one that
would unleash the ultimate horror on an unsuspecting
world...

0-8439-2185-4

Price: $3.75 US/$4.50 CAN

THE FELLOWSHIP

Mary C. Romine
Aden F. Romine

BEWARE
THE BROTHERHOOD
OF BLOOD!

The marriage of Ken DeVane and Karen Scribner begins happily enough—until Ken discovers that Karen has fallen under the spell of Anton Marek, the master of The Fellowship, a worldwide cult of vampires. At first unable to believe in Marek's supernatural powers, Ken is soon totally convinced, his skepticism replaced by the horrified realization that his adversary is indeed immortal. Desperate to save Karen and Marek's other victims, he is forced to pit his puny human strength against an ageless force for evil, a being whose power seems invincible...

0-8439-2142-0   Price: $3.75 US/$4.50 CAN

WOLF TRACKS

David Case

THE BEAST WITHIN

The girl had literally been torn apart. What sort of creature could have mutilated her so horribly? Lab tests identified wolf hair and saliva on the corpse, and it appeared that the girl had been attacked by a savage beast. But a reliable witness swore he had seen a man overpower her. Then another mutilated body was discovered, and another. The city began to panic. The police issued calm assurances to the public, but the mangled bodies had been ripped apart with an inhuman ferocity. And in the darkest corner of everyone's mind lurked the word no one dared utter – *werewolf*.

0-8439-2166-8   Price: $3.50

Make the Most of Your Leisure Time
with
LEISURE BOOKS

Please send me the following titles:

Quantity	Book Number	Price

If out of stock on any of the above titles, please send me the alternate title(s) listed below:

Postage & Handling _____

Total Enclosed $_____

☐ Please send me a free catalog.

NAME_____
(please print)

ADDRESS_____

CITY_____ STATE_____ ZIP_____

Please include $1.00 shipping and handling for the first book ordered and 25¢ for each book thereafter in the same order. All orders are shipped within approximately 4 weeks via postal service book rate. PAYMENT MUST ACCOMPANY ALL ORDERS.*

*Canadian orders must be paid in US dollars payable through a New York banking facility.

Mail coupon to: **Dorchester Publishing Co., Inc.**
6 East 39 Street, Suite 900
New York, NY 10016
Att: ORDER DEPT.